AVENGED

HOSTAGE RESCUE TEAM SERIES

KAYLEA CROSS

AVENGED

Copyright © 2015
by Kaylea Cross

* * * * *

Cover Art & Formatting by
Sweet 'N Spicy Designs

* * * * *

ISBN: 978-1514673812

Dedication

This one goes out to all our military, law enforcement and other emergency personnel, who put on their uniforms and try to make this world a safer place for all of us every day. Thank you for your service!

Kaylea

Author's Note

I'm really excited about Schroder's story, one because he's a former PJ, and two, because I just LOVE his and Taya's backstory. You guys know how I adore my PJs, and Schroder is no exception. Hope you enjoy this one!

Happy reading!

Kaylea Cross

Chapter One

It was getting worse instead of better.

Special Agent Nate Schroder cracked his eyes open as the roar of the explosion echoed in his ears. Heart pounding, he rolled over onto his back and let his arms flop to his sides against the sheets. His skin was clammy with sweat as the nightmare slowly faded and he came back to reality. The ceiling fan overhead came into focus, turning in languid circles that sent a wash of cool air over his damp, bare upper body. He shivered.

Virginia, not Afghanistan. His own bed, not the hard, sun-parched ground of Anbar province. There was no blood here. No death. No haunted, steel gray eyes staring at him.

Not while he was awake, at least. Not anymore. These days the flashbacks were less frequent, and only came when he was asleep.

He released a slow breath and blinked to clear his vision. Faint light filtered into his bedroom around the edges of the heavy blackout blinds he'd had installed on his windows. He could hear birds chirping from the branches of the cherry trees currently blooming out in front of the upscale apartment complex. The cheery sound did nothing to ease the leaden sensation in his chest.

Gradually his pulse slowed and the phantom images in his head faded. He lifted his head, aware of a slight soreness in his muscles, and tried to remember what he'd been doing last night. At the sickly sweet floral scent of a woman's perfume on his bedding and the sight of the empty condom wrappers on the bedside table, a wave of self-disgust washed over him.

Unfortunately, the once foreign sensation was becoming all too familiar these days.

He dropped his head back against the clammy pillowcase with a mental groan. Snippets of last night came back to him as he lay there staring at the ceiling fan, breathing in the cloying scent of the perfume. From the blonde he'd picked up last night at a club.

Hell, this had to stop. This time he couldn't remember her name, could barely even recall what she'd looked like, other than the shape of her curves under his hands, his body. And that wasn't even the worst part.

No, far worse was that he'd been stone cold sober when he'd brought her back here, and he still could barely remember anything about the encounter except that she'd liked using her teeth on him. And none too gently, either.

Letting out a weary breath, Nate scrubbed a hand over his sweaty face, wincing a little as his fingertips trailed down to a particularly tender spot on the side of his neck. Jesus, had she been trying to draw blood, or what? He was sure he'd find several more marks on him if he checked in the mirror before he got into the shower.

You weren't complaining last night.

Whatever her name was—Carly? Karen?—he vaguely recalled her leaving around three in the morning. She'd texted him her number soon after that, saying she'd love to see him again later today. But he wouldn't be calling her. He rarely called any of them once the night was over, and if he did, only to hook up for a few more days at most. At last count his current record was six straight days with the same woman before he'd left town on a training mission.

He hadn't told her where he was going, and he'd never contacted her again. He never told any of them that he was part of the FBI's Hostage Rescue Team, or even with the FBI at all, and not just for security reasons. Yeah, his issues ran way deeper than just the regular garden-variety paranoia that came with military training and being a combat vet. He'd spent years as a student in the school of hard knocks growing up, and that kind of upbringing left its mark on a person. Invisible scars no one else could see.

Shelving that uplifting thought, Nate pulled in a deep breath and glanced over at his bedside clock. Six-thirty a.m. In just ninety minutes he'd be with some of the guys and be able to breathe easier, relax and unwind, pretend everything was fine. It was so much easier to lie to himself when he wasn't alone.

With a groan he climbed out of bed and headed to the adjoining bathroom. He flipped on the light and yep, his suspicions were confirmed by a glance in the mirror. Half a dozen purplish teeth marks on his chest and stomach, a few on his arms and a big one on the side of his neck. He'd have to wear a collared shirt today when he went dirt biking with a few of his teammates, otherwise they'd ride him about it all day long. His extracurricular activities were an endless source of amusement for the guys these days.

Because they don't know the reason why you can't go more than a few days without hooking up with someone.

None of his teammates knew. Not yet, anyway, and

he was going to make sure they never figured it out. He was pretty sure they all thought he was just horny all the time, and that was fine by him. Well, everyone except Tuck, his team leader. Being former Delta, that guy didn't miss anything. Lately Nate had the increasingly uncomfortable feeling that Tuck knew something was off with him, even though he hadn't said anything.

The opening bars of AC/DC's *Hell's Bells* sounded from his bedroom, jerking him from his bleak thoughts. He rushed back to grab his phone from his dresser and answered Cruz's call with a brusque, "Hey."

"Hey, Dr. Feelgood," he said cheerfully. "You up and at 'em?"

Nate mentally winced at the nickname some of the guys had taken to calling him in recent weeks. "Yeah, what's up? Couldn't wait until eight to hear my voice, huh?"

Cruz snorted. "Keep on dreaming, man. Change of plans for today. Just got a call from the boss man. He wants us to report in ASAP. I told him I'd call you."

Nate frowned. His assault team was currently on a three month long support cycle, rather than on training or ops. So DeLuca wouldn't call them in on a Sunday morning unless something was up. "What's it about?"

"Dunno. Want me to swing by and get you on my way in?"

"Yeah, sure. Gimme ten to shower." Cruz lived just a few minutes' drive from him.

"You have another sleepover last night? I wouldn't want to show up too early and embarrass her." His teammate's voice was dry.

"I'm alone," Nate muttered, though his annoyance was mostly directed at himself. He'd more than earned his dubious reputation as a player. "See you when you get here." He disconnected and headed straight for the shower.

The hot water pounded over his back and shoulders as he scrubbed himself clean of last night: the blonde's scent, the sweat and the nightmare, everything. A sense of relief stole over him as he rubbed the soap into his wet skin. He felt cleaner, both inside and out.

Back in front of the mirror as he brushed his teeth, he paused when he glanced up at his reflection. What he saw there made him lower his toothbrush to the edge of the sink as sudden tension slid through his body.

Haunted, hazel eyes stared back at him, dark circles underneath. Physical proof that he hadn't been sleeping much lately. But it was the look in them that scared the shit out of him.

Gazing into the mirror now, for just a moment he saw his mother's eyes staring back at him.

It made him feel fucking ill.

He broke eye contact with the mirror and bent to spit the toothpaste into the sink before rinsing his mouth out and splashing cold water on his face for good measure. When he lifted his head and met his gaze once more, all traces of his mother were gone. The hollow sensation in his gut remained.

His mouth tightened. "I'm not her," he said to his reflection, the muscles in his arms and chest tensing under the strength of the denial crashing through him. "I'll never be like her."

You already are like her, his conscience whispered back.

God, was it true? Nate ran a hand down his face. He'd been telling himself he wasn't using the women he fucked, because he treated them well while they were with him and he always made sure they got off in bed. And he was always clear he was looking to hook up, nothing more.

The ugly truth was, though, in a way he *was* using them. Somewhere along the way they'd become his drug of choice to escape from what was happening inside him. He'd become a junkie, always looking for his next fix. Just like his mother.

No. No more, he vowed. He wasn't going to end up like her. He wouldn't piss away everything he'd fought for, the hard-won opportunities he'd earned.

Shaken, he dressed and went outside to wait for Cruz, needing air. The scent of freshly mowed grass and pavement damp from last night's rain greeted him. A silver SUV turned the corner at the end of the street and pulled up in front of him.

Nate slid into the shotgun seat and adjusted his sunglasses, glancing at the two to-go coffee cups resting in the console. "Hey, you shouldn't have," he said, taking one.

"I know," Cruz answered, shoulder checking before pulling away from the curb.

Nate took a sip of the hot coffee and hummed appreciatively. "Black, one sugar. You remembered."

A smirk pulled at Cruz's lips. "What can I say, I'm sentimental that way."

"So who else got called in, do you know?" he asked as Cruz headed for the highway.

"Vance and Tuck, I think."

Vance was Cruz's closest buddy. "But not the others?"

"Not that I know of."

Huh. "Wonder what's going on?"

"Guess we'll see soon enough."

When they arrived at Quantico they found Supervisory Special Agent Matt DeLuca in his office seated behind his desk, Tuck and Vance seated across from him. "Hey," their commander said. "Shut the door behind you."

Curious, Nate did as he was told then slid into a chair between Cruz and Vance while DeLuca pushed aside some paperwork and leaned back in his seat.

"As you guys may or may not already be aware, Nassar Qureshi's trial starts next week."

Taken off guard by the mention of the name, Nate went rigid, realizing belatedly that his hands had curled into fists.

Yeah, he was more than fucking aware of the upcoming trial. He'd been following the details carefully in the media since the bastard had been captured trying to enter the U.S. from Canada seven months ago. Evil sonofabitch hadn't been satisfied with his reign of terror in Afghanistan; he'd wanted to come wage jihad on U.S. soil. The DEA had picked him up during a drug bust just two weeks before the plot to blow up half of D.C. was supposed to be carried out.

Nate had just never imagined being involved with the trial in any way, but now it looked like his past and present were about to collide.

In the few seconds of silence that followed DeLuca's announcement, he was aware of both his commander and Tuck watching him. He forced himself to take a slow, even breath, uncurl his fingers to lie flat on the armrests.

"Given the number of supporters he's attracted here and abroad and all the media attention on this case, we've been tapped to provide extra security at the trial if necessary," DeLuca added.

"What about the others?" Nate asked, relieved that his voice sounded normal and didn't betray the way his heart rate had shot up. His three remaining teammates were involved as well.

DeLuca's green gaze cut to him. "They'll be briefed separately. You three," he pointed to him, Vance and Cruz, "are going to be working together if we get the call."

Nate and the other two looked at each other, Vance and Cruz appearing as surprised by the news as he was. It was rare for the team to be split up during an assignment.

DeLuca grabbed a couple of files from a pile on the corner of his desk. "We won't know for a few days yet, but let's go over the basics."

Nate's mind raced as DeLuca reviewed Qureshi's history. A rich Yemeni national who'd first funded AQAP before attending one of their training camps in eastern Africa and then going on to lead one of his own cells. Within a matter of a few years, he'd controlled millions of dollars' worth of equipment and called the shots on attacks throughout the Middle East and south Asia.

Including Afghanistan, where Nate had seen the results of his sick, sadistic work firsthand. It still had the power to make his gut twist.

The ghosts swirled in his mind again, making his heart pound and his palms clammy. He could hear the rattle of the AK fire they'd taken that day, see that last image of O'Neil alive in front of him, burned so clearly into his memory.

Nate shook it away, focused on what DeLuca was saying.

A few minutes later, after he'd outlined the charges Qureshi faced, DeLuca fell silent for a moment and arched a dark eyebrow at them. "Any questions?" When no one said anything, he nodded. "Cruz and Vance, you're dismissed."

Nate froze in the act of rising from his chair and met DeLuca's gaze. Not him or Tuck?

DeLuca indicated him and Tuck with a jerk of his chin. "You two stay."

Ignoring Cruz's and Vance's questioning looks, Nate lowered his weight back into the chair, a sense of foreboding sweeping over him. When the door shut behind Cruz, Nate spoke. "Something wrong?"

"Not exactly." DeLuca shifted his gaze to Tuck. Nate followed suit, watching his team leader study him for a long moment.

"Tell me straight, Nate. You up for this?" Tuck asked.

Nate nodded, heart knocking against his ribs. "Yeah, of course."

Tuck shared another glance with DeLuca before focusing back on him, and Nate's stomach muscles grabbed. "We reviewed the latest evaluation reports last week."

Oh, shit. His most recent psych eval had been in there.

Nate kept his expression blank, but inside he was panicking. What had the results said? Had he not been able to cover up what was happening to him?

"What's going on with you lately?" DeLuca asked calmly.

Nate automatically shook his head. "Nothing. Nothing's going on."

Reaching over to grab a folder from the pile at the side of his desk, DeLuca dropped it in front of him. "This evaluation says otherwise." He tilted his head, his relaxed expression and tone making it clear that this wasn't an accusation. He was willing to give Nate the benefit of the doubt, no matter what the Bureau shrinks said about him. "I wanna know what you think."

"What does it say?" He couldn't help the defensive note to his tone. Thankfully his commander didn't take offense.

"It says you've been pulling off an Oscar worthy performance to bury whatever shit's going on in your head."

Nate swallowed as a flash of panic swept through him. They couldn't sideline him by taking him off active duty. The team, the guys, were everything to him. They were his family, the only family he had, and he'd die for every last one of them. If DeLuca pulled him… "I don't—"

"Stop. Before you insult us by lying to our faces," Tuck interrupted, his expression flat, "anyone looking at you can tell you're not sleeping, and I'm betting that's just the tip of the iceberg. Am I right?"

He couldn't get pulled from the team. "I'm…" What? *Fucked up and trying everything I know to hide it.*

"Tell me you've at least been talking to someone about whatever's going on," DeLuca said quietly.

Nate pulled in a deep breath and exhaled it slowly. He hated to admit that he needed help, but even he'd realized he couldn't beat this by himself. "Yeah. I've been seeing a therapist for a couple weeks now. Privately." He'd paid for it on his own dime strictly because he'd wanted to avoid the Bureau's shrinks and having it wind up on his permanent record.

"And?" DeLuca prodded.

God, this was humiliating. DeLuca had been a decorated Marine Scout/Sniper for years before joining the FBI, making the HRT and rising to command it. And Tuck, shit, the guy had served with Delta for years before coming here, becoming team leader within two years of making the HRT.

They'd both served multiple combat tours in Iraq and Afghanistan. Both had dealt with serious personal shit in the past few years. DeLuca had lost his wife and Tuck had lost his dad. On top of that, they'd both recently gone through scary shit with the women they loved, yet they were both functioning fine.

What the fuck was wrong with Nate that he couldn't deal with his own shit, which was minor by comparison? It made him feel weak. He hated it. "And…I'm working on it," was all he could say.

DeLuca gave him a level look. "You're being straight with whoever it is? Full disclosure?"

Nate hesitated. "I've only seen her a few times." And no, he hadn't been a hundred percent truthful with her about his unresolved issues so far. He'd been working up to that.

DeLuca sighed. "That's not cutting it, is it?"

He didn't know what to say to that, except, "Look, I'm dealing with it." He frowned at his commander, unable to shake the worry inside him. Had he messed up somewhere and not realized it? "Have my performance scores slipped? Have any of the guys said I'm not cutting it—"

"If any of the guys had complaints about you, you'd have heard it from me a long time before now," DeLuca said. "Your test scores and evaluated performance are all solid, except for this." He tapped the psych eval in front of him.

When Nate didn't say anything else, DeLuca leaned forward, placing his forearms on his desk. "Look, I'm well aware of what's in your personal file, and I know what tomorrow's date signifies for you."

April second. A day that would haunt him until the day he died.

DeLuca's expression softened. "Look, it's understandable that things would get tougher around the anniversary of something like that. Ever since my wife died, every year I dread the Fourth of July, and I probably always will. I get it, and all of us know what PTSD looks and feels like. That's not my issue here. What I need to know is whether you or any of my guys are at increased risk by having you beside them on an op right now."

"They're not." The words came automatically out of his tight throat. He was desperate for DeLuca to believe him. "I would never let anything distract me on the job. I'd never do anything to jeopardize one of the guys. If I didn't think I could handle myself out there, I'd come to you and pull myself before putting any of them at risk. You gotta know that." He stared at his commander, willing him to believe it.

DeLuca glanced over at Tuck. "Your team. Your call."

Tuck held Nate's gaze for a moment, then gave a satisfied nod. "Okay."

Nate blinked. Okay? Just like that? They must know he had every reason to lie just to safeguard his position on the team.

Tuck shrugged. "Like Matt said, your scores are solid. I haven't seen anything in your performance that concerns me in regard to the team's welfare. But I am concerned about you, Nate. We're family here, yeah?"

Nate nodded. "Yeah."

"And so we look after each other like family. We look after our own. But whatever's going on with you, you need to deal with that shit immediately, understand? I'd hate like hell to lose you, you're one of the best assets on this team, but I won't hesitate to pull you if I think for even one second that you're a liability. I've gotta be clear about that."

Relief flooded him. He nodded again. "I understand."

"Good." Tuck's gaze shifted to DeLuca. "Gonna tell him the rest?"

The rest? Nate watched as DeLuca pulled a different file from the pile and dropped it atop the psych eval. "This is the other reason I wanted the others to leave," he said, and opened the folder.

Nate leaned forward as DeLuca turned the papers around and pushed them toward him.

"I said we'd potentially be called in for added security at the trial. What I didn't say is that we'd be pulling protective service detail for some of the key witnesses. Here's the list of potential candidates."

Nate scanned the list of names. A few were vaguely familiar. Then he came to one near the bottom and his heart careened in his chest.

Unbidden, her face flashed into his head, her gunmetal-gray stare locked onto him, piercing his soul. The face he'd been struggling to forget these past five years.

Taya Kostas.

Chapter Two

One week later

*Y*ou'll be just fine, sweetheart. You'll be glad when
all this is behind you.

Taya kept her father's parting words firmly
in mind as she gathered her carry-on items from beneath
the seat in front of her. Being "glad" to have this behind
her once and for all was an understatement. And yeah, she
would be fine. She was a different person now, stronger
than she'd ever been and ready to face this on her own.

More than anything, she wanted this final chapter of
her nightmare over with so she could go home to take care
of her father and truly be free for the first time in five
years.

"You ready?" the federal marshal who'd
accompanied her from Raleigh asked beside her. He
hadn't said much since showing up at her father's place
that morning, where she'd been staying for the past few
weeks during his convalescence.

Don't really have a choice, do I? "Yes."

Already her hands were growing damp and her heart was beginning to beat faster. She had an aisle seat because it lessened her sense of claustrophobia, but being wedged in such a tight place with all her fellow airplane passengers as they waited to deplane wasn't her favorite thing. She'd worked long and hard the past several years to conquer the anxiety disorder she'd developed during her time in captivity. It hadn't been easy—it *still* wasn't easy to control her innate reaction to stressful situations. But she wasn't going to let it stop her from doing what needed to be done.

Gearing up for another round of stress at being stuck in a crowd, Taya took a steadying breath and let it out slowly before ducking out into the narrow aisle behind the marshal. Once she got out into the airport waiting lounge it was better, but being surrounded by noise and people in this kind of setting was never going to be easy for her after what she'd been through.

Stay centered. Just breathe.

Traveling across North America and even Europe for speaking engagements on behalf of Amnesty International had severely pushed the boundaries of her comfort zone enough. What she was here to do in D.C. was a whole other ballgame, and it had her stomach twisted into a giant knot.

The marshal—Rick Duncan—stayed right at her side as they walked through the terminal. His left hand lifted to his ear and tapped, activating the earpiece he wore. "Package is on its way," he murmured. "We just left the waiting lounge."

Taya hurried alongside him, taking comfort from his presence even though being referred to as the "package" made her uneasy. She had some lingering trust issues with government employees because of what she'd been through, but Duncan had been thoroughly vetted and introduced to her by his boss before this assignment, so that helped ease her mind. He was dressed in jeans and a collared shirt so he didn't stand out, the shoulder holster he wore concealed by his dark jacket. The way he moved and the way he kept scanning their surroundings made it obvious he was highly trained and taking her safety seriously.

God, she was so sick and tired of having to look over her shoulder everywhere she went, needing guards to accompany her whenever she traveled. But she wasn't stupid. She didn't have a death wish, either, so when the Department of Justice had assigned federal marshals to act as bodyguards on this trip, she hadn't argued.

"You need a pit stop before we move downstairs?" he asked without looking at her.

"No, I'm good." She just wanted to get to the hotel and prepare for her meeting with the prosecution in a couple hours.

He nodded. "All right, just stay close."

Duncan stepped in front of her, acting as a human battering ram to make a path for them through a crowd at a bottleneck in the terminal. Taya stayed within a half step of him, willing her heart to slow down as the wall of people closed around them, making it seem harder to breathe all of a sudden. It had been crowded like this that day in Kabul. She'd been there on a short assignment with the Red Cross and had gone to the U.S. embassy to file some paperwork.

When the gunmen had burst in and taken her captive, she'd been thrown into a living nightmare instead.

You're fine. You're fine.

She focused on drawing even breaths, the past few years of relentless meditation and other calming exercises allowing her to stop her busy mind from spiraling out of control and into full-blown anxiety.

Duncan pushed through the large knot of people, got them into the clear, and picked up speed. Taya held her head high and lengthened her stride to keep up. She wasn't a victim anymore, she was a survivor, and damn proud of it. Her father had wanted to come with her, to lend moral support and be a familiar face in what would no doubt be a packed courtroom once she took the stand, but she'd refused to let him. He was only six weeks post heart attack and though she knew he'd do anything to help her, the stress would only set back his recovery. She wanted him home and safe, as relaxed as possible.

He and her brother, Kevin, were the only reason she'd declined to enter the WITSEC program after returning to the States. She'd insisted Kev look after their father while she was gone. This was hard to do alone, but it had to be done. She was testifying not only for herself, but on behalf of the others who had suffered at Qureshi's hand. People who hadn't been as fortunate as her during her captivity. And others who hadn't survived the rescue attempt.

Like Hassan.

All these years later, Taya still had deep and conflicting feelings about him. He'd treated her well, at least when compared to the other kidnapped women handed out to Qureshi's men. Given the risks he'd taken to get her out, he deserved justice as much as she and the others did. Whether their suffering was by Qureshi's own hand or through others acting on his orders, didn't matter. As a key witness for the prosecution, her testimony would be a critical part in getting the terrorist convicted. And hopefully result in him getting the death penalty.

Rounding the corner, the escalators leading to baggage claim came into view. Duncan pulled his phone out of his pocket, gave the screen a cursory glance before tucking it away. "Everybody's in place and waiting for us. We'll have you out of here in no time."

She appreciated their professionalism, and that he seemed to understand her unease of being out in the open in this kind of environment. The airport was safe, but the embassy in Kabul should have been a safe place for her too, and it hadn't been. "Okay."

She already knew they wouldn't be stopping at baggage claim. Someone else would wait for her suitcase and bring it to her hotel later on. Once she and Duncan got downstairs to meet the two other marshals assigned to her detail she'd be taken straight out to a waiting vehicle parked at the curb. From there her security team would drive her to her hotel downtown, where she'd meet with the prosecution team.

Duncan slanted her a grin, the change in his remote expression making him look years younger than the late thirties she'd had him pegged at. "You've been a champ so far," he said, a note of approval in his voice.

"Well, I'm tougher than I look." Lucky for her.

"I have no doubt about that," he murmured, his alert gaze moving back and forth, scanning the area around them while they kept their brisk pace toward the escalator. When they reached it, Duncan put a hand on the middle of her back and set her in front of him. "They're over at the far left, against the wall at the bottom. Both wearing jeans and leather jackets," he murmured so only she could hear. "See them?"

She spotted the two men, who were dividing their attention between the escalator and the people in the baggage claim area. "Yes."

"One will lead the way outside and the other will follow us."

"Okay." She felt perfectly calm as they descended the rest of the way. Three trained, armed men were watching out for her. Even if someone was looking for or following her, they'd never get close enough to be a threat.

As they reached the bottom of the escalator, the blond marshal glanced their way before pushing away from the wall and heading for the door. Taya followed, noting when the brown-haired marshal stepped out behind Duncan.

People swirled around her but she didn't look at any of them, focused instead on the agent in the lead. She saw his lips move and knew he was speaking via his earpiece to whoever was waiting for them outside. At the automatic sliding doors out front, he paused. Taya stopped a step behind him.

On the other side of the door, a group of five people were heading toward them. The man in the lead was carrying what looked like a guitar case over one shoulder while juggling a heavy suitcase and carryon bag.

A bronze-skinned man at the back of the group suddenly stepped out to pass by the slower passengers. Then his gaze locked on Taya.

His eyes lit with recognition. A ripple of unease shot through her.

She stared back at him, frozen, barely aware of Duncan's strong hand closing over her right shoulder.

Before she could move, the blond marshal veered in front of her. The bronze-skinned man's face tightened. He rammed his shoulder into the passenger carrying the guitar case, causing it to swing around, knocking over its owner and making the others around him trip. The man's dark eyes stayed glued to her.

Taya took a step back, instinctively started to whirl. In her peripheral she caught the flash of a weapon appear in the man's hand.

"Gun!"

Duncan's shout reverberated in her ears as he tackled her to the ground. Her elbows and knees took the brunt of the impact on the hard, cool tile. Frightened cries rose around them. She caught a flurry of movement ahead of her as the other two marshals tackled the man with the gun.

Pop, pop, pop.

Three shots rang out in rapid succession. The blond marshal screamed and grabbed his thigh, his body tangled with the attacker. Blood pumped out from beneath his hands, flowing onto the granite floor while his partner smashed his fist into the gunman's face. Panic erupted around them.

People screamed and started running, some diving to the floor and covering their heads. A mother lay curled over her young son outside the automatic doors, her terrified gaze locked on the gunman as the wounded marshal lurched up to help his fellow agent subdue the shooter.

"Come on," Duncan barked at her. He lifted up just enough to grab her beneath the armpits and started dragging her over to the far wall. Taya scrambled to her feet and ran with him, her heart pounding an erratic rhythm against her ribs. A second later he had her flattened against the wall, shielding her with his body as he relayed rapid-fire updates to someone about what was going on.

Her legs began to shake. It was just like the embassy all over again.

But there were no more shots, no more gunmen storming the building. Duncan pulled her back toward the escalators. She risked a peek around his shoulder.

People were either huddled on the floor or running away from the doors, some shouting. Security officers rushed toward the attacker. He was still fighting the marshals, screaming garbled words as they pinned him down and kicked the weapon from his grasp. It skidded away from them. Blood slicked the tiled floor, covering the man's hands, his chest. At least one of those shots had come from the marshals.

"Team's about to storm the entrance," Duncan warned her, the solid grip on her upper arm propelling her to move faster.

From across the room the man's dark stare snagged on Taya. Her steps faltered. His eyes were glazed with pain, burning with hatred. She stared back at him, frozen, heart drumming in her ears. Who was he?

His movements faded and his voice grew weaker, carrying through the brittle silence filling the air. It took a moment for his words to penetrate the haze of fear fogging her brain.

He was speaking in Pashto, the language of her captors in Afghanistan.

You will still die, American whore!

The words slammed into her like a sledgehammer, and her blood went cold.

Four well-built men burst through the automatic doors, weapons drawn and trained on the gunman. More marshals, probably the ones who'd been waiting outside with the vehicle.

Standing over the attacker, now immobilized on his stomach with both arms wrenched behind his back, one of them looked up at Duncan and nodded.

"Let's go," he bit out, his fingers curling around her upper arm in a hard grip as he rushed back toward the escalator. Taya's shoes pounded over the tile.

Airport security guards were converging on them now from all directions. One of them raced over to them, listened while Duncan showed his ID and explained who she was, then escorted them to a side entrance.

Duncan shoved the release bar and stayed her with an upraised palm while he ducked outside, weapon in hand. Once he'd verified it was clear he reached back to grab her by the arm and push her toward the black SUV with tinted windows idling at the curb. "Get in."

The right rear door popped open. Taya ran for it, scrambled across the seat a second before Duncan jumped in beside her and slammed the door. "Go," he ordered curtly.

The driver shot away from the curb and drove toward the front of the terminal, only to slow in the snarl of traffic out front. Emergency vehicles were already on scene and she could hear sirens approaching in the distance. Taya swallowed as the SUV neared the door where the shooter was, hands clasped tightly in her lap. Duncan had his weapon in his hand and he was watching around them like he half expected another shooter to materialize out of the crowd.

The driver stopped when a uniformed cop blocked their way. He showed his ID and the cop waved them through. "To the hotel?" he asked Duncan as he drove past the terminal.

"Not yet." Duncan swiveled in his seat to scan behind them. "Drive south for a while first, then double back. I want to make sure no one's following us."

Shaken, Taya couldn't help looking out the rear window. Was someone else out there, coming after her too? Her throat was dry, tight.

"Got it."

The SUV picked up speed as they cleared the terminal, leaving the chaos behind. Taya darted a glance at Duncan, who was frowning as he dialed someone on his phone. "What about the other marshal, is he—"

"Medics are already treating him on scene, he'll be okay." He paused in dialing to meet her gaze. "Feds are coming to secure the scene. Did you recognize that guy?"

Taya shook her head. "No." But she'd never forget his face or the look in his eyes. Pure hatred.

She wrapped her arms around herself, suddenly chilled to the bone. *It's not like last time. You're okay.*

Except the nightmare just kept following her. Sometimes it felt like she'd never escape it.

She clenched her jaw to keep her teeth from chattering. Who the hell was that guy, and how had he known she was flying into Dulles this afternoon? He'd come to shoot her down in cold blood. He had to be connected to Qureshi somehow, or at least the trial.

Her story had been in the media again lately because of it. The unwanted attention was proving to be yet another threat to her security. That man had to have known she'd be here with federal protection. Which meant he'd clearly been willing to die for the chance to kill her. The realization sent a fresh wave of cold through her.

"How did he even find me?" she said when she trusted her voice.

"No idea," Duncan muttered. He put the phone to his ear, his expression grim. "But I know someone who can find out." He spoke to someone for a few minutes, giving a condensed version of what had just happened. "Yessir. I'll stay with her in the meantime." After ending the call he looked over at her. "That was my boss. They're sending some Feds to the hotel to meet with you. Gonna beef up your security detail for the remainder of your time here in D.C. I'll stay with you until they get everything set up."

Turning to stare out her window at the passing scenery, Taya wondered if she'd ever feel truly safe again.

****

Ayman Tuma checked his phone messages as he gathered his mail from the apartment building's mailroom. He'd just gotten off work.

There was a call from his mother, asking him when he would be able to come over for dinner. One from his eldest sister, asking him the same. He erased both of those and listened to the third and final message—from a contact here in D.C. The call he'd been waiting on for the past five days.

"I've found what you've been looking for," the man said in heavily accented Arabic. "Gets in to Dulles this afternoon at one-twenty. I'm meeting her."

Ayman jerked his left arm up to check his watch. Damn. He'd missed the chance to be part of the welcoming committee by almost two hours.

Ignoring the three other people at the mailboxes— just as they ignored him—he turned and jogged up the stairs to the fourth floor, since the derelict apartment's elevator was broken yet again. At the end of the hall he turned left and unlocked the door of the third apartment from the end.

The traffic noise here was loud and the living space was in bad shape, but it was only a few blocks' walk from the Italian restaurant he worked at where he made enough to split the rent with his roommate, Jaleel. His parents weren't happy about him moving out on his own two months ago—they worried he would get into trouble. One more reason why he needed space from them.

They were right to be concerned. Ever since moving out he'd been training with Darwish, a lethal operative of The Brethren. The ironic part was that he hadn't become "radicalized" until he'd come to America. He was now an expert shot, knew how to handle explosives and was good at hand-to-hand combat. Darwish had taken him out on several operations already and deemed Ayman ready to begin hunting targets.

Ayman couldn't wait for the opportunity. He was nineteen years old, a full-grown man who no longer had to answer to his father, even if his family didn't see him that way. His father had dragged Ayman, his mother and two sisters here three years ago to escape the constant warfare in Syria, and Ayman hated it.

They'd come here, to America, a place Ayman despised, because his father insisted it was the best move to provide opportunity for his children. Instead, they'd all been reduced to taking menial jobs that paid only minimum wage, and subjected to a cost of living that ate up every cent they earned. It didn't matter that they all spoke passable English or that all but his mother and youngest sister had gone to college back home.

They'd gone from a life of affluence and respect in their homeland to becoming yet another poor immigrant family in the land of "liberty". Everyone thought America was a beacon of hope and prosperity, but Ayman knew that was all bullshit.

The only opportunity he'd found since coming here was through his mosque, meeting like-minded people who were sick and tired of letting the United States call the shots. It sickened him that he had to live here, in the very country that had declared war on Islam and had killed hundreds of thousands of Muslims around the world with their constant meddling.

Something had to be done, and Ayman was determined to be a part of the answer. Though he hated to cause shame for his parents, he wouldn't back out now. This was his chance to make something of himself and even the score against the country that had given him and his fellow Muslims nothing but misery. He stood to make a good bit of coin, too. If he pulled off this job he'd get a hundred thousand dollars deposited into his account, from an offshore company filled by donations from supporters of The Brethren around the world.

The hot, cramped apartment smelled musty and of last night's fish dinner that Jaleel had cooked on the hotplate. All the threadbare blinds were pulled over the windows, creating deceptively cooling shadows. He shut the door and strode to where the ancient TV sat in the corner of the main room. The tattered, stained couch cushions sagged beneath his weight as he sank onto them and turned on the news. They couldn't afford cable but using his tech skills Jaleel had been able to piggyback a connection from the apartment below them.

The breaking news headline was at the bottom of the screen, and he recognized Dulles airport in the background.

Gunman killed in apparent suicide attack at Dulles International, it read.

Ayman shoved upright and stared at the screen, heart pounding as the reporter detailed what had happened. FBI agents were on scene to investigate and the airport was still on lockdown. The lone gunman had been killed by security agents.

Lone gunman? There should have been others. At least three more, from what Ayman had heard. Even though Ayman hadn't known the dead man personally, he felt a pang of sadness and said a silent prayer for him. *Peace be upon you, my brother. May Allah welcome you into paradise with your fellow warriors.*

The reporter droned on and on about what was happening at the airport. All outgoing flights had been suspended, and all incoming ones grounded until further notice. Ayman shook his head in annoyance. Who cared? What about the woman the gunman had gone there to kill?

After five more minutes and no mention whatsoever of any other casualties besides one security agent, Ayman got his answer. She was still alive.

He shut off the TV and rubbed a hand over his face. Now what? Ayman had memorized everything from the file The Brethren had assembled about her. His network had been plotting Taya Kostas's death for weeks now, and even with the help of an insider their attempt had failed. They'd held off on targeting her until she arrived in D.C. for the trial, wanting to coordinate the attack as close to the others as possible.

We should have killed her when she was vulnerable at home.

The burner phone he'd picked up two days ago rang

in his pocket, startling him. He was surprised to see the number on his display. The elders had never contacted him directly before. "Hello?"

"Did you hear?" the man, an elder at his mosque, asked in Arabic.

"Yes. Just." He pushed out a frustrated breath. "What do you want to do now?"

Mahmoud gave an impatient grunt. "Find her and the others. We already know where both men and one of the women are. Now that the whore is in the city it will be even easier to find her."

"But now they'll have more security on her," Ayman pointed out. Federal agents.

"That doesn't matter. Our people aren't afraid to do what must be done, regardless of the threat. Unless...*you're* afraid?"

Ayman frowned at the man's tone, the threatening edge to it. Mahmoud was not a man who took disappointment well. Ayman was fully prepared to take this on and had no intention of crossing him. "I'm not afraid."

"Good. Find her. Let me know when you do."

The line went dead. Ayman set the phone down on the battered table in front of the sofa. So The Brethren had already located both male witnesses—both former mujahedin who had fought with and then for Qureshi before betraying him. They'd agreed to testify against him to spare their lives after the Americans had captured them in a massive raid in New York State a few months ago.

Mahmoud had said they knew where one of the other women was too. All witnesses' days were numbered now, just as the whore's were. Ayman and the others were all acting on direct orders from Qureshi himself, funneled through his network from the high security prison he was in, and his instructions were clear. Kill the people who would dare to testify against him in the upcoming trial, and free him at any cost.

Ayman was skilled with weapons, but he needed help on this one.

He got up and grabbed his thrift store leather jacket on the way out the door. His feet ached after a ten-hour shift at the restaurant but he had to begin hunting and he couldn't do it alone. He'd go to Darwish for assistance and have Jaleel use his hacking skills to find out where the whore was staying in the city.

That American bitch had been married to the traitor who had cost Qureshi everything. He was long dead of course, ironically killed by his own at the end, in a friendly fire incident during the botched rescue attempt five years ago.

His widow was unfortunately still alive, but not for long. She would pay dearly for daring to speak against Ayman's hero.

Chapter Three

N ate entered the hotel lobby and strode straight for the stairs, unwilling to lose even the few seconds it would cost him to wait for the elevator. He held his phone to his ear as he jogged up the first flight, anxious to get an answer. Even still, he was somewhat surprised when Celida Morales, the FBI investigator engaged to Tuck, answered after only one ring.

"I'm kind of in the middle of something here, Schroder," she told him, her voice dry.

"I'm on my way up," he said without preamble.

A surprised pause filled the line. "Did DeLuca assign you to her?"

"No." Not officially, anyway. "But he assigned Cruz and Vance. They're on their way over."

"Okay. I'll tell security you guys are coming."

She disconnected without asking anything else and he was glad, because he didn't know how to explain himself without sounding crazy. Being here probably wasn't the best idea, but right now he didn't give a shit about protocol.

When the story about the shooting at the airport had

broken, he'd been on the treadmill at the gym. The details coming in had been sketchy and he wouldn't have thought much of the incident except Taya's flight had been due in shortly before the incident had taken place. He knew exactly what time her plane had touched down, because he'd checked online.

Immediately he'd shut down the machine and called DeLuca. Within fifteen minutes his CO had called him back with the response he'd been dreading—Taya had been targeted. She was unhurt at least, and that's the only thing that kept him sane as he raced up to the seventh floor.

Outside her room, two agents wearing FBI windbreakers stood flanking the door. One of them called out to him, hand resting on the weapon holstered at his hip. "Show me your ID."

Nate slowed his pace a little and held out his open wallet, showing his badge and ID. "Special Agent Nate Schroder. Agent Morales is expecting me."

The guy who had called out to him gestured for him to approach. When he got a good look at the ID, he nodded. "Go ahead." He stepped aside while Nate moved in front of the door and knocked twice.

Inside he could hear faint voices and his heart thudded hard against his ribs as he waited. Taya was in there. The first time he'd ever seen her was that morning long ago at dawn, when he and the rest of the quick reaction force had rendezvoused with Hassan, the man they'd been tasked to go in and rescue from hostile forces. They'd been told he might have his wife in tow, but nothing else.

Nate would never forget his shock when he'd seen her frail form struggling toward them over the harsh terrain. When she'd finally removed the veil of her Burqa he'd been stunned to see her fair skin and gray eyes, hear the pure American accent with just a hint of the South in her voice.

An American woman, held captive for many months by Qureshi. Married off to Hassan against her will.

It still filled him with fury.

The rescue op had been a total disaster, to say the least. But she'd survived. He'd worried about her afterward, thought about her way more often than he should have ever since. As incredible as it seemed, in just a few seconds he'd be seeing her face-to-face for the first time in five years.

The door swung open to reveal Celida standing in the threshold. She was dressed in her usual business attire, signaling she was here as an investigator rather than in a security capacity—a gray pencil skirt and suit jacket. Stepping back to let him inside, she raised one dark brow, the scar from a bullet graze on her right cheek pulling slightly with the movement. "Hey. Care to tell me what this is all about?" she asked in a low voice as she shut the door behind him.

Nate looked past her toward the back of the suite. From the entryway he couldn't see who was there. But with Taya literally just feet away from him now, seeing her was all he could focus on.

"Nate."

Celida's tone was calm, but it was definitely a command. He wasn't getting past her to see Taya until he explained himself. And if it had been anyone else but her, he knew he wouldn't have even gotten inside the room, HRT member or not. He shifted his gaze to her and drew a deep breath. "I know her."

She nodded and folded her arms. "I gathered that. How?"

Her not knowing surprised him. "Tuck didn't say anything to you?"

"No. You know how he is with that kind of thing. If he considers it someone's private business, then that's the way it stays."

Yeah, that sounded like Tuck. And that strong sense of integrity was just another reason why Nate admired the guy.

Celida was going to find out about the botched rescue op soon anyway, once she started digging into Taya's past more. He'd rather give her the abbreviated version in his own words. "I was part of a CSAR mission five years ago, back when I was still in the Air Force. She was one of the principals we were sent in to extract." Sounded so tidy and benign when he worded it like that.

She searched his eyes for a moment before speaking. "Is that it?"

"No," he admitted. "There's more." The official version was far less pretty, and if he knew Celida, she'd be looking into it as soon as she left the hotel.

"And it's personal," she guessed, narrowing her eyes in suspicion.

He nodded, not bothering to deny it.

"She must be pretty important to you, given the way you raced up here. Have you had contact with her since the op?"

"Not really. A couple e-mails here and there for a bit. But I haven't talked to her since I joined the FBI." Four years ago now. He'd stopped communicating because he'd thought it was for the best, for both of them. Given the traumatic circumstances of their ordeal behind enemy lines together, he'd wanted to prevent either of them from forming an unhealthy psychological attachment to the other.

You mean you were afraid the feelings you had for her were as fucked up as you are, a snide voice in his head whispered.

Celida nodded thoughtfully, oblivious to his inner turmoil. Or maybe not. "Okay. So if you haven't talked to her in years and you're not here as part of her detail, why exactly do you want to see her?"

Good question. He was wrestling with the answer to that himself. All he knew was that he'd never met a woman like Taya, and that no one had ever affected him as much as she had. A dozen different emotions swirled inside him as he thought of how to answer. Guilt, grief, loneliness. And...a yearning he'd failed to conquer. "I just need to see her."

Her interest sharpened. "Let me guess, it's complicated?"

"Yeah." Very. "Look, I just want to see her. To make sure she's okay. She's been through a lot already." More than anyone should have to endure, let alone a female civilian who'd survived the kind of hell she had. God, she was amazing, to rise above what life had dished out to her.

Celida's expression softened a little and she sighed. "Understood. All right, wait here. I'll check if she's okay with seeing you."

Nate kept his mouth shut as she left him. He understood and agreed with the protocol, but it had never even occurred to him that Taya might not want to see him. If she didn't, he'd have to leave. And then he'd go nuts.

He heard female voices murmuring around the corner. A minute later, Celida reappeared. "All right, you can go ahead." She gestured for him to follow her.

Letting out a relieved breath he hadn't even realized he'd been holding, Nate strode for the back room, bracing himself for the sight of the woman who'd haunted him for the past five years. He could hear a man speaking in the other room, and when he rounded the corner was unsurprised to find Agent Greg Travers sitting there. The middle-aged agent turned in his seat and acknowledged him with a nod but Nate barely glanced at him.

He stopped in the threshold, his gaze immediately locking on the woman across the room. Long, dark brown curls, bronze skin, gray eyes. Seeing Taya again was like a punch to the diaphragm. In that instant the five-year gap since he'd last seen her fell away, leaving his heart raw and bleeding.

A weird sensation filled his chest, as if his lungs were suddenly both empty and yet too full at the same time.

"Nathan!" Her face lit up, her eyes wide with what seemed like delight as she shot out of her chair and started toward him.

Nate had only a second to steel himself before she was right there in front of him in a long, stretchy blue dress that hugged curves he couldn't help but admire, and reached her arms up to twine around his neck. Ignoring everyone else, unable to stop himself, Nate wrapped his arms around her back and hugged her. Hard.

Oh, Christ.

He struggled to hide his reaction but the feel of her in his embrace after all this time was almost too much. He closed his eyes for a moment, fighting back the painful tide of memories rushing at him, and allowed himself to breathe her in. The sweet scent of cinnamon and vanilla filled his nostrils. Her curls pressed against his cheek as she rested her face in the hollow of his throat, her breath hot against his skin.

God. Nate breathed in deeply, feeling almost dizzy. She was warm and soft and so damn *vibrant* compared to the last time he'd seen her. She'd filled out since he'd last seen her too, her body now at a much healthier weight. Having those womanly curves pressed tight to him filled him with a peace he hadn't experienced since that final day on the CSAR op when his world had changed forever.

All too soon she unlocked her arms from around his neck and eased back to stare up at him. Nate let her go, stuffing his hands into his jeans pockets so he wouldn't be tempted to reach out and touch her smooth cheek. He wanted so badly to trace his fingertips along the thin scars marking the left side of her jaw that extended halfway down her neck. He knew there were more on her back, her ribs, and down her arm. And there wasn't a day that went by when he didn't think about what had put them there.

Taya smiled up at him, tiny laugh lines creasing the skin at the outer corners of both eyes. He thought they were endearing, and hoped she'd had lots to smile about since he'd last talked to her. "What are you doing here?" she asked.

He couldn't stop drinking in the sight of her. "I live down in Quantico. When I heard about what happened at the airport, I made a call to find out where you were and drove straight here."

Her smile disappeared as quickly as it had formed and he felt bad for mentioning the airport attack. "Oh. You're with the FBI now?"

He nodded and searched her eyes, unable to look away from that penetrating gray gaze. She had seriously beautiful eyes. "You look great, but are you all right?"

"Yeah, I'm okay." She lowered her gaze. "Just a bit shaken up."

"No kidding." He glanced at Celida, who was now standing beside Travers. Both of them were watching him with interest. He could all but hear the gears in Celida's clever head turning, trying to piece together the mystery of what had happened to him and Taya on that fateful CSAR mission.

He shifted his focus back to Taya, doing his damnedest not to stare when all he wanted to do was drink her in. "Here, sit." He gestured toward her chair.

He took the one across the glass coffee table from her, leaving Celida to sit beside Travers. Taya had a plate of fruit and a bottle of water in front of her but he noticed she hadn't touched either. He spoke to Celida. "Have you talked about her security team yet?"

"Briefly." She watched him a second longer before clearing her throat and addressing Taya. "We've gone over the most important things we needed from you already. Agent Travers and I have other sources to look into, and considering your security team's on its way here and Nate knows both guys personally, I think we'll leave you two to catch up for a little bit. Your meeting with the prosecution is still scheduled for five. You okay with all that?"

"Yes, that's fine," Taya answered, her voice and demeanor completely calm despite what she'd been through little more than an hour ago. That air of tranquility she projected was damn near spellbinding.

He'd seen glimpses of it before, during the long, grueling days when they'd been awaiting rescue deep in enemy territory. Even back then, when she should have been at her worst, Nate had recognized that stoic inner core she drew from. Looking at her now, it was even more evident. How the hell had she managed that with everything she'd gone through?

Celida murmured something to Travers, who was still staring at Nate, then gave him a nod and left. Travers followed a moment later, leaving him alone with Taya.

Watching her across the small table, Nate set his palms on his thighs. "So what happened today?" he asked, strung too tight inside at the moment to even attempt small talk. He knew the main details of the attack but he wanted to hear it from her point of view.

"Whoever the shooter was, he wanted *me*," she replied, one hand picking at the fruit before her. "He was looking right at me and yelling in Pashto. He shot one of the marshals who was there to meet me." She met his eyes again. "Agent Morales told me he's going to be okay, but the shooter died. They didn't get the chance to question him."

Nate nodded. That was pretty much the story he'd been told too. "But you're okay?" Of all people, she knew she didn't need to pretend with him.

"I'm okay." She didn't look away from him as she said it, didn't fidget or give some other "tell" that indicated she was lying. But while Nate could see she was physically okay, he knew emotionally it was impossible. That attack had to have dredged up memories of the hell she'd lived through already. There was no way it couldn't have.

He spread his fingers out, gripped his lower quads. "I'm sorry it happened at all, but you'll be safe now. The guys assigned to be your security detail are two of the best, and they'll make sure nothing happens to you. And after today, security surrounding this whole trial will be tightened even more."

That steel gray gaze of hers traveled over his face, his chest, down to where his fingers dug into his thighs, then back up. "How long have you been with the FBI?"

"A few years."

"And the guys coming to guard me—how do you know them?"

"I work with them."

She gave him a measuring stare before continuing. "Agent Morales said they'd be FBI SWAT members. But something tells me they're not regular SWAT members, are they?" She tilted her head slightly, her expression curious. "And I don't think you are, either."

There was no reason to lie to her and she already knew exactly what his background and skillset was, since she'd seen him in the field firsthand. He couldn't help but smile at her perceptiveness. "No, you're right. We're all members of the Hostage Rescue Team."

At that her eyes widened in apparent recognition. "Oh. Wow, that's…good for you, Nathan." A little smile tipped up the corners of her mouth. "I'm not surprised you made it, though."

God, he loved the way she said his name. She'd always called him by his full name, never Nate. And her faith in him was so damn humbling. "Thanks."

"And you're not allowed to be part of my detail because we know each other personally?"

"Technically." Sort of. He hadn't asked DeLuca to be part of the detail because he knew he was essentially on probation and he was afraid that his impartiality was shot to shit where Taya was concerned. He owed her too much, was too attached to her in ways he didn't want to examine that closely. "But the guys assigned to you are great, I promise. I trust both of them with my life."

"Well then that's good enough for me." Another soft smile, just for him.

Having her look at him with such trust and affection pierced him. He wasn't sure he deserved that look. He'd been the one to let contact fizzle out between them, and if he was honest, he'd done it because he felt like his head was messed up where she was concerned.

Looking at her now, he could all but feel the ghostly memories swirling in the air between them. Seeing her again brought all his demons to life in full fucking Technicolor. How could it not be the same for her? How could she sit there, so calm and serene even after the attack today, when his heart was thudding like crazy and his palms were damp, his mind trapped back in what they'd been through, what they'd lost?

"So, how've you been?" she asked him, reaching out to pluck a grape from the plate before her. "I always regretted that we lost touch, but I got the sense you felt it was best we stopped talking, even though you never came out and said as much."

Nate barely resisted the urge to rub a hand over the back of his neck. It shook him a little, to know she'd read him so easily. They hadn't known each other very well, even back when they'd been e-mailing each other.

Except we knew each other in all the ways that matter, he reminded himself. After four days on the run with her in the unforgiving mountains of the Hindu Kush, he knew the most important things about her. She was strong and loyal. Determined. Deeply caring, despite what they'd done to her during her captivity. It broke his heart.

He forced his mind back to the present. "Yeah, I just thought it was better to let go, you know? For both of us." Christ, did that sound as lame to her as it did to him? "Try to move on, put everything behind us. Hopefully forget, in time." It had seemed easier that way at the time.

She nodded, a knowing glint in her eyes. "And how did that work out for you?"

It didn't.

Not by a long shot, and now he wondered what the fuck he'd been thinking back then, to imagine he could ever forget her.

He shrugged, forced a smile to avoid answering because he couldn't sit there and lie right to her face. "And to answer your other question, I've been good. Busy." *Busy getting laid every chance I get lately, that is. Mostly to try and forget you and what happened out there.* "How's your family?" He could do this. Sit here and shoot the shit, pretend he wasn't way more psychologically and emotionally attached to her than he actually was.

Her hand paused with the grape halfway to her mouth. "My dad had a heart attack a few weeks ago."

He hid a wince. She and her dad were super close. Nate had spoken to the man over the phone only once, at Joint Craig theater hospital at Bagram after she'd come out of surgery. It was the one thing she'd asked of him on the tense flight back to base, and no matter how beat up he'd been or how heavy his heart, there was no way he could have denied her that simple request. "I'm sorry."

She nodded, popped the grape in her mouth and chewed. All that did was draw his attention to her sexy mouth and make him wonder what it would feel like beneath his, or moving over his naked skin. He felt guilty as hell for thinking it, but man, he'd fantasized about her plenty over the past five years.

"It was bad," she continued. "Nearly lost him. He wanted to come with me but he's still recovering, so my brother, Kevin, is there looking after him. I had to order him to stay put, otherwise he'd have been here with me too."

"And how's he doing?" He knew Kevin was slightly older than Taya, and that he was a wounded combat vet.

"Good. Well, better than he was, anyway. Hasn't been easy, but we've all stuck close to each other and managed to do a lot of healing together over the past few years."

Nate nodded, a sudden tightness squeezing his throat. That was the difference he sensed in her now, he realized. That calmness she exuded came as a result of healing, something he hadn't even begun to do. Not really. How had she managed it?

The peacefulness that surrounded her was damn near mesmerizing. Even now, tangled up inside and tamping down a dozen emotions rolling around inside him, he could feel it reaching out to him. A warm glow he wanted to wrap himself in.

She lifted her shoulders in a slight shrug. "It's a process, as I know you're aware. Without my family I'm not sure what I would've done once I came home," she admitted with another gentle smile. "What about you?"

His thigh muscles twitched beneath his hands. He didn't want to go there. "What do you mean?"

She gave him a look that said she saw right through him. So wise, way beyond her thirty-four years. She was only six years older than him, but when she looked at him like that he felt like a damn kid in comparison. "I mean, was your family there for you? After Afghanistan? Or when you got out of the Air Force?"

She couldn't know that was a sore spot with him, and

a topic he never talked about. "I don't have contact with my family. Not since I was eighteen and enlisted."

"Oh. I'm sorry."

Nate wasn't sure if she was sorry for asking, or if she felt sorry for him. He hoped it was the former, because he couldn't stomach the latter. "It's all right. It's for the best, believe me." His white trash upbringing was something he was still embarrassed about. Not because he'd been poor, but because his mother and half-sister were drunks and master manipulators of both people and the system that gave them their welfare checks every month.

Cutting ties with them had made him a better person in the long run though. He'd vowed to himself at thirteen to leave that kind of life behind him and never look back, and he'd done just that.

Taya plucked another grape from its stem and popped it into her mouth before picking up the plate and offering it to him. He shook his head and she set it back down. "Sounds like there's quite a story there. Maybe you'll tell me about it sometime." The way she said it, without pressure or judgment, eased the tension gnawing at him.

"Maybe I will." It would be easy to talk to her. Her quiet sincerity made him wish they could spend hours and hours together alone so he could just be in her company. She'd seen him at his lowest point and still admired him. He felt safe enough with her that he knew he could tell her he *wasn't* okay, because she'd understand.

Part of him desperately wanted to do just that. The saner part made him keep his mouth shut.

Despite everything she'd gone through, and a lot of that shit had been far worse than what he'd been subjected to in SERE school, Taya had clearly dealt with the past far better than he had. He didn't want her to see what a fucking mess he'd become. Bad enough that DeLuca and Tuck and maybe some of the other guys could tell he was slowly unraveling. If Taya knew it too, the shame alone might kill him.

He eased back in his chair, thought about all the things he'd wanted to tell her over the years. "I've watched some of your speeches online. You're an incredible speaker." Her quiet strength, her resolve while on stage as she recounted her ordeal in Afghanistan, had floored him. So many times he'd watched the video clips and ached to reach out to her, re-establish communication.

But he'd known it was selfish to even think about it, so he'd left it alone. He was too fucked up and fighting a daily battle to not let it show. She deserved better than to be tainted by that.

Her gaze lifted to his, surprise clear in her eyes. "You watched me speak?"

He shrugged. "You told me in one of your e-mails that you were going to do some speaking engagements for Amnesty International. I looked you up."

She smiled again, this one brighter than all the others, making her eyes crinkle adorably at the corners. "Well, then, I'm flattered."

Nate shook his head in admiration. "Man, that took guts, Taya. After all that, getting up on stage, traveling all over the world to talk about what happened? Seriously brave." He was in awe of her ability to overcome things that would have crippled most people.

Her gaze lowered to the table. "I can see how you'd think that, but the truth is I did it as part of my healing process. Every time I got up on stage to speak to an audience, I was scared to death but I knew the story wasn't just about me. I thought about the other girls, about Hassan. I was doing it for them." Her lashes lifted and she gazed directly into his eyes. "And I did it for you and O'Neil, too."

At the mention of his fellow PJ's name, Nate's stomach balled up into a hard, searing knot below his ribcage. His mind immediately flashed back to a memory of his buddy. O'Neil laughing in their barracks at Bagram just minutes before leaving for the mission with the quick reaction force. They'd been doing a weapons check when someone had made a wisecrack. O'Neil had thrown his head back, mouth open as that contagious belly laugh rolled through the room and rang off the plywood walls, making everyone chuckle in turn.

Then, as suddenly as it had appeared, the image morphed into a snapshot of O'Neil's pale blue eyes gazing sightlessly up at the clear sky above him, his entire face covered in blood.

Instantly Nate was transported back to that rugged mountain terrain. He could taste the dust in his mouth, smell the burning cordite as he stared into Taya's ashen face across O'Neil's lifeless body. Her eyes were blank with shock and pain. One delicate hand was pressed hard to the side of her neck in an attempt to slow the blood pouring out from beneath her white-knuckled grip...

Nate sucked in a breath and broke eye contact, giving himself a mental shake. Shit. Shit, it was so fucking vivid.

He was up and out of his seat without even realizing it, needing to move, escape the memory, his heart halfway up his throat, his lungs burning.

"Nathan."

At her soft voice he stopped and looked back at her. She was reaching for him, her forehead creased in concern, one hand stretched toward him.

Nate dragged his gaze away from her and cleared his throat, forced himself to exhale and pull in a breath. Dammit, he'd known coming here was a risk, that seeing her might trigger everything. "I'll just check in with the guys, find out what their ETA is," he mumbled.

She opened her mouth to say something else, then closed it and nodded, easing back into her chair. "Okay."

Pulling his phone from his pocket, he was startled

when it buzzed in his hand. But it wasn't Cruz or Vance texting him, it was the woman who'd crawled out of his bed in the middle of the night a week ago. Her fourth attempt to contact him. He withheld a groan of frustration.

You free tonight? Would love to hook up if you don't have plans.

Jesus, she was persistent, he'd give her that.

Not interested, he texted back, then deleted her message, just as he'd done with all the others, and this time blocked her number. He was annoyed at her continued attempts to contact him, but that wasn't really fair of him. Eight days ago he would probably have taken her up on the offer, but the morning she'd left had been a wakeup call and he'd made up his mind to stop using meaningless sex as a crutch.

The truth was, he wouldn't have been interested in any woman who'd contacted him this past week. Not since he'd heard about Taya coming to town. And now that he'd seen her and talked to her again, the idea of hooking up with some random woman just so he could use sex as a Band-Aid turned his stomach.

Refusing to read too much into that, he faced her, hands on hips. "You need anything else while we wait?" Because he'd love an excuse to leave the room right now.

Taya shook her head, her frown melting away. But her eyes told him she knew exactly what had just happened to him a minute ago. "I'm okay, thanks."

He was saved from saying anything else by three sharp raps on the door. "It's Cruz," a familiar voice called from out in the hallway.

"That's them," he said to Taya. Grateful for some space and a minute to collect himself, he strode to the door and opened it. Vance's wide shoulders all but blocked the light coming in from the hallway as he followed Cruz inside, nodded at Nate.

"DeLuca told us you were already here," Cruz said.

Nate could see the questions in his teammate's light brown eyes, but thankfully all Cruz did was lift his dark eyebrows and say, "Care to introduce us to our principal?"

Chapter Four

After making the introductions, Nate moved off to the side of the room and stayed there, one shoulder propped against the wall and his arms folded across his chest as his teammates took over. He felt like a loser, having nearly lost his shit in front of Taya like that, but he wasn't going to leave her yet.

Cruz laid out the nitty-gritty of what he and Vance would do to keep Taya safe in the coming days. For his part, true to his easy-going nature, Vance merely nodded on occasion and spoke up only when necessary.

Through it all, Nate observed Taya's reaction. She was quiet as she absorbed the new security protocol, waiting until Cruz had finished before saying anything.

"So basically I only leave the building when necessary, and when I do you guys will be with me."

"Right," Cruz answered. "Either with you directly, or tailing you and another security team you might be with, usually by vehicle."

"And when I'm here?" She indicated the hotel room with a quick glance around.

"The FBI will post guards outside your room, just like they are now."

A slight frown appeared between her eyebrows. "And after what happened today, how do we know that no one followed me here from the airport?"

Cruz didn't try to downplay the threat; instead the former MARSOC Marine inclined his head in acknowledgement of that possibility. "Investigators are double checking everything now, using CCTV footage and satellite feeds, eye witness accounts, things like that. If anyone followed your team here, we'll know real soon and take care of it."

She didn't appear too comforted by the rundown, and Nate didn't blame her. "All right." Then she turned her attention on him, her eyes full of questions. "Will you be assigned to a detail for one of the other witnesses?"

Did she sound disappointed that he wouldn't be with her, or was that just wishful thinking? "Maybe. My commander hasn't given me an official assignment yet." But damn, he wanted to be on Taya's detail. She brought out all his protective urges, true, but it was more than that.

He *needed* to protect her, personally, and to do everything in his power to ensure she was safe. Hell, after what it had condoned and allowed to be done to her, the government fucking owed her at least that much. And so did he.

He shifted against the wall, fighting the urge to cross the room and sit next to her, put himself between her and anyone else, even his teammates. Which was crazy. They were here to help her.

Shit, maybe he *should* ask DeLuca for permission to join the detail. His commander might allow it if Nate could back up his request with solid reasons.

Cruz and Vance were both watching him now. Nate caught the white flash of Vance's teeth against his deep brown skin as he fought a grin. Nate shot him a quelling glare. "What?"

Vance covered his mouth with one big fist, masking his chuckle with a cough. "Nothin'."

Nate shifted his gaze to Cruz next, whose eyes danced with amusement, and raised his eyebrows in silent demand. *Problem?*

Cruz merely grinned before turning his attention back to Taya. "Any other questions or concerns on your mind right now?"

She snorted softly. "Well, yeah, but the rest can wait until we know more, I guess."

"Sounds good. Can I have your phone for a minute?"

Taya entered her passcode and handed it to him. "I'm putting in mine and Vance's numbers," he told her, then slid a teasing, sidelong glance in Nate's direction. "And Schroder's too, I guess," he added. "If something comes up, call or text one of us. We'll contact you the same way."

"Perfect, thanks," she said as he handed it back to her.

When a knock sounded on the door, Cruz and Vance both stood. "That'll be the lawyers," Cruz said and strode toward the foyer.

Taya shifted in her chair and smoothed her hands over the front of her dress. To Nate she looked suddenly weary. He wished she didn't have to sit through another meeting with strangers right now, alone.

Voices came from the foyer and Cruz reappeared with three men and one woman dressed in business suits, all carrying briefcases. "Security's cleared them all," he told Taya, then nodded at Vance and Nate. "Shall we?"

Taya stood to shake hands with the lawyers, but then her gaze strayed to Nate. "Will you excuse me for a minute?" she said to the group before turning to follow him to the foyer. Nate paused to wait for her as his teammates headed for the door.

Cruz and Vance glanced back at them questioningly, and Vance smoothed over what could have been an awkward moment by saying, "See you both later." Without another word he opened the door and both men walked out into the hall.

Nate faced Taya and slid his hands into his pockets so he wouldn't be tempted to touch her again. She put on a smile for him. "Sorry we didn't get to talk longer."

"It's okay, this is more important right now," he said, nodding toward the other room where the prosecution waited.

"Well maybe we'll get another chance to catch up while I'm here." Her gaze moved over his face, almost as if she was cataloguing his features. Awareness and longing tingled up his spine. "It was great to see you again, Nathan."

"You too. And look, what Cruz said is true. If you need anything or want us to check on something or your gut says something doesn't feel right, contact one of us." Though he wanted to be the one she reached out to if anything was bothering her.

She nodded. "I will."

For a moment he stood there, fighting the urge to reach for her, but she ignored his hesitation, stepped forward to close the distance between them and slid her arms around his back. "Thanks for coming to check on me," she murmured against his shoulder. "I appreciate it."

He gathered her close, trying and failing to ignore the way his body reacted to the feel of her soft curves pressed against him. He'd thought about holding her this way so many times. Just the two of them, away from prying eyes. He didn't care that others were waiting for her in the next room. Nothing mattered but her standing so trusting and warm in his arms. "You don't have to thank me for that," he said. "And I meant what I said. Anything comes up that you're not sure about, call me."

"Okay." She pulled back and put on a brave smile. "See you later?"

"Yeah." Even if he didn't end up on her detail, he still planned to see her again. Whatever it was he was searching for to slay his personal demons, closure maybe, he knew Taya was the key. But now he was beginning to think he wanted a whole lot more than just closure, and that was dangerous. For both of them.

He was still thinking about her an hour and a half later when he entered his kitchen from the garage. His phone rang while he was fishing a beer out of the fridge. With the bottle in one hand he pulled out his phone and checked the screen. DeLuca.

"Hey," he answered, phone wedged between his ear and shoulder as he twisted the cap off. "Perfect timing, I just got home. Taya was meeting with the prosecution when I left."

"You need to come in to HQ," his commander said. "Rest of the team is on the way down, including Vance and Cruz."

Oh, shit, this had to be bad, for him to pull everyone in. Nate straightened and set the beer down on the counter, a sense of foreboding sweeping through him. "Why, what's happened?"

"Three of the prosecution's star witnesses have just been kidnapped at gunpoint in broad daylight. Their security details are either all dead or wounded."

His heart rate shot up. For the attackers to locate witnesses in WITSEC and then take out the U.S. marshals assigned to them, they had to be incredibly well trained.

He gripped the edge of the counter, his fingers curling around the cool granite. "What about Taya?" he blurted. If the attackers had gotten to the other three—two of whom were supposed to have been in special holding facilities that were heavily guarded—then it stood to reason that they either knew where she was staying, or had a pretty good idea. And if Cruz and Vance were being called in to HQ, that left only regular FBI agents to guard her. That wasn't good enough, not for Nate.

"She's fine, no incidents reported at her hotel. Celida's already placed an extra detail there and everyone's on alert."

No. Nate shook his head, concern for her overriding everything else. "She can't stay there—"

"I know. Her temporary detail is moving her out of the hotel shortly. I'm gonna have Vance and Cruz swing by to meet them and bring her down here with them until we can decide what the plan is."

Nate breathed out a sigh of relief. "All right. Have you let her know yet?"

"No. I thought it'd be best if she heard it from you. She's got a temporary burner phone." He gave Nate the number.

"Okay, thanks." He was glad DeLuca was letting him be the one to break the news. "See you in ten." As he rushed for the garage he dialed Taya. She answered in a groggy voice that told him he'd woken her. "Hey, it's me."

A short pause, then, "Nathan?"

God, hearing his name in that sleep-husky voice had him imagining her sitting up in bed, her curls all tousled. Did she sleep in anything, or naked? "Yeah, sorry to wake you."

Sheets rustled on the other end. He pictured her pushing her curls out of her face with one hand. "It's okay. Is something wrong?"

"There's been some recent developments that I can't go into over the phone," he explained calmly. "Cruz and Vance are going to head over and pick you up soon, then bring you down to our headquarters in Quantico."

"What happened?" There was no mistaking the sudden tension in her voice, even if she sounded calm.

"Intel's still coming in, but the guys will fill you in with what they know on the way down. For now, get dressed and repack your suitcase, okay? They'll be there within the next few minutes or so."

She blew out a breath. "Nathan, you're scaring me."

Ah, God, he hated to give her anything more to worry about. "Don't be scared. We're moving you as a precaution, that's all." He was thankful two of his teammates were going to be there to watch over her and make sure she was safe, but he didn't like knowing she was at risk, and not being there to guard her in person. "Stay in your room until they get there, and don't leave with anyone but them." If attackers had managed to locate and kidnap protected federal witnesses, then he couldn't rule out the possibility that WITSEC had a security leak somewhere.

"I won't." He could hear her moving around the room now, probably grabbing her clothes.

"That's good. Everything's gonna be fine. We're just erring on the side of caution."

She made a sound that let him know she was listening. "Are you going to be there? At headquarters?"

The hope in her voice made him ache inside. He looked down at his free hand, gripping the edge of his truck's doorframe. Shit, he was so compromised when it came to her, but he couldn't shut his feelings off. *He* needed to be the one making sure she was safe, period. It would drive him nuts otherwise. "Yeah, I'll be there."

"Good," she said on a sigh of relief.

He was quiet a moment, listening to the sounds of her opening and closing drawers, the rasp of a zipper, probably on her suitcase. "You okay?"

"I'll be better once I know what the hell's going on," she muttered, the annoyance in her tone making his lips twitch. She wasn't scared, she was pissed that he was withholding information from her. But he wouldn't talk about this latest incident over an unsecured phone line. His phone was encrypted, but if anyone was listening in on her end, he didn't want to tip them off.

"Soon, I promise. Just get your stuff together and be ready when my guys get there."

"I will."

"Want me to stay on the line with you?"

"No, it's fine."

There was no reason to continue the conversation, but he found himself stalling, searching for an excuse to keep her talking, just to hear her voice. And he wanted to take her mind off the situation a bit, ease her anxiety level. "I'm just hopping into my truck. Wanna keep me company while I drive?"

She huffed out a small laugh. "Guess that means you don't want me to turn on the news while I wait, huh?"

"Damn straight."

"Sure then. I'll pack, you drive."

"Deal." He got into his truck and turned on his hands-free system. "You still with me?" he asked as he backed out of the garage. The street out in front of his building was quiet, just a few people out talking on the sidewalk or walking their dogs.

"Still here, almost packed."

"How did the meeting with the lawyers go?"

"Fine, everything was about what I expected. Mostly they wanted to go over the details of the plot I learned about when I was Qureshi's prisoner. They're going to focus mostly on that, rather than the human trafficking, weapons and drug smuggling, but they'll bring all that up to paint a picture for the jury. They took pity on me and cut things short in deference to what happened today though."

"That's good. I bet you were glad to get the extra downtime." He heard a faint knocking in the background, a muffled male voice calling out.

"It's Cruz," she said.

"Check through the peephole first before you answer."

She didn't answer, but he could hear her moving around the room. Then, "Yeah, it's Cruz and Vance." The distinctive turning of a deadbolt followed. "Hi. I'm just on the line with Nathan."

"Hi, *Nathan*," Cruz chimed in, the singsong voice making the use of his whole name into a verbal dig. Then in his normal voice he added, "You mind hanging up and letting us do our job now, brother?"

"All right," Nate said to Taya. "Tell them to take good care of you."

"He wants me to tell you to keep me safe," she said to the others.

"Goes without saying, Doc," Vance's deep bass voice called out in the background.

"Well, I guess I'd better get going," Taya said to Nate.

"Yeah. I'll see you soon, okay?"

"Okay. Thanks for the distraction."

"Anytime. Bye." He disconnected, relieved that his guys were taking care of her, and keyed up about the coming meeting with DeLuca and the others. He'd likely have an argument on his hands, but his mind was made up. He'd say or do whatever it took to be put on Taya's detail, starting tonight.

Chapter Five

—————⌒—————

Taya wished she knew more about the HRT, aside from the basics and that their headquarters were inside Marine Base Quantico, Virginia. She'd only done a little bit of research before exhaustion had forced her to get some sleep. Agent Cruz stopped the SUV at the gate and showed his ID to the armed Marine standing guard.

The Marine nodded at Vance, looked at her through the window, and smiled before speaking to Cruz again. "Have a good night, sir."

She looked out at the base as Cruz drove them to headquarters and parked out front. She felt better being here, partly because she was closer to Nathan. After learning that some of the other witnesses had been kidnapped, she needed all the reassurance she could get.

"Here we are," Cruz said, gathering a folder and his jacket from Vance. "We'll get you a coffee inside while you wait. It's not Starbucks or anything, but it's decent. Our meeting could take a while."

"Sure." She gathered her purse and exited the SUV, then followed them up the walkway to the front entrance.

She noticed both men seemed much more relaxed than they had been when they'd picked her up at the hotel. Neither of them was scanning the area, which made sense, since they were in the middle of a military installation. Cruz had also doubled back several times on various streets near the hotel before hitting the highway down here, to ensure no one was following them, and Vance had been watching the mirrors carefully too. The chances of anyone tailing them here were low, and the chances of someone attacking her while on base were pretty much nil.

She hoped.

The scent of coffee greeted her when she stepped inside the brightly lit building, Vance holding the door for her. It was after midnight now, so it wasn't a surprise that the place was so quiet. "Thank you."

"No worries." The incredibly muscular agent waited for her to precede him and follow Cruz down a hallway. Taya looked around, absorbing every little detail. So this was where Nathan worked. He must spend a lot of time here on base.

Before falling asleep after her meeting with the lawyers, she'd Googled the Hostage Rescue Team. What she'd read was impressive, not to mention eye-opening. It didn't surprise her that Nathan had made it through selection and had been given a spot on one of the teams. After seeing him in action in Afghanistan, watching him work under pressure while under extreme duress, she knew what a skilled operator he was.

She'd never forgotten him or what he'd done for her. In fact, she'd thought about him maybe too often over the years. In particular his protectiveness and the kind way he'd spoken to her, keeping her calm even while her life lay in his capable hands.

And his touch while he'd tended to her. Skilled, firm, but also gentle with her. She'd thought about that plenty as well, had wondered what it would be like to feel his fingertips stroking all over her naked body.

Stop that. Bad Taya.

She couldn't stop thinking about those hugs earlier though. Having his arms around her that way had been amazing, and remembering the feel of that hard body was only going to torment her now.

After getting her a coffee, Vance left her to wait in a staff lounge and headed out to his meeting. She waited for nearly half an hour before footsteps sounded at the end of the hallway, along with two male voices. Taya set down the news magazine she'd been reading and sat up straighter, relaxing a little when Nathan appeared in the doorway next to a good looking middle-aged man with short, dark hair. Not as good looking as Nathan, mind you, but still easy on the eyes.

"Hey," Nathan said to her with a sexy smile that set off a burst of warmth inside her. With his dark auburn hair just long enough for a woman to run her fingers through and a few days' growth of stubble on his jaw several shades darker than his hair, the man was ruggedly sexy.

She stood, returning the smile. "Hi." She looked at the other man, who stepped forward and offered his hand.

"I'm Supervisory Special Agent Matt DeLuca," he told her, his grip firm but not painful. "I'm sorry we had to drag you down here in the middle of the night on top of everything else."

Nathan's commander. "No, it's fine. Did you find out anything more about the missing witnesses?"

DeLuca nodded. "Come into my office and I'll tell you what I can."

She didn't like being kept in the dark about any of this, but knew she had no say in the matter. "Okay."

Taya fell in step with Nathan as they followed DeLuca back down the hallway and into the second room on the left. She felt small next to him, but in a nice, fluttery way that made her hyper aware of her femininity. And he smelled good too, the subtle, clean scent of cologne emanating from him as he moved. The attraction wasn't unwelcome, but it was more intense than she'd imagined it would be, and she had no idea if it was mutual or not.

You're too old for him, Taya. He'd never think of you that way.

DeLuca made his way behind the large desk that dominated the far side of the room and typed some commands into his computer. When he was ready he looked up at her and motioned for her to approach. With Nathan at her back, she walked over and took a look at what was on screen.

"Two of the missing witnesses are male," DeLuca said to her, easing back for her to get a better look. "I think you might recognize them."

Taya's breath caught when she saw the pictures of the two men. She swallowed. "Yes. I know them." They'd both been in Qureshi's most trusted inner circle. And both had taken their turn beating her when she'd first been captured. All in an effort to break her.

They'd failed.

She straightened, fighting her body's innate flight response to seeing the men's faces. "Those aren't the names I knew them by though," she added, reading the unfamiliar names beneath the photos.

"No. You knew them by their noms de guerre," DeLuca said. "After they were captured they both agreed to testify for the U.S. government against Qureshi in return for a reduced sentence. They were attacked along with their prison security teams in two separate locations during a routine transfer tonight."

"The attackers are acting either for or on Qureshi's orders?" she guessed, not liking the possibility that a homegrown cell or cells had been activated for the purpose of eliminating the witnesses and disrupting the trial.

"That's what we think so far, yes."

Taya nodded, still staring at the screen. She rubbed her hands over her upper arms, suddenly feeling chilled. "So are the witnesses presumed dead at this point?"

DeLuca nodded. "If they're not already, they will be soon. There's no way Qureshi's network would capture them and then let them live. If they do, we think it'll be for propaganda purposes."

She was acutely aware of Nathan standing at her back, and had to fight the urge to step closer to him, enough to feel the warmth of his body against her spine. Taya took a deep breath. "And what about the third witness?" From the way DeLuca had worded it earlier, she knew the third one was a female.

"This might be a shock for you," DeLuca warned.

Taya glanced at him sharply, her heart thudding hard against her ribs. "Who is it?"

"You sure you want to do this right now?" Nathan asked, shifting to stand beside her. Taya looked up and met those warm hazel eyes, saw the concern written there. "It's been a long day for you already."

Oh, God, who was the third witness? Her stomach muscles tensed. "Just tell me."

Nathan shared a look with DeLuca, then let out a deep breath and relented with a muttered, "Okay."

Taya looked at the screen while DeLuca pulled up another page. Her heart plummeted when she saw the familiar face looking back at her. "Chloe," she rasped out. She straightened, one hand flying to her mouth as she turned away from the sight.

Nathan's big hand caught her shoulder. His warm fingers curled beneath her chin, tilting it up until she looked into his face. "I'm so sorry, Taya."

She couldn't answer, could barely even breathe as the horror of it sank in. The male witnesses dying didn't bother her except that it might now delay the trial and Qureshi being brought to justice for what he'd done. But Chloe? Until now Taya hadn't even known she was still alive.

She struggled to swallow the lump in her throat, lowered her hand from her mouth. "She got out." Her voice sounded strangled, but that's exactly how she felt, like an invisible fist was closing off her airway.

To his credit, Nathan didn't look away. He gazed straight back at her, nodded. "Yeah. A year after you did. She went straight into the WITSEC program. That's why you didn't know. Her story was kept secret from everyone, even her own family."

She could feel her lips trembling, her body beginning to shiver. Chloe had chosen WITSEC to keep her safe, had sacrificed yet again by missing out on the support of her friends and family, and for what? In the end, even that hadn't saved her from Qureshi. "Who got her out?" she managed to ask, hating that her voice shook but unable to stop it.

"A team of Delta operators."

Taya pulled free of his gentle grip and wrapped her arms around herself. "I can't believe it." She turned away from both men, struggling to get hold of herself. This was too much.

It was too awful. Just too goddamn cruel to think of what her young friend had gone through. At twenty-two, Chloe had been captured from a refugee camp near the Pakistani border where she'd been working as an aid worker. She'd endured an even longer captivity than Taya had, only to come home and be taken by people working on Qureshi's orders, here where she was supposed to have been safe. Now she was either dead or about to be executed.

"How did they get to her? WITSEC has a good reputation. How did they even know where she was?

There's no way anyone should have known where to even find these witnesses, let alone be able to pull off multiple, successful attacks like this," Taya said.

DeLuca nodded. "I've heard from a trusted source that the attackers got help from an insider at WITSEC. One of their agents. That's what it looks like for now, anyway, so they're taking care of it on their end. He's been arrested and if there's enough evidence against him, he'll be charged and prosecuted accordingly."

God, she was so thankful she hadn't volunteered to enter the WITSEC program.

Taya shook her head, adamant. "This is unbelievable." God, she hoped that man was put to death after the trial.

"I'm sorry," DeLuca said.

She rubbed her fingers over her burning eyes and nodded, not trusting her voice. If they had the resources and manpower to get to Chloe and the others, then Taya and the remaining witnesses were all facing a significant threat of their own.

"I'll give you two some privacy," he said in a quiet voice. "If there's anything I can do, let me know."

Unless he could find Chloe and rescue her before her kidnappers ended her life, no, there was nothing he could do for Taya at the moment.

The door shut quietly behind him. She released a ragged breath.

"Taya…"

She turned back around to face Nathan. He was watching her, his green-gold hazel eyes full of torment. The lump in her throat suddenly magnified, all but choking her. She didn't care that they were in his commander's office or that he had a professional distance to maintain from her. He'd seen firsthand how she and the other female captives had been treated, and he knew Chloe's story. He understood Taya's pain better than anyone else could have.

Taking a step toward him, she exhaled a shaky breath of relief when he reached for her and pulled her close. Warm, strong arms closed around her, one banded around her ribs, his other hand cradling the back of her head. Taya leaned into him and held on, letting his heat and strength soothe her. When he held her like this she felt truly safe, for the first time in forever.

Tears burned the back of her eyelids as she focused on regulating her breathing, using every technique she knew of to find her center. Concentrating on Nathan's clean scent and the strength of his body helped calm her.

But after a few moments she became all too aware of all the hard muscles pressed against her. She melted a little when he began stroking her hair, his fingers catching in her curls.

Tingles spread out across her skin, spiking her pulse rate and making her nipples tighten. The pull she felt toward him was powerful, and not something she could hide for long if she didn't put some distance between them. Gently easing away from him, she immediately regretted the loss of his warmth.

Rather than step away he surprised her by reaching out and brushing an errant curl from her cheek. "Just to play it safe we're gonna get you out of town for a couple days, okay?"

She frowned up at him. "We?"

He nodded. "Me, Cruz and Vance."

"You're on my detail now too?" She hoped it was true.

Nathan exhaled and nodded. "All the guys have been placed on protective details for the remaining witnesses when they arrive in town during the next few days. I spoke to Matt and my team leader about things, and unless you have any objections, I've been added to your detail, along with Cruz and Vance. You'll have the three of us for the time being, and we have the option of adding in more guys later on. The trial's going to be delayed, we just don't know for how long."

She got the feeling there was something more to it than he was telling her. There had to be rules and protocol about this kind of situation, him protecting a witness he knew personally. Was he volunteering out of a sense of obligation? "You've already done more than enough for me, Nathan. You don't need to do this." DeLuca was aware that they knew each other on a personal level, and she didn't want to be the cause of any sticky situations for Nathan that might either hurt or jeopardize his career.

His mouth tightened and he shook his head. "Yes, I do." He dragged a hand through his hair, looking slightly agitated. "Cruz and Vance are both more than capable of guarding you, but you're too important to me to stand back and do nothing. I need to make sure you're safe."

He thought he owed her, she realized. She shook her head, adamant. "You already saved my life in Afghanistan. You don't owe me anything."

"Yes, I do, but that's not what this is about." He paused, searching her eyes. "Unless you don't feel comfortable having me on your detail."

The uncertainty in his eyes took her by surprise. She wouldn't let him doubt her trust in him for one second. "Of course I am. I've put my life in your hands before and I wouldn't hesitate to do it again."

His smile was so full of relief and maybe even gratitude, it made her heart ache. "Then come on. I've got someone I want you to meet."

****

Special Agent Ethan Cruz slid his arms into the sleeves of his clean T-shirt and held his phone to his ear with his shoulder as he took his sidearm from his locker.

The briefing had finished ten minutes ago and all the guys were headed out. He and Vance were going to the Virginia coast with Schroder to guard Taya, after a little pit stop at DeLuca's place.

"Ethan!"

He couldn't help but smile at his mother's excited voice. "Hey. Sorry I didn't call you back last night. Been busy."

"But you're all right?"

She liked him to check in with her at least every couple days when he was stateside, just to let her know he was okay. Didn't matter that he was twenty-nine years old and a member of the HRT. He'd always be her baby. "Yeah, I'm all right. You?"

"Fine, son. Are you boys still scheduled to come down this way at the end of May?"

"Looks that way for now." They were tentatively scheduled to do a joint exercise with the DEA in Miami. He glanced over his shoulder as Vance walked in with a duffel and went to his locker, located next to Ethan's. "You sure you still want to host us all for dinner one night?"

Vance's face brightened and he paused in the act of packing his body armor. "Is that Mama Cruz?"

Ethan gave him a nod and grabbed two extra magazines for his M4 and put them in his own duffel. Before he could say anything else, his mother's delighted gasp sounded in his ear. "Is that Sawyer?"

Oh, lord. "Yeah, it's Sawyer," he said, rolling his eyes.

Vance grinned at him, all white Chiclet teeth and sparkling eyes. "Hey, Mama Cruz," he called out, loud enough for her to hear. "You're still having us for a cookout when we come down there, right?"

His mother laughed. "Tell him of course, and that I'll have his favorite bread pudding and a flan ready."

"She says yes," he grumbled, omitting the last part.

"Tell her I'll love her forever if she'd make one of those flans," Vance said, his expression hopeful. Guy was six-two and two-thirty easy, but right now he looked more like an eager puppy dog than an elite counterterrorism and hostage rescue operator.

Ethan lowered the phone slightly to cover the microphone and shot him a mock glare. "Get your own mom." Vance and his mother were ridiculous in how much they loved each other.

Vance chuckled and landed a solid punch to Ethan's left shoulder, knocking his upper body a few inches to the side. Guy had fists like a freaking sledgehammer. "You're just jealous, man, cuz you know she loves me more than you."

"You wish. You're only an honorary son," he muttered and raised the phone, turning his head when DeLuca stepped into the locker room. Their commander looked directly at Ethan and waited, sliding his hands into his pockets. "Hey, Mom, I gotta go."

"Wait, I wanted to tell you about Marisol."

Ethan frowned. He hadn't seen the little-girl-from-next-door in his old neighborhood for several years now, since she'd graduated from law school. "What about her?"

"I was speaking to Soledad today, and she said Marisol's coming back into town in a few weeks to work on a big case she's landed with the U.S. Attorney's Office here in Miami."

"That's great," he said, not sure why his mother was telling him this.

"Yes, something to do with a big drug lord who was arrested by the DEA a few months ago."

Ethan straightened as he filled in the blanks. "Diego Fuentes?"

"I think that's him, yes. Anyway, Soledad is very proud. It's a big honor for someone who just started

working for the U.S. Attorney. She said Marisol will be
around when you come down, so maybe you'll see her."

"Yeah, maybe." The "ice princess" would probably
go out of her way to avoid him as she had the past few
times he'd gone home for a visit, but he still didn't love
the idea of her prosecuting someone like Fuentes. That
asshole was ruthless, and his network extended far
beyond Miami. In fact, word was, he'd controlled most of
the drug trafficking throughout northern Mexico and even
into the Caribbean. He also still had tentacles everywhere
throughout the region. For her own safety, Marisol needed
be aware of exactly what she was getting into with the
case. "I'll call you soon, okay? Love you."

"I love you too, Mama Cruz," Vance called out.

His mother giggled. "He's just too adorable. Tell him
I send a hug."

"Uh huh, will do. Bye." He disconnected and shot
Vance a bland look. "You're pathetic, you know that?"

Vance clapped him on the shoulder. "She sent me a
hug, didn't she?"

Ethan couldn't help his grudging grin. "Yeah."

DeLuca cleared his throat, bringing Ethan's gaze to
him. "Can I have a second?"

"Yessir, of course." He shared a look with Vance.
"I'll meet you outside." When they were alone he faced
DeLuca.

"I need you to keep an eye on Schroder," he said
without any warning.

Whoa. "In what way?"

His commander gave a casual shrug. "Couple things
have come up that we're concerned about. Just want to be
sure he's taking care of himself. If he's not, I need you to
let me know."

Ethan frowned. "Wait, like, you want me to babysit
him?" What the hell for? Doc had never done anything to
warrant supervision. Sure, he was the newest guy to the

squad and his social life with the ladies was getting a little out of control, but that was his personal biz and it never affected his performance at work. All the guys liked him, including Ethan.

"No, just let me know if you notice anything off. Being placed on this security detail might not be easy for him."

Ethan had read the file on Taya Kostas and knew she had some kind of history with Schroder from over in A-stan. This was just too fucking strange though. He'd never heard of DeLuca asking any of them to spy on another teammate. "All right," he said slowly.

"I'm not anticipating a problem," DeLuca added. "Just looking out for him."

"Sure." Ethan watched his commander walk away. Well, hell. Now he was dying to know exactly what had happened between Doc and their principal.

Chapter Six

When Ayman entered the apartment that night, Jaleel was waiting for him. His roommate sat up on the couch, muted the TV and looked over at him. "Have you heard the latest?" he asked in Arabic, eyes lit with excitement.

Ayman nodded. While he was happy about the attacks, he'd since lost most of his initial excitement. Now that reality was sinking in, he felt almost numb inside. He hadn't accomplished anything yet. His part in this had only just begun, and the consequences if he failed were too grim to think about.

"I just came from a meeting." He didn't have to say aloud that it had been with his group from the mosque. "Got the call two hours ago, right after the story broke on the news."

Jaleel turned to face him squarely, his expression tense. "And? What did they say?"

"They said taking three key witnesses is good, but if the Kostas woman is still free, then it's not good enough."

Jaleel watched him remove the pistol he'd tucked into his waistband and take out the magazine, checking it out of habit. He was always armed, even at work. Darwish had helped turn him into an expert marksman, and Ayman had to be ready to protect himself from law enforcement that might come sniffing around.

And from the men he worked for if they decided he was no longer of use to them.

"Do they know where she is?" Jaleel asked.

Ayman shook his head and opened the kitchen drawer that held extra ammo and the military-style knives he'd collected. He knew how to use those too. Close quarter battle skills were a useful part of what he'd learned during his sessions with Darwish.

He took out another magazine, examined it to ensure it was fully loaded before slipping it into his pocket. "Someone was able to follow her partway from the airport. He lost her vehicle in traffic once they got into the city but he was able to narrow the hotel she's staying at down to four possibilities. He saw the SUV stopped at an intersection and then someone took a suitcase into one of the hotels on the east side of the street. But now that some witnesses have gone missing the FBI will move her soon, if they haven't already." So now his and Jaleel's task would be even harder.

Jaleel frowned in concern. "So what now? How will we find her?"

Finding the American whore was their responsibility. Locating her, tracking her, was all up to him and Jaleel. She was their target and the currency that guaranteed their survival. "You need to find us a reliable starting point."

"They won't let her use credit cards or an unencrypted phone. I'd have to hack into the hotel's security itself."

"Perfect."

Jaleel blew out a breath and ran a hand over his closely shorn hair, clearly agitated. "They'll be able to find us, no matter how carefully I cover my tracks. Maybe not right away, but eventually if anyone gets suspicious and starts looking into the hacks. We'll have to plan out emergency actions."

Ayman's heart thudded. "But you can find her, right?"

"Yeah." He looked away, appearing deep in thought for a moment. "Once I gain access to the right hotel's registries and security footage, I can find her."

"I've got the names for you," Ayman said, pulling out his phone.

"I'll get my laptop." Jaleel headed toward his room.

"No, you can't use it."

Jaleel stopped at his sharp tone and looked back at him. "Why not? It's encrypted."

"It's not safe anymore. We'll have to go elsewhere."

Jaleel frowned at him, as though unconvinced. "So what do you expect me to use, then? The libraries are closed, and the internet cafés won't be open until morning. We can't wait that long. If the FBI is moving her, we need to find her *now*."

Ayman straightened. "What about the computer system at the office building where my father works? Would that work?"

Jaleel frowned. "How new is the system?"

"Just got upgraded a few months ago." Ayman shrugged, not seeing any other viable option at the moment. "We won't even have to break in, my father will let us inside. We'll tell him it's for an assignment you're working on for your master's thesis. That your computer's busted and you have a deadline coming up. He'll let us if he thinks it's for school."

Jaleel hesitated. "We shouldn't involve your father in this. Not even in such a small way. He's smart, Ayman, he might figure out what we're doing. And as soon as I hack in, it's only a matter of time before the FBI finds out as well. I can cover my tracks well enough, but I can only buy us time. And probably not much of it."

They didn't have any other choice, so they'd have to risk it. "He won't, because he'll be too busy doing his job." Cleaning an entire nine story building before business hours tomorrow morning.

It was one of the things that made Ayman most angry about coming here. In Syria his father had been a respected government official in their city. Now he was reduced to menial labor as a janitor, working graveyard shifts six days a week just to pay the rent and put food on the table for the rest of the family.

Ayman wanted more, wanted to strike back at the country he blamed for Syria's woes. The money offered to him only sweetened the deal. "And we'll go on the move as soon as we're done. We'll have a good head start from the FBI."

"What kind of security do they have there?"

He blew out a breath. "A few guards, but my father knows them all. Their system's password protected and whatever. And they'll have cameras. We'll have to hide our faces without looking suspicious."

"I won't know until we're in there, but yeah, I can get us in to pretty much anything. The hotel security systems are likely on an intranet network, so I'll have to use special equipment to access those, which will be a red flag for anyone monitoring the site." He licked his lips, his tension obvious as he shook his head slowly. "You and I both accepted the risks involved with this back when we joined the group, and we're prepared to go on the run. But your father...he's a good man. If it comes down to it, are you willing to let him go to jail for us?"

Ayman ignored the sudden rise in his pulse and pushed aside the guilt forming inside him. "He won't. Even if they figure out who we are and what we're doing, they won't have any evidence against him. Besides, you're the best hacker The Brethren have. If anyone can find her, it's you." Whatever the cost, whatever they had to do, they had to find her.

Jaleel didn't look convinced. "All right, if you're sure."

Ayman was already in too deep. He didn't have a choice now. "We can't back out now. You know what will happen if we do." They'd both wind up dead, cut into pieces and dumped into the Potomac as a former member of their group had been a month before when he'd balked about an operation he'd been tasked with.

Apparently the man had been about to go to the FBI to turn everyone in. The Brethren had sent a death squad after him. Men like Darwish, trained in militant camps throughout the Middle East and south Asian countries.

Men Ayman never wanted coming after him.

They were all playing a dangerous game. For Ayman, winning it was the only way out.

****

As Nathan drove them down the darkened highway, he glanced over at Taya in the front passenger seat. "You doing okay?"

She made herself nod. "Fine." It was just the two of them, which was a relief, but her mind was spinning. She couldn't stop thinking about Chloe, about the horrific ways she might have died at her captors' hands after surviving so much. The possibilities turned her stomach.

"Were you and Chloe close?" he finally asked, correctly guessing the direction of her thoughts.

That was harder to answer than she realized. "Not close in the normal sense, no. The men kept us apart from one another as much as possible, to avoid us making escape plans. But she was so young. I remember when they first brought her in, she was terrified." She shook her head, lost in memory for a moment, of Chloe's blue eyes so wide with fear that the whites showed all around the irises. "When I had contact with her I did what I could to comfort her, tried to make the transition easier for her, but it wasn't much." A kind word here and there, a hug. Stolen minutes of whispered conversation, giving her advice that would hopefully help her avoid some beatings.

Nathan made a growling sound in his throat and tightened his hands on the wheel, a muscle flexing in his jaw. "Fucking bastards," he muttered under his breath.

Yep. "The man she was given to was one of the most brutal." Her voice hitched on the last word. "She had it way worse than I did. He got off on beating her for the slightest thing, like making eye contact with anyone, or crying. Any excuse he could find to punish her."

Taya hadn't realized until later how fortunate she'd been that Hassan had chosen her. The last time she'd seen Chloe had been in one of the endless string of mountain villages they'd been moved to in an effort to escape detection by anyone searching for them. Chloe's eyes had both been recently blackened, one swollen nearly shut. She'd walked with her head down, shoulders hunched, cowering anytime one of the men came near.

'Broken. It made Taya's eyes sting to think of it.

"Goddamn it," Nathan muttered, shaking his head. "It makes me want to punch something, to know you and the others were treated like that."

Taya understood all too well the helpless fury he felt. At first after she was captured she'd assumed the U.S. government was searching for her. That they'd launch some sort of secret rescue op and get her out. But weeks had turned into months and no one had come for her. She hadn't learned the truth until after she'd come home. Turns out her own government had left her in captivity because they didn't want to risk blowing Hassan's position in Qureshi's network. They'd weighed the major bust he'd been close to giving them as more important than her life or freedom. All of that had been covered up of course, so there was no hard evidence for her to use against them in a lawsuit.

Knowing they'd abandoned her was one of the hardest things for her to get past.

So many times during those months as a prisoner she'd thought about running, risking everything just for a chance at freedom. But knowing what would happen to the other women if she did had always stopped her cold. They'd all have been tortured and then slaughtered because of her actions.

She was quiet a moment, staring out her window as the scenery flashed by in the darkness. "I think the worst part is to know she survived all that, actually made it home and got into WITSEC, and now she's gone anyway."

Nathan drew in a deep breath then reached across the console for her hand. His fingers wrapped around hers, strong and sure.

Oh, his hands. Callused at the base of the fingers, fingertips slightly rough, but so gentle on her.

He squeezed. "It's not exactly classified, but the bastard she was given to was killed when she was rescued. And whoever took her this time will get what's coming to them." It sounded like a vow.

"I hope so." She shook her head, tried to make sense of it all. "God, I hope so."

Nathan didn't say anything else, just kept holding her hand and for that she was grateful. The physical contact made her feel less alone, not as lost. This madness had to end. She would get up on that witness stand whenever she was called, and earn justice for Chloe and the others.

Let it go. There's nothing you can do for now. Let it go, before it eats a hole inside of you.

She'd lived with a giant black hole inside her for the

better part of two years after coming home. She refused to let it take over her again.

With effort she exhaled and sought her center, focused on everything she had to be grateful for. Her health. Her father and brother. Finding Nathan again after all this time.

"So where are we going?" she finally asked as he drove west away from the base.

He'd left his truck parked there and taken an unmarked SUV instead, in case anyone was looking for them. He'd explained that the hotel security cameras would have both of them on video, so there was a chance someone would be able to see them coming and going from the hotel. Cruz was in another vehicle not far behind them and other agents were on call as well, available to them if they wanted extra backup. Nathan had told her they might use a rotating team, or just stick with him, Cruz and Vance, depending on what intel came to light in the next twelve hours or so.

"My commander's house," he answered.

She glanced over at him in surprise. "Are we staying there?" She understood that she would have people guarding her during this trip, but she still wasn't comfortable with the idea of going to someone's home—she didn't want to put DeLuca or anyone else at risk. Too many people had already been in harm's way to protect her, and now Nathan was as well. If anything happened to him she didn't know if she could take it.

"No, just making a quick stop to grab a few things."

His enigmatic answer made her curious but she didn't ask anything else on the short drive over to a residential neighborhood close to base. Nathan pulled into the driveway of a white two-story house with a long porch across the front. He took the keys from the ignition just as Cruz appeared in a silver Bureau-loaned SUV behind them and parked alongside the curb. She didn't know where Vance was, but assumed he was somewhere nearby.

"Come on, she's expecting us."

Taya followed him up the short walkway and up the steps to the front porch. The door opened even before his finger pressed the doorbell. A dark-haired, fit-looking woman somewhere in her mid-twenties stood in the threshold, dressed in snug jeans and a thin black sweater. "Hey. Come on in." She stepped aside to let them enter and closed the door, locking it behind her. "I'm Briar."

Taya noticed that the woman didn't offer a hand to shake, so she kept her hands at her sides. "Taya."

"Nice to meet you."

"You too." Taya shot a questioning look at Nathan. Was this woman DeLuca's... daughter? No, that couldn't be right, unless he'd become a father in his teens. Niece maybe?

"Briar's my commander's better half," Nathan told her in an amused tone.

"Oh." She covered her surprise. There was a pretty big age difference between them, but having known Briar for all of six seconds, Taya could already see the razor sharp edge to her. Similar to that military bearing Nathan and his teammates had. It made her seem much older than she looked.

"Thank you for that," Briar said to him, a smirk on her face as she turned and led the way into the kitchen. "I've got everything ready in here for you."

What did she mean by *everything*? When Taya came around the corner she saw the items laid out on the kitchen island. Clothes, makeup.

"I wasn't sure how big a transformation you guys had in mind, so I've laid out some stuff you can choose from," Briar said. She settled her gaze on Taya, and this time Taya recognized the timeworn look in those dark eyes. Whatever had happened to Briar in the past, she hadn't lived an easy life. "Wig or hair color?"

Taya glanced at Nathan for help. "I…"

"We'll just take a bunch of options with us," he said to Briar, reaching past them to grab some items and put them into a bag she'd left on the countertop. "You got the ID ready?"

"It's here." Briar gathered up what looked like a driver's license and maybe some credit cards. "I digitally lightened her hair color in the pictures, so she'll have to go lighter too."

"Perfect."

"And you'll need this," she said to Taya, picking up a new cell phone. "It's encrypted. Have you made or received any calls from the burner phone?"

"Yes, from Nathan."

She nodded. "I'll transfer all your contacts and whatever else you need into the new one, and you'll leave that burner with me so I can take it apart and make sure no one can trace anything."

Holy. "Wow, okay then."

Briar grinned and shrugged. "Tech stuff isn't my area of expertise, but I can handle this kind of thing."

"Just what is your area of expertise?" Taya asked, unable to contain her curiosity.

A slow smile stretched Briar's mouth, and a satisfied gleam entered her espresso-colored eyes. "Long guns."

Long guns? "You mean…rifles?"

Briar gave a terse nod. "Yes."

"What it means is, she's one of the best shooters in the world, she's just not gonna say that out loud. She can outshoot most military and law enforcement guys I know with a sniper rifle, including me," Nathan interjected, his voice shaded with a hint of amusement and a whole lot of admiration. "Except for maybe her other half and the shooters on our sniper teams. But she holds her own with them too on the range."

Whoa. Taya eyed her with newfound interest, trying to imagine this trim, petite woman as capable of being that lethal. "Okay, now I'm fascinated. And a little intimidated, to be honest."

Briar's cheeks turned pink and she frowned as though uncomfortable with the praise, and shot what seemed like a censoring look at Nathan. He obviously wasn't supposed to have told Taya that much, and she wondered why. "Everybody's got their own strengths," Briar said, waving a hand away in dismissal.

"Actually, you two have a lot more in common than you might think," Nathan said to Taya now. "Maybe after the trial's over and things have settled down you guys can do lunch or something. Briar's got some very interesting friends she might decide to tell you about. And if you're lucky, she'll even let you live afterward." His eyes danced with amusement as he said the last part.

Now Briar shot him a warning, narrow-eyed look. He just grinned at her, managing to look both sexy and adorable at the same time. Then Briar shifted her gaze to Taya. "Anyway, enough small talk. Let's get your phone set up so you guys can hit the road."

Fifteen minutes later she was back in the SUV with a new phone and a bag full of things to change her identity. Nathan plugged his phone into the charger in the center console before wandering down to the curb to talk with Cruz for a minute and Taya took the time to gear up for these next few days. She'd have to dye her hair as soon as they got to the hotel.

The phone in the console rang. Taya tensed and glanced at it, prepared for more bad news. It was almost midnight. She expected an unknown number or maybe a picture of one of his teammates to show up on screen. Instead a twenty-something blonde named Jennifer appeared.

Taya frowned. Seemed weird, but maybe someone

he worked with. Had to be important, if she'd called at this hour though.

Or it could be his girlfriend.

Taya flushed, a sudden sinking feeling in her gut. The way he'd jumped in and volunteered to guard her had somehow convinced her he was unattached, but now she realized that was stupid. A man like him wouldn't be wanting for female company. A sharp spike of jealousy streaked through her, taking her by surprise. She had no claim on him.

Nathan climbed back into the vehicle and started the engine. "You hungry? Want me to stop to grab something before we head out of town."

"No, I'm good. Someone named Jennifer just called you, by the way."

His expression froze for an instant, then he looked almost uncomfortable. "Thanks," he muttered, but made no move to check his messages or call her back. Not work related, she guessed. And for a woman to call at this time of night, they had to know each other pretty well. So, either girlfriend or a hookup.

Nathan didn't offer an explanation and she didn't ask. It was none of her business, she reminded herself. "Where are we going?" she asked instead when he pulled out onto the road, not wanting to think about Nathan and whoever he was seeing at the moment.

"Out to the coast. We're booked in a small inn just south of Virginia Beach."

An inn? It didn't seem like the most secure choice, but she supposed it made sense in terms of decreasing visibility. And she'd have three highly trained and extremely capable HRT members to watch over her. "For how long?"

"A few days at least, until we've got a better idea of what's going on. But we won't be moving you back into D.C. until the night before you take the stand. Maybe not even until that morning. Normally we'd use a safe house but there wasn't time to secure one and this place has been well vetted so we're staying there for the time being."

She nodded, but inside she was thinking about all the things that were out of her control right now. She didn't like it, but there was nothing she could do to change that. When the quiet grew oppressive, she searched for a change in topic. "Briar seems like a very interesting woman."

"Yeah, you could say that," he said dryly. "She and DeLuca have only been together for a few months, but I can't imagine him with anyone else now. She's badass, for sure, but she's also pretty quiet and on the shy side. Introverted, like you."

Taya made a humming noise. She hadn't always been that way. Before she'd been kidnapped she'd loved to go out to clubs with her friends where she'd dance the night away. Now her social circle consisted solely of her dad, brother, and a handful of long-term girlfriends. "Guess she'd have to be if she was a sniper."

"A lot of them are wired that way, but not all. She's been on her own for a long time before she met Matt, so this is a big change for her. The guys like to get together for barbecues and dinners from time to time and I know at first it was really uncomfortable for her to be thrown into the middle of that."

"Now, see, being in the middle of that much testosterone would intimidate me, but I doubt it would faze Briar."

Nathan shot her a sidelong glance. "I don't think it would intimidate you either. I don't think much could, actually."

It was true that her tolerance for stress was much higher than it had been. Little things that might have bothered her before didn't even register on her radar anymore. But since she didn't know how to respond to the praise in his voice, she changed the subject. "Everybody seems to call you Nate or Schroder, but I've always called you Nathan. What would you prefer I call you?"

He shrugged his broad shoulders, drawing her eyes to the swell of muscle beneath his shirt. She'd love to glide her hands over them, explore every dip and hollow, find out what spots made him purr when she kneaded his muscles. "Whatever you want to call me is fine. But I like the way you say my name."

There was no mistaking the sexual undercurrent to his tone on that last part. It surprised her for a moment, but when he glanced over at her this time she felt the invisible currents of heat flowing between them. Was he seeing anyone, or not? She'd told herself it was none of her business but dammit, she wanted to know whether or not she had a chance with him once his bodyguard duty was over.

Not wanting to make things awkward between them, she didn't ask, but she planned to eventually. They kept the conversation light, mostly about her family, and then let a comfortable silence descend after a few minutes. "You must be tired," he said, reaching into the backseat to grab something and came up with what looked like a jacket. "We've got another two-and-a-half hours or so on the road. Fold this up and use it for a pillow if you want. Get some sleep."

She took the thick hoodie from him with a murmur of thanks and rolled it up into a makeshift pillow. It smelled like him and laundry detergent. Setting it between her head and the window, she closed her eyes and breathed in the clean, spicy scent, wishing it was his chest her head rested upon instead. Feeling truly secure for the first time all day, she put her safety in his hands and let herself drift off.

Chapter Seven

Taya wasn't sure how long she'd been asleep but the next thing she knew she was opening her eyes to find Nathan parking the SUV out front of a pale yellow Victorian-style inn.

"We'll wait here until Cruz checks us in," he said, watching as his teammate entered via the front porch.

"Where's Vance?"

"He'll stay in an unmarked car down the street. We'll all take turns rotating through various roles."

Taya secretly hoped that Nathan would be spending more time with her than the others. "I'm not complaining and it's beautiful, but why this place?" This wasn't a holiday, she was a federal witness.

"One of our teammates, Bauer, is a former SEAL and he knew about this place. The innkeeper's got a good rep in the Spec Ops community. Her son is an active duty frogman stationed out of Virginia Beach, so she knows all about security and discretion. A lot of Spec Ops guys come to stay here when they want a few days away with their wives or girlfriends or whatever. We didn't have a lot of time to find a good location so Bauer called to set it up and she put her two guests up at another inn just to make room for us."

"That was nice of her." She stared through the windshield at the pretty inn, the front verandah wrapped with strands of white lights and a pair of gas lanterns flickering on either side of the wide front door. A few minutes later Cruz stepped back out onto the porch and held up a key.

"All right, let's go," Nathan said.

As soon as he opened the passenger door, the rhythmic sigh of the surf reached him. Standing beside the vehicle, Taya closed her eyes for a moment and took a deep breath of the cool, salt-tinged air. Almost as though she was savoring the experience.

Nate took her suitcase from the back and stayed at her back while she walked up the front steps to meet Cruz. The other agent gave her a small smile and handed her the key. "Pleasant dreams."

"Thanks. You too." The response was automatic, but immediately she realized it sounded stupid. Both he and Nathan would likely be up most of the night, keeping watch and doing investigative work and whatever else being on a security detail involved.

"Let's get you settled," Nathan said, leading the way up the wooden staircase to the second floor, Cruz right behind her. Nathan held up a hand in a silent command for her to stay put while he and Cruz went in the room first to look around.

Cruz walked out and gave her a nod, then Nathan stuck his head around the doorway a moment later. "Okay. I put your suitcase on the ottoman over in the corner."

"Thanks." She walked past him into the room and tucked a lock of hair behind one ear, trying not to stare at him as he shut the door, the action sending her heart rate up a notch. Over by the bed the leaded glass lamp on the nightstand cast a warm yellow glow that brought out the rich red highlights in his hair and lined his broad shoulders. He was an inch or two over six feet and his presence in this cozy, feminine room seemed suddenly intimate somehow.

Blocking the path her train of thoughts wanted to follow, she searched for a safer topic. "Should I color my hair now, or…"

"In the morning's fine. Get some sleep first. We'll probably eat downstairs, but not all together. One of us will be with you whenever you leave your room." His warm hazel eyes seemed to caress her face for a moment, then settled on her eyes. "Just remember you're safe here. And I'm right next door if you need anything."

He might not have meant the double entendre intentionally, but there was no mistaking the sudden leap of heat she read in his eyes as his words registered. She'd caught flashes of male awareness and maybe even appreciation from him a few times today, but this was the first time she'd been sure the pull wasn't one-sided.

Staring up at him, Taya caught her breath at the answering flare of arousal that sparked inside her. Their history was already problematic, all tangled up with strong emotion forged in the most difficult of circumstances. Knowing he was guarding her only intensified her attraction to him. If it had been just physical, she could have ignored it easily enough. But it wasn't.

Nathan was strong and protective and capable, but he also had a softer, incredibly caring side to him that had stolen a piece of her heart long ago. She'd seen him fight through his grief to do his job while under fire and mourning the loss of his fellow PJ, in the field and on the chopper ride to base.

She'd felt his skilled touch while he tended to her, keeping her from bleeding to death, then again later after she'd come out of surgery at Bagram. His face had been lined with exhaustion as he'd leaned over her bed. He'd cupped the side of her face in one hand, just above where the bandages stopped, smiled down at her and said, *You're going home today, Taya.*

She remembered tearing up instantly, her voice scratchy because of the recent intubation. *Because of you.*

No, he'd said, shaking his head, his expression fervent. *Because you're a survivor.*

Just the memory of it made her heart swell.

All those things together made him impossible to forget. Him stepping up to guard her today, now standing only feet away alone in this room with her, made him irresistible.

Nathan cleared his throat and looked away. "Well. See you in the morning." He started for the door, took two steps then paused and turned back to her. His shoulders were tense and while she couldn't read his expression, she could tell he had something important on his mind.

"What?" she asked softly, heart beating faster.

"I need to know," he began, then stopped. "I need to know if—" He pulled in a deep breath, let it out, and his hesitation told her that whatever he was about to ask, it had been bothering him for a while. "Did Hassan hurt you? Did he…" He let the sentence trail off, though there was no mistaking what he was asking.

The mention of her tribal husband's name caught her off guard for a moment and doused the flames of desire slowly licking at her insides. But she understood why Nathan asked her, given what she'd said about Chloe earlier. She should have expected him to ask more.

Holding his gaze, Taya considered her answer carefully before speaking. "He treated me better than any of the other men treated their wives."

Nathan stared back at her in silence, his eyes full of torment as he put together what that probably meant and filled in the blanks on his own.

Taya wished she could say something to ease his mind about it, but she couldn't. And she refused to lie to him about this. "He was an undercover DEA agent, born to parents who emigrated to the U.S. from Tajikistan before he was born. I didn't know any of that until later though. In fact, the first time he ever spoke English to me was the night he took me from Qureshi's camp and ran."

She'd been confused and terrified, woken from a sound sleep when Hassan had come into her tent and clapped a hand over her mouth, stifling her scream. He'd been rigid with tension.

No time to explain, he'd said. *If you want to live, we have to leave right now.*

As the shock wore off she'd become furious. He'd lied to her the entire time, put her through nine months of hell, using and manipulating her as much as Qureshi had.

In time, she'd come to understand why he'd done it. "His life depended on his ability to play his part without ever giving himself away, and maintaining his cover no matter what. So he did what he had to do to make our marriage look real."

Not rape in the violent sense that most people would assume she'd endured. More of an awkward, uncomfortable joining that she'd been too afraid to protest. It had been awkward for him too. He'd cared about her on some level. But even if she'd protested it wouldn't have mattered.

She could feel herself flushing as she went on. "It would have been suspicious if he hadn't. And it was only once." Once in nine months as husband and wife, to make it official. She swallowed. "He didn't have a choice. Two of Qureshi's men were in the room as witnesses."

That was the hardest part to get over, that awful, crawling mortification she'd felt as they witnessed that humiliating act. Hassan had treated her gently and gotten it over with as fast as possible. It was by far the worst thing she'd endured during her captivity. Bruises and cuts healed. Her soul hadn't recovered as easily.

Nathan drew in a ragged breath but didn't say anything. She could feel his stare boring into her, feel his horror and outrage.

As difficult as this was to say to him aloud, she shrugged. The past was what it was, and couldn't be changed. Twisted though the reasoning behind Hassan's decisions and actions might have been, she accepted it all now. Looking back, she realized now that he'd actually protected her from a lot of things during the nine months they'd been "married", at least as far as tribal custom was concerned.

"I found out later that he planned several times to get me out before that, but his attempts always fell through for various reasons. The government wanted him to stay until he had what they needed against Qureshi and his network. It wasn't until Hassan's cover was blown that he was forced to risk everything and run that night in an attempt to reach friendly lines before Qureshi's men caught up with him. He could have left me behind, but he didn't, even though he knew I'd slow him down. He ended up giving his life to save mine, and I'll always be grateful to him for that."

Nathan looked haunted now. "Jesus Christ, Taya." His voice was hoarse, full of anguish.

She knew how it sounded. Her first therapist had told her she suffered from classic Stockholm Syndrome, but in Taya's opinion, that was a copout, bullshit description. Her relationship to and feelings toward Hassan were so incredibly complex, no label any psychologist could come up with would ever fit the real description.

She swallowed, wishing she knew what to do to comfort Nathan, erase that terrible look in his eyes. "Like I said before, compared to the other women, until then I had it easy."

He shook his head, apparently at a loss for words.

Taya continued, needing to at least try to explain her reasoning to him. "It's complicated, and I won't pretend that part of me still feels betrayed by what he did. But once I got home, after a while it dawned on me that I had a choice to make if I wanted to move on with my life. Just because our pasts are part of us, it doesn't mean they have to define us. I refused to give my past that kind of power over me. So I chose to let it go."

When he didn't respond, just kept staring at her, she stayed silent to let her words sink in. She'd seen the way he reacted back at the hotel when she'd said O'Neil's name, and even without a psych or medical degree it was obvious to her that he hadn't come to terms with what had happened that day. If she could spare him any more pain by offering the solution that had helped her overcome her past, she'd gladly give it. Only she wasn't certain he was ready to accept it yet.

After a moment a slight frown marred his brow but then he nodded, and his silent acceptance gave her the courage to continue.

"I mean, it wasn't easy, not by any means, but in the end I realized I couldn't change the past and only had control over *me* and what happened going forward. I made the decision to make peace with everything and move on," she said softly.

He was silent a long moment, studying her in the expanding silence. "How could you let that go?" he asked, his tone and expression incredulous. "How could you let that go after what he did to you? What *they* did to you?"

"Forgiveness," she answered. She knew it sounded overly simplistic and probably cheesy, but that's exactly what had helped her break from the past. "Hassan saw himself as a patriot, first and foremost. He did what he had to in order to accomplish his mission, and did what he could to protect me at the same time. It's why he married me, so I was off limits to the others." She was thankful for that too, in hindsight. The alternative was beyond bearing.

"He risked everything to get me out of that hellish situation, and wound up paying for my freedom with his life." Taya paused to pull in a slow breath. "I've forgiven him for the rest of it. I had to, to be able to go on. But I didn't forgive him for *his* sake. I forgave him for mine." She needed Nathan to understand the difference. "Forgiveness was what earned me my true freedom."

He was quiet a moment. "Well then, you're a better person than me," he said in a low voice, his eyes burning with emotion. Confusion maybe. And pain. So much pain buried beneath the calm, easy façade he wore, even if he thought no one else could see it. Taya saw it. She desperately wanted to help him unlock it, let it go once and for all before it ate away at him like a cancer.

But she couldn't, not unless he wanted the help. And he wasn't ready yet. He might never be ready.

Taya shook her head, unwilling to let this go just yet, disturbed by the hint of self-loathing she detected in his tone. "No. Not at all. And I think the person you need to forgive is yourself." She said it gently, but she swore he flinched before he looked away, but not before she read the flash of guilt on his face. Did he blame himself for O'Neil's death?

The need to wrap her arms around him, try to at least ease his torment, was so strong it was all she could do to stay where she was. And she wanted his arms around her again too, with a strength that frightened her.

It had been more than six years since she'd craved a man's touch. She hadn't dated anyone since coming home five years ago, just hadn't been interested, and she'd always assumed her captivity was to blame.

She'd been wrong. Because standing here now in front of this incredible man, she was forced to acknowledge the hard truth of why that was.

Deep down, all this time, on some level she'd known she only wanted Nathan.

Taya sucked in a soft breath as the realization slammed through her. The six-year age difference between them wasn't even a consideration for her, and she didn't think it was for him either. Right or wrong, emotional transference from the trauma in Afghanistan or not, she wanted him. And she was pretty sure he wanted her too, even despite the things she'd just told him.

Long seconds ticked past as they stared at each other across the room. The charged silence seemed to crackle with the electric potential of what would happen if they touched.

Taya caught the way his nostrils flared and heat kindled in his eyes as her gaze roamed over his face and down his neck, over the T-shirt stretched across the solid muscles in his chest and stomach. A powerful tide of need and hunger rose inside her. She thought of the woman who'd called him earlier and felt stupid. God, how she wished things were different.

If he was available, not here guarding her in an official capacity and possibly risking his career for her sake, she would have walked past him to lock the door and turned back to face him, letting her actions tell him exactly what she wanted.

Him.

More than anything right now she wanted to take his face in her hands and kiss him with all the pent-up longing she'd locked away for so long. But she couldn't. And for his sake, she *wouldn't*.

Realizing she was still staring, Taya blinked and looked away, a flush of embarrassment creeping up her neck. "Well. That's enough unsolicited advice from me for one night, huh? Thanks again, for everything."

Nathan didn't move. After a beat of silence she

looked up at him once more. As if the eye contact was exactly what he'd been waiting for, he held her gaze as he spoke, so strong it almost felt like a physical touch. "I don't want your gratitude, Taya. And there's nothing I wouldn't do to keep you safe."

His words echoed through her, resonated deep inside her heart.

Then his gaze traveled over her face like a caress, lingering on her mouth for a long, sizzling moment before coming back to settle on hers. And Taya knew in that moment if he hadn't been her bodyguard, they'd have been making good use of the queen-size bed behind her.

Heat swept through her body, tightening her nipples. She wanted to feel his hands and mouth on her, feel the weight of his strong frame as he pressed her down into the mattress. Nathan would cherish her with his strength, not violate her.

That only made the heat burn hotter.

"Sleep well, little warrior," he murmured instead, then turned to go.

Little warrior. The unique endearment, the admiration and respect in his voice as he said it, made her throat tighten. Before she could respond, he was gone.

Taya stared at the closed door, feeling like her heart had just been torn wide open.

Chapter Eight

*" **I**ncoming!"*

The shouted warning penetrated Nate's brain a split second before his body reacted. The man next to him was already dead, having bled out from multiple bullet wounds. Nate dove to the ground behind a low rock wall and covered his head with his arms an instant before the impact.

When the earth settled and he looked up, O'Neil was gone.

Nate woke in the darkness with his heart in his throat. Immediately he shot up in the bed, confused for a split second as to why he was still dressed and on top of the covers. Then he saw the red digital display of the clock on the night table and the muffled roar of the waves crashing against the beach outside reached him.

Virginia Beach. Historic inn. Guarding Taya.

He inhaled deeply, forced the air out slowly and ran a hand over his damp face. *Jesus.*

O'Neil had died out there, right in front of him while Nate had been helpless to stop it. Nate had walked away with barely a mark on him. That would always bother him.

Since the room was empty, Cruz must be downstairs either in the kitchen or living room. Nate only had twenty minutes until he was due to relieve Cruz anyhow. He'd switch places with Vance the next shift after that.

He got up and went to the bathroom to splash water over his face and neck, then crept down the old wooden staircase to find his teammate standing at the kitchen counter, facing the water, the thin moonlight the only illumination.

"Not a bad gig, huh?" Cruz murmured to Nate without turning around.

"Could be worse," he agreed, and walked over to help himself to some coffee he smelled from the half-full pot on the counter. "How old is this?"

"I just made it an hour ago." Cruz set his cup in the sink. "No calls since we checked in. She doing okay?" He nodded toward the ceiling, indicating Taya.

"Yeah, she's doing amazingly well, all things considered." Helluva lot better than he was, which he found sadly ironic.

He was the one with the advanced training. The government had spent hundreds of thousands of dollars on him to ensure he was as capable of taking a life as he was of saving one. He'd been through freaking advanced SERE school and too many other psychological courses to name, all meant to prepare him for the worst. He should be able to handle things better than anyone, yet Taya was light years ahead of him in terms of being able to cope with the mental and emotional trauma that came with seeing combat.

Man, talk about a kick in the ass.

"That's some seriously twisted shit she went through," Cruz muttered, shaking his head. He and Vance had read her file after the briefing back at base.

Nate nodded. Even he didn't know the fine details,

but he could imagine well enough what she'd gone through and it made his skin crawl. "So fucked up that an undercover American agent would do that. Force her to marry him and live under those conditions just to maintain his cover. She said she was well treated compared to the others and that he protected her from a lot of stuff, but all that tells me is that he didn't protect her from other stuff." It infuriated him.

Cruz turned and the moonlight cut across him, showing the disgusted face he made. "No doubt." He shifted his stance, putting his back to the counter and leaned against it. Folding his arms across his chest, Cruz gave him a level look that made Nate's stomach tense. "So out of curiosity, what did you wind up saying to Matt to get him to agree to you being on her detail?"

Nate ignored the niggling guilt and shrugged. "Just that I figured she might be more comfortable with me being assigned to her. She knows me, trusts me already to some extent."

Cruz's eyelids lowered to half-mast and one side of his mouth quirked up. "Uh huh. And it had absolutely *nothing* to do with personal reasons on your behalf, right?"

His teammate's bland tone told him Cruz was teasing. Still, the question made Nate defensive. "So what if it does? I feel like I owe her, and it's the least I can do to make sure she's safe while she testifies against that asshole. After we talked, both Matt and Tuck agreed that I had more motivation than anyone else to keep her safe, so I got the green light." Did Cruz have a problem with it or something?

His teammate nodded, his light brown eyes watchful. "You're into her though."

Nate felt the back of his neck flush and was grateful for the few days' worth of stubble covering the lower half of his face, even though it was fairly dark in here. But he didn't bother denying it. "You worried I can't get the job done?" And dammit, he couldn't help the defensive edge in his voice.

Cruz shook his head. "Nope. If I was, I would've said so to Matt and Tuck earlier. Just trying to be real with you, bro. You've been strung pretty tight lately." Even though Cruz didn't say it in an accusing way, it still embarrassed him. "Is she part of the reason?"

Nate made a sound of disgust. "Christ, since when did you go to shrink school?"

Cruz merely grinned. "No, seriously, I'm curious. Because the way you look at her makes me feel like I'm intruding when I'm in the same damn room with you both."

Nate rubbed the back of his neck and poured the damn coffee. It was too fucking early and he was too strung out to have this conversation right now. "Look, I care about her, okay? But don't worry about me not being focused. I'm tight."

"Not worried about that, man, I already told you. So let's drop it." He stepped forward and clapped a hand on Nate's shoulder. "You good to take over now?"

"Yeah." He took a sip of coffee, covered a wince as the scalding liquid burned down his throat.

"See you at oh-six-hundred then."

Nate nodded and slipped his earpiece in. When he was alone in the kitchen he expelled a deep breath and let his shoulders relax. Shit, he hated feeling like he still had to prove himself to the others. That was on him, he knew it was, since the guys had been nothing but good to him since he'd joined the team.

He just wanted this so badly—wanted them to respect him as much as he respected them. And he couldn't help feeling like he was on the verge of losing that if he didn't pull himself together. Part of him kept thinking that maybe this job guarding Taya would help him kick the baggage he'd been holding onto. God knew seeing her again had stirred up all kinds of shit in his head, but being around her also soothed him in a way he hadn't expected.

He glanced toward the ceiling, thought of her curled up in that antique four-poster bed upstairs. Was she sleeping soundly? Or did she have nightmares still like he did? The way she'd looked at him earlier in her room, like she'd been imagining what he tasted like, had been a special kind of torture. Even now he wondered what it would feel like to slide his hands into her curls and kiss her, sink into her. He got the feeling if he did, he'd be drawn in so deep that he'd never be able to pull free.

And for some reason that didn't scare the shit out of him like he'd thought it would. Taya was different from all the women he'd been with. Losing himself in her wouldn't be about escaping his issues; it would be about mutual respect and healing. He hoped for both of them.

Needing to collect his chaotic thoughts, Nate slipped outside onto the back porch, shutting the French door quietly behind him. He walked to the railing and eased one hip onto it, staring out at the rolling waves as they crashed against the shore, illuminated by a sliver moon peeking out from behind a bank of clouds. The damp, salty breeze ruffled his hair and went straight through his jeans and T-shirt.

Taya's words about forgiveness and not letting the past define her kept coming back to him. She was absolutely right. He had to find a way to make peace with, or at least become at peace with what had happened in Afghanistan, and during his childhood. He was a grown-ass man. Time to own his shit and deal with it.

He just wasn't sure how to.

Vance's deep voice came through his earpiece. "Single vehicle approaching from the east. Silver minivan."

96

Nate sat up straight. "Roger that."

"Parking near the front walkway. Looks like single occupant. Driver's getting out. Single male, carrying a stack of something in his hands. Maybe magazines. Can't see a weapon. Want me to follow?"

Could be hiding something in the magazines. "I'll check it out. Stand by. Cruz?"

"I'm on it."

A slight shuffling sound broke into his thoughts. He was on his feet in an instant, staring toward the left side of the house where the sound had come from.

Footsteps. Barely audible over the sound of the waves.

Nate tapped his earpiece. "Footsteps coming from out front now. Vance, he still alone?"

"That's affirm. On his way up the walkway."

Nate reached back for the weapon he'd placed at the small of his back and moved into the deep shadows hugging the wall, all his senses on alert. His boots were silent on the wooden floorboards as he slowly made his way to the corner of the building and paused. The man was moving around out front.

There's no way anyone could have found us. None.

The FBI had booked all four rooms at the inn, paying double the usual rate with a Bureau credit card just to ensure they'd be alone and have plenty of privacy over the next few days. And there was no way anyone had followed them here. He, Vance and Cruz had been hyper vigilant.

Weapon lowered in front of him but at the ready, Nate eased around the corner and started for the front porch. This was probably nothing, but he wasn't leaving anything to chance. He'd take any principal's safety seriously, but especially Taya's.

The lamps mounted on either side of the front door were still on, illuminating the front of the inn. He caught sight of the man moving on the porch and stilled, just out of sight, then eased his head forward enough to see. As if he sensed someone watching, the man looked up and froze.

Nate took in the shock on the middle-aged man's face, and the stack of newspapers in his hands. He was bent forward slightly as if he'd been about to place them on the doorstep, frozen as he stared back at Nate.

Nate tucked his weapon away out of sight and nodded to him as he fished out his badge and held it out for him to see. "You're out early."

The man straightened, watching Nate warily. "I always deliver this time of the morning. Nancy likes her guests to have their papers first thing, in case they get up early for coffee."

Nate nodded. "I'll take one."

The man hesitated for a second, then stretched out an arm and handed one to Nate. "Have a good day."

"You too." Nate stayed there until the man walked down the pathway and out to his car parked near the end of the walkway. When the headlights swung in an arc and the car drove away, he did one more sweep of the property just to be sure.

"We're all clear," Vance reported from down the street.

"Copy that."

Cruz was waiting for him at the side of the porch when he got back. "See anything?" he asked, holstering his own weapon.

"No, all clear." Nate glanced down at the newspaper in his hand and unrolled it. On the front page, the headline read Shooter Targeted Qureshi Trial Witness and showed a picture of the federal marshals tangled on the floor with the dying shooter. Below it, embedded into the article was a picture of Taya, dressed in a business suit, smiling on stage during an Amnesty International speech.

"Fuck," he muttered, and handed it over to Cruz.

His teammate scowled at the front page. "Greeeeaaaat," he drawled sarcastically before lowering the paper. "Makes our job so much easier, to keep her hidden now that everyone from here to D.C. knows she's in the area."

Nate sighed. "I'll call DeLuca. You go on back to sleep."

"All right."

Alone, Nate headed back around to the rear porch. A slight movement caught his attention as he neared the French doors leading off the kitchen. He stopped as the handle turned and then a head of dark curls appeared in the opening. Taya glanced over and gave a tentative smile when she saw him. "Cruz said it was okay for me to come down."

She was wearing some sort of long, knit coat that came to her ankles, over what looked like yoga pants and a snug top that hugged the ample curve of her breasts. She wrapped her arms around her middle, cutting off his view of her breasts, for which he should probably be thankful.

He unstuck his tongue from the roof of his mouth. "Yeah, it's fine, but you should still be upstairs sleeping."

"I heard someone on the front porch."

"Just the paper delivery guy."

"I know. Cruz left it on the table at the bottom of the stairs. Not the first time I've made the front page."

Hell. "To them it's business as usual. All they care about is their story and selling papers. They don't think about what the consequences of the material they print might be for others."

Taya looked out at the ocean, then over at the porch swing at the end of the deck before coming back to him. "Can I sit out here with you for a while?"

He'd planned to go back inside but if she wanted to stay out here with him, he'd allow it for a while, but not out in the open where he couldn't guarantee her safety. "Uh, sure."

He indicated the porch swing, set with its back to the far wall of the enclosed porch. She walked over to the swing, her curves highlighted by the moonlight filtering beneath the eaves of the porch. And just like that, a fantasy took shape in his mind.

He envisioned her standing naked in front of him, her back to him, his hands mapping the shape of her body from her shoulders and down her ribs, to the indent of her waist. He'd slide his hands around her hips and hold her steady while he bent to nuzzle the vulnerable spot at her nape, just beneath where those enticing curls began.

She'd been violated by a man before, by someone she'd been forced to rely on for protection and survival. Nate longed to worship her, burn away those memories with his touch, his mouth, his body.

He'd nibble and nip his way down her neck to her shoulder, feeling every little shiver and gasp, kiss and lick at the thin scars there, then follow the indent of her spine, touching his mouth to every little mark the shrapnel had left on her body. Savor her the way she was meant to be savored.

When he reached the base of her spine he'd let his hands wander over the backs of her thighs, then up the insides, before sliding his fingertips in between. And when she was wet and needy he'd bend her over at the waist, hold her hips tight and use his mouth on her most sensitive place until she writhed and begged for more.

Taya sank onto one end of the swing and looked up at him uncertainly. Nate shook away the erotic image, feeling guilty for even imagining it. And shit, now he was half hard and had to sit out here pretending she was nothing more than a principal on a job to him, when she was already so much more than that.

She wrapped the folds of her sweater coat tighter

around herself. Nate grabbed a folded up quilt from the top of a chest near the railing and shook it out. "Here." He settled it around her, tucking it over her shoulders for good measure. Not only would it keep her warm, it would give him another layer between them.

Taya offered him a little smile. "Thanks."

"Sure." He sank onto the opposite end, leaving about eight inches of room between them.

Taya tucked her feet up underneath her and breathed out a soft sigh. "It's peaceful out here, listening to the waves."

He nodded, half his attention on her and the other half watching and listening for anything going on around the perimeter. He was still on the clock and he wasn't going to let his guard down fully, not even out here alone with her in the darkness.

"How do you think that reporter found out about me?"

He grunted. "Who knows? Could be something as simple as paying off a bystander who happened to get a picture of you at the scene. Or someone who worked at the airport."

"Do you think they know where we are?"

"*No.*" No way.

Her shoulders relaxed. "That's good."

He resisted the urge to wrap an arm around her shoulders. "I don't want you to worry about things like that. Not with us here."

She sighed. "I know, and I don't want you to think I don't trust you guys and your abilities. It's just hard for me to put my safety into anyone else's hands in light of everything that's happened. Both before and now."

"I can understand that. But you leave everything security related to us and use this time to recharge. Think of it as a kind of vacation."

A slight nod as she stared out at the waves, and the

hint of a smile played around the edges of her mouth. "I'd be lying if I said I wasn't worried about the trial."

"Have you been prepped for it?"

"Mostly. The prosecution wants to meet with me a few more times before I take the stand. But it's not testifying or security concerns that bother me the most."

Nate watched her, waiting for her to continue.

"It's seeing Qureshi for the first time in five years, and worrying that my testimony won't be enough to put him away."

"It will be. With you and the others, there's no way it won't be." And he admired the hell out of her for standing up and doing what she could to see the asshole brought to justice.

Now she turned her head and met his gaze. In the soft moonlight, her eyes seemed to gleam bright silver. "Whenever it happens. The attacks today could delay it weeks or months, or even more."

"We'll know soon enough. And if it's going to be a while, I think you should consider going into WITSEC."

She stared at him. "Because that worked out so well for Chloe."

The devastation in her eyes sliced him inside. Unable to stop himself, he wrapped an arm around her shoulders. "I'm sorry about what happened to her."

Her lashes lowered. "Yeah, I am too." She huddled deeper under the blanket. "Can we talk about something else?"

"Sure. Like what?"

"Like, what did you get your degree in? I read that all HRT members are Special Agents or higher, and therefore have to have a four-year degree at the minimum. And that you have to serve with the FBI for at least two years before you're eligible to try out for the HRT."

"You Googled us," he said with a grin.

"Of course I did. Last night I was insanely curious

about the HRT all of a sudden."

He chuckled under his breath. "Criminal justice."

"Really? Mine was in inter—"

"International studies," he finished for her. "I know."

She quirked a brow. "You checked me out too?"

"Something like that." Initially after the CSAR op he had, but now he'd read her official file the Bureau had compiled on her. He was sure she'd at least guessed that. With one foot on the porch floorboards he set the swing into motion. The slight creak mixed with the sound of the waves pounding against the sand in the distance.

"Can I ask you something?"

At her soft question he glanced over at her. Damn, she was pretty with the breeze tousling her curls around her face. Her expression was serious, her eyes nearly silver in the moonlight. "Sure."

"Did what I told you about Hassan change the way you see me?"

What? Now she had his full attention. "No, not at all. Why would you think that?" Had she seriously been worried about that?

She moved her shoulders in a taut shrug. "I just… I know how it must have sounded to you. Like I was a victim."

"You *were* a victim. But that's not how I see you, and it's not how you present yourself. Not at all. Like I told you before, you're a survivor."

A slight smile tugged at her mouth. "If that's true, then I'm relieved."

"It's true. I think you're one of the strongest people I've ever known." His hand tightened around her shoulder. He needed her to believe him. If he'd said or done something to make her feel otherwise it would slice him up inside.

She gave a slight nod and focused her gaze on the quilt spread across her lap. "I'm working on it."

Sweetheart, compared to the rest of us, you're already way ahead of the game.

"Since coming home, I haven't uh, haven't gone out much." She shot him a sideways glance, as though gauging his reaction.

Nate sifted through her words, trying to figure out what she was getting at. "You mean in general? Or do you mean with guys?"

"Guys. I haven't…dated since then."

He stared at her in surprise. In five years? This gorgeous, brave, accomplished and sexy woman hadn't been on a date in five fucking years because of what had been done to her? "Well that's… I can see why you wouldn't have wanted to." God, what the hell had that fucker Hassan done to her? His free hand curled into a fist, his entire body tensing.

"What about you?"

He blinked, forced himself to relax. "Pardon?"

"Well, here I show up in town and suddenly all hell breaks loose, then you volunteer to be part of my security detail. Am I going to have to worry about a jealous girlfriend or two coming after me as well?" Her tone was teasing but her words struck deep. And suddenly Nate felt dirty. Cheap.

He jerked his gaze away, focused on the rollers crashing on the sand because he couldn't take the scrutiny of her stare any longer. "No. No girlfriends." Just a string of faceless, nameless lays that made him feel like the worst kind of player. He was done with that lifestyle though.

Shame rose up, thick enough to choke him. Taya would be disgusted, at the very least disappointed if she knew the truth. He couldn't stomach the thought of her looking at him like that. "But even if I did, you wouldn't have to worry. Legally I couldn't tell anyone about who I was working security for," he added.

"Oh. I guess that's good, then. Because I've got enough on my plate to worry about at the moment." When he didn't answer or respond to her wry attempt at humor, she sat up straighter. "Hey. What's wrong?"

He shook his head. "Nothing." *Just that I hate who I've become. I don't want to be that guy anymore.* Looking over at her, he forced a smile. "It's just... Seeing you again has inspired me to want to be a better person."

She searched his eyes. "I think you're a very good person. One of the best I've ever known."

Only because you don't really know me. "Trust me, I could stand some improvement."

Taya didn't say anything for a long moment. The breeze picked up, colder than before. She shifted, trying to huddle deeper beneath the quilt. Nate saw his chance and took it.

"Cold?"

"Yeah. And getting sleepy," she admitted.

"Come on," he said, pulling her up from the swing. "Time for you to go inside and get back to bed. Sun'll be up before you know it."

"What about you?" she asked as he led her to the French doors.

"I've got some work to do. I'll see you at breakfast." He shut the doors behind them. Immediately he felt warmer, the sound of the surf muted now.

"Okay." She stopped at the threshold of the kitchen, glanced back at him with those too-wise eyes. "I'm really glad you're here, Nathan."

"I'm glad too." And he truly was. It was almost a miracle that they'd met again. There was no place on earth he'd rather be right now than here, watching over her.

He listened to the creak of the stairs as she went up, alone. Standing in the shadowy kitchen, he wished like hell he had the right to follow her there. He wanted to crawl into her bed beside her and hold her tight in his arms

105

all night, keeping the monsters at bay.
Especially the ones in his head.

Chapter Nine

Ayman dragged himself out of bed and stumbled to the shower after allowing himself a brief half hour nap. He and Jaleel needed to get away from the apartment but he'd been so exhausted he couldn't have functioned without at least some sleep.

He was supposed to be at the restaurant well before breakfast service started, but he'd already called in sick a couple hours ago. He had more important things to take care of, and the money he wanted depended on him carrying out The Brethren's orders.

Though it was still dark outside and he was beat, he couldn't afford to sleep anymore. They'd been up all night trying to find a lead on the whore, and all they'd managed to find so far was a short video clip of her entering the hotel yesterday afternoon with some big, government security-type guys, then her leaving late last night with a different team.

That was it. No location, no clues that would help narrow the search. There were no cell phone accounts or credit card transactions to tip them off. All the searches they'd run, all the websites Jaleel had managed to hack into, all for nothing. And his father had asked way too many questions when he'd let them in last night. It made Ayman extremely nervous. If his father suspected something was up, he wouldn't let it go.

The hot shower did little to help clear his brain. He walked out of the steam-filled bathroom and into the living room to find Jaleel dead asleep in his seat at the desk shoved into the far corner of the room. His laptop was still on, a bunch of coding Ayman didn't understand typed onto the screen. Jaleel lay with his cheek on the corner of the desk, a pair of headphones covering his ears, his body slumped over in what looked like a really uncomfortable position.

Ayman let him be for the moment, heading instead to the kitchen to put on the second-hand coffee maker he'd bought when he moved in. As it perked he stuck a container of leftover pasta in the microwave, his eyelids drooping as he watched it go round and round on the glass tray inside. His phone rang in the middle of the third rotation, startling him.

Recognizing the number, he kept his voice low as he answered in Arabic. His pulse beat faster, nervousness curling in his gut. "Yes."

"Have you found anything?" the man demanded.

Ayman dragged a hand through his hair. "No."

A frustrated sigh came from the other end of the line. "And what are you doing about that?"

"We've looked everywhere we can think of," he responded, a bite to his tone. "We were up all night trying. I only got thirty minutes' sleep and—"

"*Sleep*? You think you have time to sleep? You were told to find what we need, and you haven't done it yet." The man made a sound of outrage. "Get out of there and meet me at the usual place in forty-five minutes. You're putting us all at risk now. Understand?"

"Yes," he bit out, but an undercurrent of fear

threaded through him at the man's words.

The line went dead. He shoved his phone back into his pocket, then turned to face his roommate as the microwave beeped behind him. He couldn't be sure, but based on that conversation he got the feeling that The Brethren knew something he didn't. Maybe they'd discovered that the FBI were already hunting them. Ayman could practically feel the seconds ticking past, slipping away like grains of sand through an hourglass.

"Jaleel." He didn't stir. "*Jaleel.*"

His friend jerked upright and winced, putting one hand to the back of his neck as he blinked wearily and looked around. "What?"

"We have to go. Another meeting."

Jaleel made a face. "Now?"

"*Right* now." He wasn't messing around with these guys. Part of him wanted to run as far and as fast as he could before he got in any deeper with them. But he knew the situation was already beyond that. The Brethren had contacts and resources all over the country. If he ran, they'd find him, and kill him. And maybe even his family, too.

More guilt squirmed inside him, blending with the growing anxiety.

"Gimme a few minutes to shower, at least," Jaleel grumbled, and headed for the bathroom.

"No, just delete everything you've been doing there," he said, waving a hand at the computer.

His roommate turned widened eyes on him. "What? Are you kidding me? It took me almost four hours to program that code."

"Do it." If anyone intercepted them between here and the meeting, Ayman didn't want anything on that computer to incriminate them.

"No, because that's just stupid. This thing is totally encrypted and if anyone besides me tries to login, everything gets erased anyhow."

"Yeah, that's great. And you think that's gonna keep an FBI or NSA analyst from being able to access your stuff?"

Jaleel raised an eyebrow. "Yeah. Happy?"

"No. Get moving and grab your stuff. We're on a tight deadline."

While he waited for Jaleel, he loaded another pistol for his friend and poured himself a cup of coffee. His phone rang again. He thought of ignoring it, expecting it to be The Brethren again. Instead it was his father.

Ayman frowned. His father had likely only just finished work a little while ago. He'd been far too observant and almost suspicious last night when they'd used the computers at the office building. Why the hell was he calling Ayman at this hour? He should have been headed home to sleep.

For a moment he worried that something terrible had happened, maybe with his mother or sisters, but that was unlikely. And he sure as hell didn't want to speak to his father right now.

Unless...

He paused with the coffee cup partway to his mouth, then lowered it as a sickening possibility occurred to him. Had someone at the office building figured out what Jaleel had done last night? Maybe some internal system had detected the hack. Had they somehow gained access to the history Jaleel had opened, even though he'd sworn he'd erased it all along with the surveillance camera footage and was an expert at covering his tracks?

The coffee rolled in his stomach, suddenly bitter and acidic. Ayman dumped the remainder into the sink and pocketed his phone, not about to call his father back. Jaleel reappeared from his bedroom a moment later, carrying a large backpack. "You're sure you erased the search history last night, right? And you made sure no one could detect your hacks?"

Jaleel threw him an insulted look. "You're kidding me, right? You're seriously joking."

"I'm just checking to make sure you covered our asses."

"Erase my history," he muttered in disgust, rummaging in the cupboard and coming up with a protein bar. "You think that's gonna stop people from tracking us?" He snorted. "What I did is a little more complicated than erasing history, Ayman. For the hacks, it's harder, but I did what I could. There's only a small chance anyone would notice that we were in their system, and it would take a lot of digging to uncover what we were searching for."

But someone knew they'd been up to no good. Cold settled into Ayman's belly. "He knows," he murmured to himself.

Jaleel's expression froze. "Who? Who knows?"

"My father." As he said it his phone buzzed with a text message. Ayman didn't want to look.

"What did he say?"

"I didn't answer." *And I'm not going to.* His father was smart. If he suspected something was going on—and Ayman was pretty sure he had—there would be hell to pay.

He sighed, ran through their options and came up with nothing. Of all the scenarios he'd envisioned about getting caught, none of them had involved his own father. "Make sure you've got enough packed to last you at least a week. We won't be coming back here for a while." If ever. "And take this." He handed him the loaded pistol. Jaleel wasn't nearly as good a shot as he was, but his friend definitely needed to be armed now. Ayman would protect him if necessary.

Jaleel nodded, all visible traces of fatigue now gone. He tucked the weapon into the back of his waistband, pulled the hem of his hoodie over top of it. After a couple minutes to pack he followed Ayman to the door. Together they stepped out into the empty hallway that smelled of stale cigarette smoke. The entire building was silent as a tomb at this hour, most of its tenants either fast asleep or still not home from their graveyard shifts.

They took the stairs to the lobby. Ayman unlocked the front door and pushed it open, the brisk, damp breeze instantly clearing his head. He took one step up the sidewalk and froze, his heart careening in his chest.

His father stood a dozen feet away against the brick wall, arms folded across his chest, clearly waiting for him. Ayman's mind went blank.

His father eyed the two of them, taking in their backpacks. "Where are you going?" he demanded in Arabic.

Ayman's mouth was dry, his pulse thudding in his neck. He didn't want to do this. Not now, not ever. He could feel Jaleel hovering uncertainly behind him. "A meeting."

Those shrewd black eyes studied him critically. "With whom? It's not even five o'clock in the morning."

"It's an interview for a different job. For both of us." Not exactly a lie. "We wanted to make sure we left early so we arrived in the city in plenty of time to find the building." He blurted it all out.

"That's strange." The hard look on his face made Ayman's stomach pull into a knot. "I was hungry so I stopped at the restaurant on my way home but they said you'd called in sick at about three this morning. Which would have been soon after you left the office building." He paused. "But you seemed fine then. And you don't look sick to me now."

Oh shit. Ayman's heart jackhammered against his ribs. "I'll make up the hours later. We have to go now, father. We can't be late."

At that his father's expression transformed into a frightening mask of outrage and alarm. "There is no interview, is there. *Is there?*" he demanded, taking the two steps between them and grabbing Ayman by the lapels of his beat-up leather jacket. "Answer me! There isn't one. You're going to meet those men from the mosque, aren't you?" He shook him once, hard, fury and fear stamped all over his worn features. "The ones who have poisoned your mind and heart against everything you've been taught."

Ayman automatically gripped his father's fist and leaned back, trying to hide his panic. This was something he'd never anticipated. Right now Jaleel was the key to this operation. They needed his skills to find their target. Once they did, Ayman was prepared to take the woman out, any way he could. He couldn't let anything jeopardize their operation, not even his family. And their lives could be at stake just as much as his was. "No, I—"

His father's face contorted. "Don't you lie to me! I know what you've been doing!"

How did he know? *How?*

People on the street were staring at them now. A few stopped in their tracks and watched them warily. Ayman's face began to burn. Even though chances were none of them spoke Arabic, this scene was humiliating enough.

His father shook him again, the rage on his face making Ayman cringe inside. "What are you involved in? Huh? What are you doing that makes you lie, skip out on work and avoid your own family? I'll tell you what—evil things. They are *bad men*, Ayman." He shook his head sharply, the disappointment in his eyes much harder to take than his rage. "I raised you better than that. I gave up everything to bring you and your sisters here to make something of yourselves, not so you would throw your life away on a bunch of brainwashed radicals! What is *wrong* with you? How could you be so stupid and selfish?"

113

"Selfish?" Shaken, Ayman tore free of his father's grip and stumbled back a step, panting from all the volatile emotions racing through his veins. "You're the selfish one, dragging us here where we are less than nothing. I'm tired of being nothing!"

"Nothing?" his father said, eyebrows rising in disbelief. "You're *alive* and *free*, Ayman, which is more than you would be back in Syria right now, and more than most of our friends and relatives there are. At least here you have a chance. Don't be stupid and throw it away."

Before he could protest, his father turned on Jaleel, pinning him with a withering look. "And *you*. I trusted you. What would your mother think of you if she knew about this?" He shook a gnarled finger at him. "She's broken her back working two jobs to give you a better life than she had, and look how you repay her. It would break her heart to see you involved with something like this— going against everything Allah teaches us."

Jaleel cut Ayman a pleading look out of the corner of his eye, clearly not knowing what to do, already half turned as though he was going to bolt.

Years of pent up anger and resentment suddenly detonated in Ayman's chest. He would not stand here and be scolded like a disobedient child for doing something he believed in.

"Enough," Ayman snapped. His father's eyes shot to him, narrowed in warning at the blatant disrespect in his tone, but he didn't care. And now that his father knew, he could be at risk from The Brethren. "I'm a grown man and I will determine my own path. I no longer answer to you."

Under the low light from the nearby streetlamp his father paled visibly, his mustache quivering with his outrage. "How dare you," he whispered. "How *dare* you speak to me that way after all I have sacrificed for you? I am still your *father* and the head of this family. You will answer to me!"

"Not anymore." The answer was automatic, spewing out of his mouth from years of repressed resentment. Guilt pressed down on his chest, so heavy it hurt to breathe. He had the awful intuition that he was about to step off the edge into an abyss from which there was no return. But he couldn't rein in his frustration, or his pride. And as angry as he was, he didn't want his father paying for the choices Ayman had made.

"I'm done with you and the others—*all* of you. Get out of my way." He shoved past his father, knocking him aside with his shoulder, something he would never have dared to do before now.

The violence of the action shocked even him, freezing him in place for a split second.

His father reeled back at the impact, the stricken look on his face like a knife through the heart as Ayman stalked past.

He caught himself against the rough brick exterior and scrambled upright as Ayman strode away. "Ayman, no. No, please, I beg you. *Listen* to me—"

But he was done listening.

His father's pleading voice followed him for half a block down the sidewalk until he finally stopped calling after him. Shameful tears blurred his vision as he fled from the man he'd idolized his entire life, but he refused to let them fall. The confrontation had shaken him far more than he'd realized. He was prepared to hunt down a woman and kill her in cold blood, yet what he'd just done left him queasy and bathed in sweat.

He'd just destroyed the only remaining bridge leading back to his family, cutting off his last means of escape from what awaited him. There was no escape for him. He knew too much, they'd never let him go. There was only one path left for him.

A path that seemed more and more likely to end with him either in jail or an early grave.

"Ayman," Jaleel began in a shaky voice, hurrying beside him.

"Shut up," he growled and kept walking, moving faster. There was no going back now. Not for either of them. His father was a strict, law-abiding man. He wouldn't hesitate to turn his own son in for being involved with The Brethren. Especially after this.

"He'll call the cops on us, and maybe the FBI." Not to turn on him out of vengeance, but to save him. Hoping the FBI and other law enforcement agencies would be able to find and arrest him, stop him from putting his life at risk. His father loved him that much.

The fingers wrapped around his backpack strap curled into a fist. "We can't go back and we have to cut ties with everyone else now." They were fugitives on the run, depending upon a group of dangerous strangers to help them. "We have to go to The Brethren, and we have to find the woman in the next few days. We *have* to, Jaleel." Their lives depended on it.

"Okay, I know."

First he had to calm down, focus. Sucking in a deep breath, he took comfort from the feel of the weapon hard against the small of his back, and concentrated on what he needed to do. Go to the meeting, draw on whatever resources they could find to help narrow the search until they could locate the target.

He'd wanted his independence from his family, to stand on his own merit without them. Now he had his wish. And it scared the hell out of him.

He'd never felt so alone in his life, even though Jaleel walked beside him.

He was fully committed now. All in, for better or worse.

God help me for what I have done and for what I'm about to do.

Chapter Ten

Taya sat cross-legged on the patchwork quilt on her bed at the inn, holding her phone to her ear with one shoulder as she fiddled with her hair. "Sorry this has to be such a short conversation, but they don't want me on the phone long for security reasons. Been a long day, so I'm looking forward to some quality time with my pillow."

"Yeah, I'll bet you are," her brother said.

"You know how I love my sleep." She tugged her ponytail higher up on her head. Normally she wore her hair down but her thick, newly straightened hair was slippery and kept making it slide down toward her nape.

Right after waking up she'd used the hair color Briar had given her, turning her from a dark brunette into a golden brown one. It wasn't a great dye job and the roots would show within a week or so, but it did the trick for now. Once the trial was underway they could hire a professional to come to her hotel room and do a better job. After it dried she'd taken a flat iron to it, and the resulting transformation was startling, even for her. Anyone looking for her would be hard-pressed to recognize her unless they got up close, and that was the whole point.

"You sure Dad's doing okay?" she asked.

Kevin snorted. "You know how he is. Stubborn as a fucking ox and twice as thick-headed. Insists he can do everything on his own, same as before the heart attack."

So like her father. "Wow, sounds like someone else I know," she said in a wry voice.

"Yeah, well, at least when I was being stubborn it wasn't gonna get me killed."

"No? What about all the blood clot scares you had while you were at Walter Reed, and you flat out ignored all the medical advice telling you to scale it back and rest, hmmm?"

"Whatever, you know what I mean. But other than that, yeah, he's doing fine. We're both worried about you though, especially after the airport attack. How are you doing?"

"I'm all right. Except, did you hear about the female witness?"

"Yeah. Did you know her?"

"Yes."

"Hell, Tay, I'm sorry. Damn, I wish there was something I could do."

"I know. I'm doing the best I can, and I've got a crack security team with me. Including the former PJ who got me to Bagram," she added after a pause.

Kevin sucked in a breath. She'd told him all about Nathan when she'd come home. "No fucking way."

"Way. He works for a different agency now, heard about what happened and volunteered to be part of my detail." She didn't feel right telling her brother that Nathan was now with the HRT. She'd wait until later, when it was safe to talk in person, and she could divulge more. "Anyway, there are three guys keeping a very close eye on things here."

"Good. That takes a load off my mind."

Taya smiled. Kevin didn't like people to know it, but he had an incredibly soft side when it came to people he cared about. Speaking of which... "Have you talked to Michelle lately?"

A pause. "Yeah, she called yesterday when all this news broke. Why?" He sounded a little suspicious.

"Just wondered. If you could pass on the message to her that I'm okay, I'd appreciate it." She didn't feel like talking on the phone to anyone else right now. And she had an ulterior motive in wanting her brother to call her best friend.

The change had developed slowly, so slowly even Taya hadn't noticed right away, but Michelle definitely had serious feelings for Kevin. Taya got the feeling they might even be reciprocated, except that every time she brought it up, Kev dismissed the idea with some muttered remark about Michelle deserving better than being with a cripple. He might be one of the strongest men she'd ever known and Taya idolized him, but losing a lower leg to an IED blast during his last tour had done as much damage to his self-esteem as it had to his body.

Afghanistan had not been kind to the Kostas siblings.

He grunted. "I'll text her once I get off the phone with you," he said grudgingly.

"You know she'll just call you if you do."

"Hell, knowing her, she'll probably show up here instead."

Taya grinned. "Such a hardship for you, putting up with the likes of her, a pretty little blonde who'd do anything for our family. My heart bleeds for you."

"She only comes around to check on Dad," he muttered.

"That's not the whole reason, and you know it." She was tired of watching her brother avoid the woman who might be the one to knock down the walls surrounding his

119

jaded heart.

Another grunt. "She's a good girl."

His wording might not sound like much, but that compliment was the highest form of praise from her gruff, macho brother. "Yes, she is." She and Taya had been besties for over a decade. Michelle had been there for her after Taya came back to the States. She was more than a friend, she was family. And Taya knew damn well her brother saw her as way more than a friend as well. "So you might think about being a little more sociable with her the next time she visits."

Kevin blew out a breath. "I told you before—"

"Yeah, and it's still bullshit, no matter how many times you say it. Make all the excuses you want about why you're not for her, but it's not going to change the reality. Don't you think it's time you stopped being a dick and quit pushing her away?"

A heavy sigh came through the phone, and she pictured him scrubbing a hand over his closely-shorn hair, his forehead creased in a deep frown. "I should go check on Dad."

"Chicken. But all right, and tell him I send a big hug. I'll try to call you again tonight, or if there's an update. You can reach me at this number if you need me, they gave me an encrypted phone so I could contact whoever I need to. Love you."

"Love you too."

As she disconnected Taya glanced at the time displayed on the phone. She'd heard at least one of the guys upstairs earlier when she got into the shower and knew the other two would be inside or near the inn at all times.

After checking her hair one last time in the mirror above the pedestal sink in the bathroom, she pulled a knit sweater over her top and headed out of her room. The rich scent of coffee and something sweet tickled her nose and made her stomach rumble as she reached the landing at the top of the stairs.

The front door opened and closed below her, just out of view downstairs, and solid footsteps sounded on the old hardwood floor.

"Well, if it isn't Dr. Feelgood," she heard Agent Cruz say. "Want some coffee, sunshine?"

"You're way too fucking happy first thing in the morning, man," Nathan's voice responded. "I ever tell you that? And yes, I want coffee."

Taya descended the stairs, keeping her footsteps light. Stepping into the breakfast nook, she found Agent Cruz at the table and Nathan standing in the kitchen with his back to her. A very broad back, the dark gray T-shirt molding to the muscles across his shoulders and down his spine. Muscles she wanted to trace and explore with her fingertips.

"Morning."

They both looked over at her but she noticed the way Nathan's gaze swept over her, taking in her new look before coming back to her face. "Wow, you look really different," he murmured, an appreciative gleam in his eyes. "Hungry?"

"Starved." She headed for the mugs laid out on the counter next to where he stood near the coffee maker.

Cruz shoved a big bite of what appeared to be a muffin into his mouth and stood, the tats on his forearm shifting as he grabbed the mug in front of him. "I'll go relieve the big man, send him in to catch some rack time. See you later."

"Later," Nathan murmured as he sipped his coffee.

Taya stole a glance at him out of the corner of her eye as she selected a mug. "You get any sleep last night?"

"A bit. I'm good. Here," he said, and took the mug from her. He filled it with coffee and handed it back. His fingers brushed against hers, sending tendrils of heat up her forearms. "You?"

He looked tired, the start of dark circles showing beneath his eyes. She knew sleep deprivation was part of his job, but she hated being the cause of it. "Once I fell asleep, yeah." She'd lain awake thinking of him for a long time after coming inside from the porch, even though she'd been wiped.

"Talk to your family yet?"

"Just before I came down. Dad's doing well, except he's starting to drive my brother nuts because he won't stay in bed like the doctors want him to."

"Ah." He skirted the edge of the counter and headed for the dining table, all without looking at her, and Taya got the feeling he felt suddenly awkward around her. Because of what she'd told him last night? Maybe because things had gotten too personal and he felt the need to distance himself now, for professional reasons?

Coffee in hand, she joined him at the table and helped herself to a piece of toast. The innkeeper had laid out different kinds of jams in little crystal dishes, the luscious ruby red of the raspberry glistening in the sunlight filtering through the sheers covering the French doors.

Nathan helped himself to his own breakfast. Only the light clink of silverware against crystal broke the quiet. Taya buttered then spread the preserves onto her toast, and the painful silence between them began to scrape over her nerve endings.

While he was in the middle of spreading peanut butter onto a slice of toast, his phone rang. He pulled it from his pocket, and she caught a glimpse of a young brunette pictured on the display. The last one she'd seen had been blonde. And if their pictures were showing up on his phone, then they had to be more than just one-night stands.

His expression turned blank and he silenced the call

before placing the phone face down on the table. He didn't look at her or say anything, so Taya stayed silent, wondering what had caused the change in him.

A few moments later his phone buzzed. He flipped it over in his hand, gave a cursory glance and turned it face-side down again, but not before Taya saw the same brunette and the bubble of a text message on the screen.

They ate together in silence, but there was a strange tension between them now, and it was definitely coming from him. She looked up at him through her lashes as he bit into his toast, tried not to stare at the way his lips moved and wondered what they'd feel like moving over hers. The way he carried himself alone was insanely sexy.

His phone buzzed again, the sound somehow more shrill with it vibrating against the table. He pushed out an annoyed breath and turned the phone back over. This time when he set it face down on the table he looked almost annoyed.

Whoever the brunette was, she really wanted to talk to him. Taya began to feel awkward, as if she'd intruded. "Do you want some privacy?" she asked him finally.

Nathan's shoulders tensed, his hand frozen around the phone. "No, it's not important." He still wasn't looking at her. Taya got the feeling he was either embarrassed or avoiding her gaze.

A sinking sensation filled her stomach as she put all the pieces together. Cruz's Dr. Feelgood remark. The young women texting and calling. Only a couple that she'd been aware of, but his reaction to them had been telling and told her there were probably more. And suddenly she was the one who was embarrassed.

Last night she'd not only admitted to this heroic, sexy man that she'd been physically used by the husband who'd been forced upon her, but that she hadn't been with a man in the five years since she'd been stateside. And here he was being pursued by women wanting a piece of him. Not that she blamed him or was surprised that he had so much female interest—for God's sake, just look at the man—but it was humiliating to have her pathetic lack of a romantic life out in the open when compared to his.

Taya lowered her gaze to her plate, aware that her face was turning hot. God, what he must think of her. Compared to the women calling him she was old and...used.

The toast she'd swallowed stuck in her throat in a dry lump. She grabbed her coffee, took a big gulp to force it down, uncaring that it scalded her entire esophagus. She felt dirty all of a sudden, as though she needed another shower.

Nathan huffed out a breath, his knife clattering to his plate. "Look, Taya, there's—"

She held up a hand to stop him and waved it slightly, unable to meet his eyes. "No, don't apologize. Your private life is none of my business." And she was such a freaking idiot to ever think he might want her when he clearly had his pick of eager young things looking to hook up. If not for this trial pulling his team into personal security duty, he'd likely be hooking up with one of the women right now.

"*No.*"

The forcefulness of the word made her glance up at him in surprise. Nathan's face was set, his jaw tense, eyes blazing with emotion. He picked up the phone and wiggled it between his thumb and forefinger, his brows drawn together in a deep scowl. "All these girls calling? Mean *nothing* to me. Zero." He paused. "But you do. This job, and your safety, *does*. Okay?"

Taya had no idea how to respond to that, didn't even know what to make of it. Again, beneath his words, she sensed the deeply buried self-loathing she'd detected before. He seemed so earnest, that it was important she believed him. "Okay," she said quietly, fairly sure he meant it.

The resounding silence in the room pressed in on her as he shifted in his chair, a muscle in his jaw working. "They don't mean anything," he said again, this time softer, without looking at her.

He was angry with himself, and clearly embarrassed. She wanted to ask him so many things but was afraid he'd clam up if she did.

His hand fisted on the table, the only sign of his inner turmoil as she waited for him to continue. "I haven't…dealt with things as well as you have," he said finally.

Taya kept watching him, hoping he'd keep talking. Things as in PTSD?

His gaze dropped to his lap, a slight flush staining the tops of his cheekbones above his dark auburn whiskers. "I'm not proud of the way I've been handling things up 'til now."

Handling things… She couldn't imagine him risking his career by abusing drugs or alcohol, and suddenly his meaning about the women was all too clear. Sex. He'd been using sex as a kind of self-medication. And he clearly wasn't proud of it.

Taya's heart ached for him, but she was also concerned. If he was ashamed by his actions, then his behavior was self-destructive. "Is this about Afghanistan?"

He gave a tight nod, uncomfortable with what he'd just admitted. Then he expelled a breath and set the phone back down, his shoulders relaxing a bit. "Mostly."

Losing a close friend like O'Neil in combat must have been hard for him. "I'm always here if you want to talk to someone," she said finally, and left it at that. If it was in fact O'Neil's death that still haunted him, maybe it would help that she'd been there. He had to know she'd understand and relate. She reached for the pitcher of freshly squeezed orange juice and poured a glass to signal she wasn't expecting an answer.

"I meant what I said last night, you know," he said. "About you inspiring me to be a better person."

Glancing up, she met Nathan's hazel stare. She could see the struggle there, the pain he tried to hide beneath the strong, impervious mask he wore. The mask he had to wear in order to safeguard his job and reputation. She wanted to hug him.

Solid footsteps sounded out on the front porch, cutting off anything she might have said to ease him.

Taya's gaze shot to the front door just as it swung open and Vance came in. The man was built like a linebacker, wearing cargo pants and a black polo shirt. "Hey, what up, Dr. Feelgood?" His deep voice boomed through the room.

Nathan grunted at him. "Stop calling me that. You want some chow before you hit the rack?"

"Yeah, don't mind if I do." He sauntered over to the table, gave her a polite nod before taking the chair beside Nathan's. "I'm guessing that coffee's not decaf, huh?"

"No," Nathan answered, glancing at Taya.

"I'll wait 'til the next rotation then," Vance said, and helped himself to some toast and the fresh-baked muffins.

A few seconds of silence passed. "Well, guess I'll go check in with the boss." Nathan stood and took his plate over to the sink. Once he'd loaded it into the dishwasher he glanced over his shoulder at her. "You've got a conference call with the prosecution team this morning, right?"

"In about an hour."

He nodded. "One of us'll be here or at least on the grounds at all times. The other two will be around. Call or text if you need anything."

It was weird, she could already feel him distancing himself from her. Was it because he was embarrassed about what he'd revealed? Or was it because of the job? "I will."

****

Nathan strode down the front pathway that led from the porch to the road, edgy as hell after what had just happened. What must Taya be thinking of him now?

At the curb he slid his earpiece in and activated it, noting the minivan parked at the end of the street. "Cruz, I'm gonna walk around the perimeter."

"Enjoy yourself, sunshine."

Despite his bad mood Nate cracked a grin at his teammate's overly upbeat tone, faced the minivan and raised his middle finger high.

Cruz chuckled. "No thanks, I don't swing that way, brother. But damn, you are hot, so I'm kind of flattered," he said in a dry voice.

"You should be," Nate teased. He turned east and started up toward the garden on the far edge of the property.

It was shaping up to be a gorgeous day, the sun warm on his shoulders, the birds chirping in the trees and the sound of the sea a soothing, constant rush in the distance. It still didn't lighten his mood.

As he walked, watching for anything suspicious, all he could think about was what a pussy he was. Those phone calls and texts Taya had been witness to had irritated and embarrassed him. After how honest she'd been with him last night, telling him secrets that couldn't be easy for her, he'd felt like he owed her the same.

Now he wished he'd kept his mouth shut. After what he'd said, she was now fully aware that he wasn't nearly as in control as he wanted everyone to think. And she also knew he'd been trying to fuck his way out of his PTSD or whatever the hell it was.

That flash of pity he'd seen in her eyes had hit him hard. She was a rape victim who'd survived degradation on a level he hated to think about, and here he'd become a man-slut, going from lay to lay in an effort to escape his issues. God, even if he'd had a shot of being with her when this security gig was over, she wouldn't want anything to do with him now. And he didn't blame her.

Realizing he'd just lowered himself to the level of having a private pity party, he pulled his phone out and dialed DeLuca. "Hey, Schroder, what's up?" his commander said.

"Just checking in. Everything's good here. Any new developments to report on the investigation?"

"Nope. No word yet on the missing witnesses, but the three remaining ones have doubled security teams on them. Nobody's sure yet how the attackers found the targets or how they pulled it all off, especially in Chloe's case since WITSEC was involved. How's Taya?"

"She's fine. Upset about her friend, though."

"Yeah, it's a shitty-ass mess. Listen, I've got Bauer, Evers and Blackwell heading into D.C. to beef up security on one of the other witnesses. You guys good down there? I can send Tuck down if need be."

"No, we're good for now." And hopefully there wouldn't be any more issues to deal with. Taya had been through more than enough. "I heard they might be pushing the start date of the trial up by a few days."

"That's the rumor. Still waiting for the official word. Given the security situation for the remaining witnesses, the DOJ wants to start things sooner and get everything rolling, minimize the risk of any further attacks."

Nate shook his head. "Security at that trial is gonna be insane."

"Yeah, and we'll likely get called in on standby for that, along with Gold Team."

Nate didn't like the thought of being pulled away

from Taya, even for a situation that warranted both HRT assault teams being present. "Who would take over witness security? WITSEC?"

"Most likely. It's a total shit-show over there right now though. Nothing like yesterday has ever happened before in the history of the program. Heads are rolling on some higher up's floor right now, I'm sure."

"I'll bet." He'd made it to the far end of the property, marked by curving garden borders filled with all kinds of flowers beginning to bloom. There were no footprints visible on the dewy grass or anything that suggested anyone had been snooping around, so he skirted the edge of the neatly trimmed lawn and began walking east toward the beach. The sun glinted off the water in sparkling strikes of silver and gulls cried overhead. "Taya's got a phone meeting with the prosecution shortly, but other than that we've got nothing going on here. I'll be in touch."

"Sounds good."

Nate slipped his phone back into his pocket and scanned the yard. A movement on the front porch caught his eye. Taya stepped out to the railing and stood facing the water for a moment with Vance, one hand shading her eyes. She glanced his way, and even from where he stood he could see the smile she flashed him as she waved.

Longing and protectiveness surged up inside him; protectiveness won out. She shouldn't be out in the open, but Vance had obviously thought it safe enough for her to come outside for a minute.

His teammate had it covered. *You're here to do a job, and you have to stay focused if you want to keep Taya safe.* That meant stepping back from her and keeping his distance.

Raising a hand in acknowledgement, he turned and abruptly walked away.

Chapter Eleven

"I think I've got something."

Ayman dropped the papers he'd been going through and sat up straight on the couch at Jaleel's excited announcement. "What?"

His friend angled his laptop so Ayman could see the screen. "Here. I've been looking at incoming and outgoing calls from her father's place in North Carolina. A call came in there early this morning from a phone with an unlisted number, but the cell tower in the area pinged it as coming from just south of Virginia Beach."

"So?"

"So don't interrupt me. I also found calls coming in to that same number this morning, about an hour afterward. When I traced the number of that caller, I got the District Attorney's office." Jaleel's expression was pure smugness. "Even though I can't trace the other number, it's fairly close to D.C., only a couple hours south. And it can't be coincidence that it called her house and then received a call from the Attorney General's office. Has to be her." A broad, cocky smile filled his face.

"I guess it could be her," he allowed, the first stirrings of excitement flashing through him. "Is there any way to narrow it down from here? Or to hack into the system and track the conversations themselves?"

"I'm still trying. But you should tell the others what's going on."

"All right." Ayman left the tiny study they'd been holed up in for the past eight hours. They were at the home of one of The Brethren's contacts, though there hadn't been any formal introductions to the other men staying here. He walked down the short hallway on the townhome's second floor and knocked on the closed door at the end.

"Enter."

He opened the door to find two mid-level members of The Brethren and their host seated around a TV, eating snacks and watching a movie. Ayman's stomach rumbled and resentment shot through him. He and Jaleel had been working nonstop since they got here without any food, and these guys were sitting around on their fat asses doing nothing while his and Jaleel's lives depended on finding their target?

He forced his anger aside. "We may have found a lead. It's not totally solid yet, but it's a good starting place. We think she might have called her family from outside of Virginia Beach, and then talked to the District Attorney soon after."

At that, Darwish stood, stroking a hand over his dark beard. "Show me." He and the others followed Ayman back to the study.

Jaleel had his headphones back on, working on some coding, and stopped to explain everything. "We know the Feds moved her, and that she's been in contact with the prosecution. Chances are good it's her."

"It's her," Darwish said, his voice laced with anticipation, a smile curling his lips beneath his heavy black beard.

Ayman's heart began to beat faster. Finally, a solid lead. "Where is she though?" he asked Jaleel. "Can you pinpoint it?"

Jaleel shook his head. "I keep trying." He typed in more commands, looked at the information popping up on screen. "The phone she's using must be encrypted because it's scrambling the signal. I can't get a lock on exactly which tower the call was routed through."

"We'll go down there," Darwish said. "That call was made hours ago so they might already have moved her. You'll keep searching on the way," he said to Jaleel. "She has to be in the area someplace, hopefully still within range of that tower. That'll give us our search radius."

Glad that they were finally taking action, Ayman strode to the couch where he'd dumped his backpack and set his extra ammunition on top. His pistol was still safely tucked into the back of his waistband. When he looked up again, Jaleel was packing up his laptop and Darwish was pulling something from the closet in the corner.

The man turned toward him and Ayman saw the automatic rifle in his hands. "You'll need this," he said to Ayman.

Ayman took the weapon, a rush of excitement ripping through his bloodstream. The Brethren were well funded and had many connections here in the States. They wanted the whore badly, and they had the money and equipment to make it happen.

Darwish gave him a knowing smile, but there was a deadly edge there that sent a warning shiver up Ayman's spine. Unlike him, Darwish would take great pleasure in the actual killing of the target, or anyone else who got in his way. He loved watching his victims suffer in their last moments. The more painful the better. "Let's go hunting."

****

Taya set aside the book she'd found in the bookcase next to the fireplace in her room and rubbed her burning eyes. After a long day of isolation and two seemingly unending conference calls with the prosecution, she was ready for a good night's sleep. Only she was pretty sure it would be a while before she'd be able to shut her mind off long enough to fall asleep.

The Department of Justice was going ahead with the original date of the trial but switching the order of witness testimony, which meant she'd be called to the stand sooner than initially planned. One more thing for her to worry about, though she'd rather just get this whole thing over with and behind her.

Since breakfast she'd barely seen the HRT agents. They'd all taken turns rotating through various positions and posts during the day. She'd mostly kept to her room but the few times she'd ventured downstairs for something to eat, the men had acknowledged her with a nod and a polite word or two, but that was all.

Nathan had been conspicuously absent all day, except for when she'd seen him this morning from the porch and when she'd caught him just as he was leaving the inn a couple hours ago. Both times he'd walked away without anything more than a wave or a smile.

She understood that he was here as a bodyguard and that he took his job seriously, but after everything they'd said to each other, this abrupt transition to him being so distant still hurt. Maybe he didn't want his teammates to think anything was going on between them. Whatever it was, she wasn't going to force her presence on him.

A sound from the adjoining room caught her attention. She'd heard Nathan go in there just over an hour ago. She focused on the door between their rooms, listening intently. It had sounded like a low cry, or maybe a muffled shout, followed by a light thump of something hitting the floor.

When she didn't hear anything else over the next two minutes she put it out of her mind and decided to get up and change into her pajamas. She paused in the act of rising from the bed when the floorboards creaked in the other room. A few moments after that she heard the sound of the shower running, the old pipes groaning in the walls.

Taya frowned. She knew he'd been out doing other things most of the day and that he'd been sent up here to get some sleep before his next watch. They seemed to work in four to six hour shifts, so he still had plenty of time before the next one started and he'd looked so tired this morning. After barely sleeping last night, he had to be exhausted. He should have been fast asleep right now.

She drew her knees up to her chest and set her chin atop them, still staring at the door between their rooms. Something was wrong, and she had a fairly good idea of what it was.

She'd meant it earlier when she'd told him he could talk to her about Afghanistan. She'd give him the option once he was out of the shower.

****

Palms braced flat on the tile wall of the shower, Nate bent his head and let the hot water pound over his shoulders and back, washing off the film of clammy sweat he'd woken covered in. He'd been dreaming about Taya, but not in a good way.

In his dream she'd died right in front of him, bleeding out while he'd desperately fought to staunch the flow, her eyes staring up at him, begging him to help her.

Just a dream.

His heart rate was almost normal again but he couldn't shake the memories cascading over him as he closed his eyes, transporting him out of his nightmare to back in time five years ago. It all played out in his head like a high-definition movie on the big screen, vivid and unstoppable.

Automatic fire cracked in the distance behind them, the three uninjured SEALs from the quick reaction force dealing with the lead element of Qureshi's force that had been chasing them for the past three days. Three damn days stuck in enemy territory with no hope of extraction due to adverse weather and logistical problems with launching the QRF waiting at Bagram.

Out front his teammate, pararescueman Staff Sergeant O'Neil led the way, checking to make sure their front was clear. Hassan was behind him. Their American-born undercover DEA agent principal was already bleeding from two bullet wounds to the torso, sustained during his escape from the village back before Nate and the others had been called in. His American wife, Taya, stumbled on behind him.

Acting as rear guard for their group, Nate had a close up view of her and his medical experience told him she couldn't go on like this much longer. She was thin and pale, covered in scrapes and bruises, and had likely endured many hardships during her time as a captive.

Hassan had a tight grip on her wrist as they scrambled up another incline, their sandaled feet slipping on the loose shale and soil. Taya fell to her knees, struggled to get up even though the man was pulling her. He was weak too, having lost a lot of blood. Nate had patched him up as best he could but the man needed surgery and several units of blood. He was going on pure adrenaline at this point.

Nate slung his weapon, ran over and grabbed Taya, putting her over his shoulder as he dug the toes of his boots into the hillside and forced his way up. His thigh muscles burned and his lungs ached from the thin air at this altitude but they couldn't slow down. The three

SEALs could only hold off a force that big for a short time, buying them maybe a few more minutes' lead-time at most. If they were going to have a shot of making it to the extraction zone where the Blackhawks were supposed to meet them, they needed air support, fast.

One of the SEALs contacted him over the radio link via his headset. "We're falling back before they overrun us. Air support inbound. Haul ass to the LZ, over."

"Roger that," he panted, then set his jaw and pushed hard to the crest of the hill. At the top he could see the area where the LZ lay in a small valley a little over a kilometer away. Still no sign of the incoming birds though, or their CAS. "Keep moving," he shouted to Hassan and O'Neil.

Hassan was lagging now, the blood loss and drop in adrenaline sapping his strength. On the other side of the ridge he went to one knee and bowed his head, gasped for breath as he pressed a hand low on his side to the bandages there. "Give me a weapon and go," he gasped out, his English perfect and without an accent despite his native appearance. He'd been living hard during his undercover op. "Take her and get her out of here." He indicated Taya with a sharp jerk of his chin, still draped over Nate's shoulder.

"No, we're not leaving you behind." She struggled on his shoulder and Nate set her down. The long robe of the burqa she wore covered her from neck to ankles. She rushed forward and grabbed Hassan's hand, pulled him. "Come on."

"Let's go, people," O'Neil shouted from out front.

Hassan gazed up at his wife, his features set, then struggled to his feet and pushed on.

But the sound of the gunfire behind them was louder now. Getting closer with each second.

"Coming up on your six," the SEAL's voice said over the headset.

"Roger," Nate responded. He waved the others forward. "We gotta move fast."

With his M4 to his shoulder he pushed them on down the slope and into a dry stream bed for cover. They'd just reached a slight bend when he heard the faint roar of jet engines approaching. The shooting behind them grew more intense, coming closer still. In the distance he spotted a single dot in the clear blue sky, breaking through the solid deck of clouds below the mountain ridge. From the sound he already knew what was coming. A Warthog.

He'd never been so glad to see an aircraft in his life.

The SEAL spoke again, his voice choppy and out of breath. "Fifty yards behind you. Pilot's bringing the rain. Get ready."

"Take cover!" Nate yelled to the others.

Out front, O'Neil looked back at him over his shoulder.

A burst of gunfire erupted from the left.

O'Neil and Hassan both went down, the second man dragging Taya with him. Nate charged forward and returned fire where he'd seen the muzzle flashes, spraying the brush off to the left.

Shots exploded from his right. He hit the ground on his belly and raised his rifle to his shoulder, searching for a target. The fuckers were trying to surround them, he realized. He could hear the SEAL over the radio as he fired, then the scream of the A-10 drowned out everything else. It dipped low above the battlefield and unleashed a barrage of 30 mm fire on the enemy from its Gatling gun as it streaked overhead.

Nate got up and ran toward O'Neil and the others. His partner was on his knees, still returning fire despite the blood soaking his pants. He'd been hit in the left thigh and was bleeding bad. Hassan was down, not moving. Taya was crawling toward them.

Nate heard the SEAL's voice again. "Incoming, danger close!"

Immediately Nate dove for cover. "O'Neil, get down!" He was too far away to reach them. The A-10 had swung around and came back for another pass as his buddy dropped to his stomach. This time the Warthog unleashed a Maverick missile.

Nate watched it streak toward the ground. Everything went slo-mo, each heartbeat a separate eternity. A huge fireball erupted in the main enemy position, the impact of the warhead ripping through Nate's body. The ground seemed to ripple beneath him, rattling his bones. Intense heat blasted over the back of him, followed a split second later by chunks of dirt and rock pelting him from above. In the wake of the explosion he couldn't hear anything. When he raised his head he saw two things.

O'Neil was lying on his back, unmoving. Taya was scrambling to her knees. She lunged for him, throwing her body over top of O'Neil's, shielding his head as more debris rained down. She was covered in blood.

Heart in his throat, Nate didn't even look around him as he surged to his feet and tore across the remaining yards between them. He spotted Hassan up ahead lying face-down in the streambed, a baseball-sized hole in his head. Without pause he kept running, intent on getting to his buddy. "O'Neil!"

His fellow PJ didn't move, but Taya did. Slowly she pushed to her knees and looked up at him. Her face white with shock, her eyes wide and glazed, one hand pressed tight to the wound in the side of her neck.

"He's hit," she rasped out, blood spilling down her throat and chest in a scarlet rivulet.

She'd been hit too, pretty badly by the looks of the bleeding. Nate tore his gaze from her and looked at his teammate. Half of O'Neil's face was missing.

"Fuck, no," he breathed.

Plunging to his knees beside him, Nate immediately set his fingers over O'Neil's carotid pulse, already knowing what he'd find but unable to accept it.

No pulse.

With an inarticulate sound of denial and grief, Nate checked to ensure he still had an airway, then stacked his hands on O'Neil's sternum and started compressions. Blood gushed out of the horrific wound with every push of his hands. He ripped a bandage from his gear and slapped it over the mangled side of O'Neil's face, holding it there as he banged out another fifteen compressions.

Off to the side Taya slumped into a sitting position, her expression dazed as blood continued to pour from her neck.

Nate shuddered, closed his eyes for a moment. O'Neil was gone, beyond saving. He knew that. He could still save Taya.

A blessed kind of numbness flooded him as his training took over.

He took his hands from O'Neil's body, hopped over him to kneel beside Taya and clamped a hand down over top of hers. "Lie down."

She did as he said without a word, her wide, frightened eyes focused on him. He could feel the pulse in her neck pounding against his palm through the bandage he pressed there, the column of her throat so fragile beneath his hand. One of the SEALs finally reached them, knelt down and started digging through his medical kit.

Over the ringing in his ears and the grief screaming in his head, Nate caught the faint sound of rotors approaching the LZ below, less than two hundred yards away. In his peripheral he could see one of the other SEALs tending to O'Neil, then backing off. Nate didn't look. If he looked at his friend's body another second he would fucking lose it.

He swallowed the boulder-sized knot in his throat, gazed down into Taya's dazed gray eyes.

"Are th-they b-both..." She trailed off, her whole body trembling, jaw jerking with the force of her shock.

Nate leaned over her, got right in her line of vision and refused to allow her to look away. "Don't worry about them, you just look right here at me. I've got you. You hear me? I've got you, and I'm not gonna let go. You're gonna be fine."

She swallowed and gave a tiny nod, her gaze locked on his as though she was afraid to look away, her blood-slick fingers gripping his wrist tight. Her resolute silence and the unspoken plea in her eyes killed him.

Please don't let me die. *Her eyes conveyed it as clearly as if she'd spoken aloud.*

She knew he was her only chance. If he loosened the pressure, if he didn't keep his hand where it was and get the bleeding under control, she'd never make it to Bagram alive.

Chapter Twelve

N ate opened his eyes and raised his head, sucking in a deep, shaky breath as the horrific memories scattered. The hot water continued to course over his body and he wished it could wash away the memories as easily as it had the sweat.

He'd straddled Taya's torso in the helo, started a large bore IV and kept pressure on the wound in her neck as he pumped her vein full of the whole blood the onboard medics had brought. That entire flight he'd been vividly aware of O'Neil's body on the other side of the hold, already zipped into a body bag.

He missed his buddy every single fucking day. Sometimes so much that his chest ached.

Taya had kept gazing up at him for most of the flight, until finally her body had given into the shock and blood loss. Ten minutes out of Bagram her fingers had slipped from his wrist, her eyelids falling closed as her body went lax on the bloodstained stretcher. For a moment he'd thought he'd lost her, but her pulse had still been palpable beneath his searching fingertips.

Somehow she'd held on through the surgery, and the

long healing process—both physical and mental—that had come afterward. Nate had no idea how she'd made it through all that, because he sure as hell hadn't.

It hadn't been until the next day at Bagram, after his second debriefing that he'd learned the truth about who she was and what had happened to her. It seemed incredible that she was here now, in the room next to his.

Her sudden reappearance in his life had made his inner demons even more visible, yet he couldn't stop thinking about her. No, he didn't *want* to stop thinking about her. She was the only good thing that had come out of his time in Afghanistan. Physical proof that he hadn't let everyone down that day. That there must be a reason that he'd lived and O'Neil hadn't. It was the only thing saving his sanity.

The old pipes groaned as he shut off the spray. He climbed out of the shower and toweled off, then put on jeans and a fresh shirt. But he was way too twisted up to sleep.

He still didn't understand why he'd walked away from that mission with barely a mark on him. Survivor guilt, they called it, but for Nate it was more than that. He and O'Neil had gone through Superman school together in the Air Force, and by the time they finished the pipeline to become pararescuemen, they'd been closer than brothers. Brothers who would do anything for each other, including give up their life for the other if necessary.

That's what killed Nate the most. Given the chance, he'd have swapped places with his buddy and died that day instead.

O'Neil had been engaged to an awesome girl back home in Michigan, and they'd just had a child together. At the funeral Nate had held the baby while O'Neil's fiancée clung to him and sobbed her heart out against his shoulder. He'd never forget that, either.

Nate started for the door with the intention of

escaping outside for some fresh air, made it three steps before he stopped. Vance was downstairs right now. There was no way Nate was up to even a friendly conversation in his current state.

Against his will, his gaze slid to the door connecting his and Taya's rooms. He imagined her curled up beneath the patchwork quilt, him twisting the knob soundlessly and crossing to her bed, then sliding in beside her and drawing her into his arms.

She touched a place inside him that no one else ever had.

He wanted to touch her so fucking badly right now it was a physical ache in the center of his chest. He wanted to hold her, feel her alive and whole in his arms, feel her curl trustingly into his body.

But he knew if he did he'd never be able to stop there. Taya wasn't like the others. He'd been using sex as a form of self-medication, but he'd never use her like that.

Closing his eyes, he exhaled hard and turned around to face the window. He'd left one side of the curtains parted slightly when he'd gone to bed just over an hour ago. Now he crossed to the window and sat on the window seat built into the wall.

Pulling the curtain a few more inches away from the edge, he stared out at the ocean. The moon was brighter tonight. The waves were restless, their white, foamy fingers clawing at the beach each time a breaker hit the shore. It should have been peaceful.

There was no peace for him tonight.

He stiffened at the sound of a doorknob turning behind him. Looking over his shoulder, he barely made out the knob on the door between his and Taya's room turning. His heart began to pound, hope and panic meshing in a chaotic mix. And when the door pushed open slowly and Taya stepped inside, dressed in the same clothes she'd been wearing at breakfast, he couldn't move.

In the dimness he couldn't see her face but he could feel the strength of her gaze on him as she stood there watching him for a long moment. Then she shut the door behind her.

His heart lurched, twin bombs of relief and dread detonating deep in his chest. His entire body tensed, the instinct to order her from the room nearly overpowering. But he couldn't force the words out. His throat was locked up.

Tense seconds ticked past as she stood there, not saying a word, and finally he couldn't take it anymore. Smothered by shame and the guilt he'd never been able to shake, he turned back to the window, part of him wanting to escape and part of him knowing he couldn't run from his demons anymore.

Her soft treads sounded on the hardwood floorboards behind him. His muscles drew tighter with each step, so taut he felt like he might shatter if she so much as laid a hand on him. "You shouldn't be here," he finally managed to grate out. "Go back to your room."

She didn't leave, instead stopping behind him. Nate clenched his jaw. He could smell her cinnamon-vanilla scent now, hear her gentle breathing and braced for what would come next.

Talk to me, Nathan. Tell me what's wrong.

Except she didn't ask him what was wrong. She didn't say a word.

Instead she sat behind him on the bench and leaned into him, slipping her arms around his waist. Her palms came up to rest over his thundering heart and she laid her cheek between his shoulder blades.

No hesitation, no tentative stroke of her hands. Just her soft, warm weight pressed to his back, her arms holding him, enveloping him in comfort and…acceptance. He felt it in her touch, in the way she nestled against him so naturally.

Accepting his silent struggle even if she didn't understand it fully. Because she'd been through hell herself and had emerged on the other side a stronger person for it.

His muscles loosened in relief. But as the tension faded, the knot in his throat expanded. The prick of tears burned the backs of his eyelids.

Goddamn it, no.

He sucked in a shuddering breath and swallowed, tried to fight them back, but it was no use. They rushed to the surface and flooded his eyes in a hot torrent of grief. Nate bowed his head and squeezed his eyes shut as they began to fall, the tightness in his chest painful.

Taya stayed with him, unmoving. She didn't murmur useless words of comfort or whisper for him not to cry. She simply held him in silence while he vented five years of pain and self-blame for the first time.

And he was so pathetically fucking grateful to her for it that he leaned his forehead against the cold glass and let the tears flow.

He didn't know how long they stayed like that, but by the time he was done his eyes felt swollen and his throat was raw from holding back the unmanly sobs he'd trapped inside him. He was leaning against the window frame now, his forehead still on the cool glass because he was too drained to move.

Gradually he became aware of a reduction in pressure in his chest. His lungs seemed to expand more and more with each inhalation as he got his breathing back under control.

That was when he realized he was naturally responding to Taya's respiration rate. Her palms were still flat against his chest, her cheek resting on his back. But she was drawing in slow, deliberate breaths, holding them for a second, then releasing the air in a long, steady exhalation. Almost coaching him.

Instinctively he followed, eventually matching the almost hypnotic rhythm. Within a minute he felt lighter. Warmer. Strangely at peace, at least for the time being.

Taya shifted against him, finding a more comfortable position for herself, then began to hum softly. Nate didn't recognize the tune, but the soft sound of her voice and the gentle caress of her hands over his chest were incredibly relaxing. Long minutes passed as she hummed the song and rubbed his chest ever so slightly. His heart began to swell, his chest now aching for a different reason.

She was a fucking miracle to him, so sweet and giving. Brave, and stronger than any other woman he'd ever met, maybe even stronger than she realized.

Wiping a hand across his eyes, Nate reached up and placed his hands over hers, holding them against his heart as he sat up. Taya fell silent and eased away from him. He missed her warmth immediately.

Don't go.

He released one of her hands to turn on the window seat and face her. The moonlight coming through the gap in the curtain illuminated her face, her smooth golden-toned skin and eyes sparkling like silver. She accepted him, and was so warm and caring it turned him inside out.

Unable to stop himself, knowing it was probably a bad idea but not caring at the moment, he gave into temptation and cupped the side of her face the way he'd been thinking about for the past five years. Taya searched his eyes, leaned into his touch as he swept his thumb across her cheek, down to the corner of her mouth. He heard her soft intake of breath, saw her pupils expand with desire.

Smothering a groan, he brought up his free hand to frame her face and slid his thumb ever so gently across her lower lip. She pressed harder into his hand and parted her lips to kiss the pad of his thumb, and he swore he could feel himself drowning in her eyes.

"Why did you cover O'Neil like that, after the missile hit?" he asked, his voice sounding rough as sandpaper. He'd always wondered what had motivated her to do it.

She stilled and lifted her face slightly. "He was wounded."

"So were you."

A slight frown wrinkled her forehead as she considered it. "I don't know, I just saw how badly he was hurt and knew he wasn't moving so I tried to keep anything else from hitting him. I didn't think about it, I just reacted."

Nate shook his head in awe. "Do you even know how brave that was? How selfless?" She'd literally covered O'Neil's body with her own, despite bleeding from a serious wound and facing the threat of more incoming fire.

Her lashes swept down as she lowered her gaze. "It was reflex. You guys had come there to save us. I wanted to help him, so we could get out. I wanted to live."

God, she was breaking his heart and didn't even realize it. "I think part of me fell for you right there and then," he said. That image of her had been permanently seared into his mind, along with the way she'd stared up at him while he'd held his hand to her neck.

Taya's gaze flashed up to meet his, surprise in those silvery-gray depths. "You did?"

Nate nodded, stroked his thumb along her cheek. *I'm still falling.* "I've thought about you so many times over the years, wondered how you were."

A soft, almost shy smile spread across her face. "Glad I wasn't the only one." Her hands came up to frame his face in return, her thumbs sweeping away the traces of the tears on his cheekbones. And Nate was done for. He was done lying to himself, trying to pretend his feelings for her weren't real, or that they'd go away.

The truth was, they were only going to get stronger.

Tilting her face up to his, he lowered his head and kissed her.

Heat punched through him at the tiny sound of need she made and the hungry way she pressed her lips to his. His fingers traced over the sides of her face, moved down to follow the line of her jaw as he kissed the corner of her mouth. Sipping, tasting with a gentle flick of his tongue. Taya hummed in approval and parted her lips for him, tilting her head to get closer.

He took the invitation and licked into her mouth, needing to get deeper, closer. Hunger roared through him, making his heart pound and blood pool in his groin. His cock hardened, pushing against his fly with a throb that was quickly becoming unbearable. He slid one hand into her hair, his fingers flexing against her scalp as he tasted her, gliding his tongue along hers. His other hand trailed lower, down her jaw to her throat and the fine, silvery scar marring the soft skin there, a place he'd wanted to touch since he'd seen her in that D.C. hotel room two days ago.

Driven by the need to erase the past, show her what it felt like to be touched by a man who cared deeply about her, he broke the kiss and angled her head back to follow the line of that scar with his mouth. Taya moaned softly, the sound vibrating beneath his lips as he licked and nibbled his way down the length of the scar. He'd managed to keep her alive that day, would go back and do it all over again, endure that hell again just to have her in his arms like this.

He felt the goose bumps rise beneath his mouth as he sucked at her skin gently, felt her shiver in his hold and wanted more. More of her skin to explore, more of her melting in his arms. His right hand slid lower, over the neckline of her shirt to caress the curve of her breast.

She sucked in a breath and grabbed the back of his

head, holding him to her. He cupped her in his palm, explored the fullness in his hand and swept his thumb across her hardened nipple. An incoherent sound of pleasure came from her and she arched harder into his hand, then grabbed his wrist.

Nate lifted his head, the soft weight of her breast still cradled in his palm. As the tide of lust slowly receded he became aware of her stillness and a low buzzing sound and realized it was his phone where he'd placed it on the bedside table earlier. He searched her eyes for a moment, hoped she wasn't assuming it was some woman calling him at this hour—dammit, even though it might be.

Releasing her breast he cupped her face between his hands once more and pressed his mouth to hers, kissing her with a fierce sense of possessiveness that felt exactly right.

When he lifted his head they were both breathing hard.

Taya shifted off his lap and stood while he retrieved the phone. He activated it, saw DeLuca's number on display. He'd just hit a button to call him back when treads on the staircase made him swing toward his door.

Knuckles rapped against the wood. "Doc. You there?" Cruz asked softly.

"I'm here." He hauled the door open.

Cruz's gaze cut from him to Taya over by the window, then flashed back to him. Nate was prepared for questions but his teammate didn't ask any. "DeLuca just called."

"I know, I was just calling him back." He stepped back to let Cruz in.

Cruz looked over at Taya as he strode in and paused inside the doorway before closing the door. "New intel just came in."

When the latch snicked shut Nate faced him. "What's going on?"

"They got a credible new threat against Taya."

Nate's muscles tensed and he saw Taya look over at him. "What kind of threat?"

"Got a tip this morning from a concerned father that his son and a friend of his are working for a group called The Brethren."

"Fuck." Those radical assholes had been in the media for months now, bragging about how powerful they were and how they couldn't wait to unleash operations in the U.S.

"You know the name?" Cruz asked Taya.

"I've read about them, yes." She wrapped her arms around her waist, calm under pressure as always, but he was starting to know her well enough to see beneath it and the anxiety she was fighting to hide made Nate want to haul her into his arms.

Cruz nodded. "FBI executed a search warrant on the kid's apartment a couple hours ago. Both he and his roommate are involved. The roommate has a computer science degree and must be pretty damn good at what he does, because the NSA tried to recruit him last year. They're digging into phone records and all that right now, but apparently last night both these guys used computers where the father worked to hack into various sites. Including surveillance video of the hotel Taya was at yesterday. Vance and I are both seen on video with her in the hallway."

"So they've seen your faces," Nate finished in a mutter, glancing toward the door to Taya's room as a phone rang in there. Would DeLuca call her personally about this?

"Pretty much. DeLuca is leaving us on the detail for now, but that could change depending on what else they turn up about these guys." He shifted his gaze to Taya. "I need to talk to Nate for a minute alone."

Nate's gut constricted at his teammate's quiet

command. He knew Cruz was going to drop something big on him once they were alone.

"Sure," she murmured, casting a lingering glance at Nate before slipping past him through the door connecting their rooms.

When the door closed behind her Nate focused back on Cruz, his mind spinning as he ran through the new intel and what it might mean for Taya. "Does the Bureau think they could have traced us here?"

"It's possible. They could have hacked into the phone transmissions. Agents are looking into that now. If the hacker is as good as they seem to think, then it could mean trouble for us. No matter how you look at it, this isn't good. DeLuca's sending Tuck down to us, and may pull some of the other guys off their details to work with us. The Brethren want Taya bad." His amber-brown eyes were grave. "Bad enough to put a million dollar bounty on her head."

A *million*? Jesus.

Nate ran a hand through his hair, his blood running cold at the thought of every radical whackjob on the eastern seaboard coming after her with guns blazing, radical Islamist or not. "Fuck." Urgency hummed in his gut. "How long do we have until we need to be out of here?" There was no way they'd endanger Taya's life by staying here if someone was tracking her.

"Fifteen, maybe twenty minutes. Vance is doing a perimeter check. I'll bring the truck around the side for you guys."

"Okay. I'll tell her and meet you down there." Nate turned toward the connecting door, reached out a hand for it but it opened before he could grasp the crystal knob. Taya stood in the opening, bathed in the lamplight streaming behind her, her face pale, eyes bright with tears.

Alarm jumped inside him. Automatically he reached out to wrap a hand around her shoulder. "What's wrong?"

151

"My father's back in the ICU," she whispered. A tear spilled over, flashed down her cheek and Nate's chest constricted. "He had another massive heart attack, and they don't know if he's going to make it this time."

Chapter Thirteen

———————⟋———————

"You sure this is the place?" Ayman asked as he slowed the vehicle at the corner of the street down the block from where the inn was located. One of the others in the group had borrowed this car from his cousin for a few days. If anyone noticed them in the area and traced the license plate, nothing would lead back to them.

"Has to be," Jaleel murmured, craning his neck to see down the road to the right. "It's the only inn listed on this street, and the signal was definitely coming from here." He'd been able to hone in on the cell phone signal's location using the computer program he'd been working on.

"I'm gonna drive around the block. Keep out of sight." Darwish was waiting with two other men a few miles away in the parking lot of a strip mall. He'd sent Ayman and Jaleel here to find out if the whore was actually here, and to see whether there was any sort of security response to their presence.

Ayman turned right and drove up to the yellow-painted historic inn then past it, careful not to slow or do anything to draw attention to them. If this was the place then there'd be highly trained FBI agents inside, and probably in the vicinity as well.

A white SUV was parked at the curb partway up the street, but all the other vehicles were parked in the driveways of private residences. It was possible they were keeping her in some kind of government safe house, but the inn made the most sense. There could be agents posted around the perimeter in plain clothes or hiding in one of the gardens lining the street. It made him uneasy. "Anything?"

"Can't see into the place from here. Turn the corner and I'll see if I can get a better look inside with my binoculars."

Ayman turned right at the next street. Trees and hedges blocked a decent view of the inn, no doubt for privacy of the guests. And it made him nervous to think that trained agents might have eyes on them right now.

"Slow down," Jaleel commanded, ducking down to peer through his window with the binoculars. Hopefully discreetly enough that a watching agent wouldn't be tipped off. "I can see into the back when there's a gap in the hedges. The curtains in one room are open a little. Maybe I can get a look inside."

Ayman slowed, glanced around to make sure no one was around to see, then shifted into reverse and backed up a bit. "I'm only giving you a second. If they've got people watching the road they might see you." The engine whined in protest as the vehicle moved backward to the slight gap in the hedge. "Better?"

"Yeah." He shifted in his seat. "I see…a guy. Big guy, with his back to the window. He's in a dining room, I think. And there's…yeah, there's a woman in there too, she just walked through." He lowered the binoculars. "Looks like our target. Long, dark, curly hair, face looks right." He glanced at Ayman.

"How sure are you?"

"Pretty sure."

"I need a percentage." Everything hinged on this, so it had better be extremely high.

"Ninety."

He nodded, somewhat satisfied. "Has to be her." Had to be, because Darwish and the others were getting impatient and wanted them to take action.

Immediately he drove away, turning left at the next corner. Excitement pulsed through him as he pulled out a burner phone and dialed Darwish.

"Yeah?"

"It's her," Ayman said, knowing that if he was wrong, they'd kill him.

"You sure?"

"As sure as I can be without giving us away. Want me to do it now?" His heart beat erratically, his pistol hard against the small of his back. The assault rifle was in the trunk, loaded and hidden beneath a bunch of camping gear, along with his special scope. As soon as he got the word to attack, he'd use it rather than his pistol to make the shot easier, and to put as much distance between him and the target. Once he pulled the trigger, he'd have only seconds to get out of there.

All he had to do was get within range of the whore, find a clear shot. One shot, that's all he needed.

If he got lucky, The Brethren would allow him to watch the place for a while longer, maybe even wait for the target to come outside. Then he'd take the shot, get to the car where Jaleel would be waiting to get them out of the area. They'd have to switch vehicles because every Fed and cop within a hundred miles would be gunning for them afterward.

After that, Ayman was done. He'd have the satisfaction of pulling off his part in this operation, and receive the money promised him. He had an escape plan in mind to evade the authorities; he just needed the opportunity to enact it.

"Has anyone seen you?" Darwish demanded.

He glanced in his mirrors. "Don't think so." But he wasn't certain and that only amplified his anxiety. Clammy sweat broke out between his shoulder blades and beneath his arms.

He was merely a foot soldier to The Brethren. At least if he carried out this attack he had a chance of survival. If he balked or ran away now, they'd kill him for sure. And maybe his family as well. Ayman couldn't let that happen.

"Find a place to hide the vehicle and wait. Keep an eye on her. If you see an opportunity, take it."

"Okay." He slipped the phone back into his pocket and put the car into gear. "Gotta hide out for a bit," he said to Jaleel. "You get out here, see if you can get another look inside the back of the house then meet me here. I'll come back for you as soon as I find a place to leave the car." And he'd have his rifle hidden in his backpack.

Jaleel looked uncertain, but nodded. "Okay. Hurry though."

After his friend climbed out and vanished into the shadows, Ayman steered the little car to the next block and turned left along the beach. The restaurants along the water were all busy and there were people out walking along the promenade. His palms were damp, his breathing unsteady as he parked in a darkened lot off the road and got out, pulling his ball cap lower on his forehead. The damp, salty breeze washed over him, clearing away some of the nerves.

This would all be over soon. He'd eliminate the target, get his money and disappear, start over in Mexico or on an island in the Caribbean.

All he had to do first was kill the whore.

****

The next few hours passed in a blur for Taya. After her announcement Nathan and the others had immediately moved into action. More agents had arrived about an hour ago while she'd stayed up in her room, packing and trying to get a handle on her emotions.

All she cared about was getting to her father as soon as possible, but this new security threat against her might make that impossible. Even though she'd made it clear that seeing her father was more important to her than her own safety, it wasn't just her at risk by going there.

Someone knocked on her door. "Come in."

Nathan stepped inside, sliding his hands into his jeans pockets. "You packed up?"

She nodded, beyond the ability of making small talk at the moment. "Any word yet?"

"DeLuca just called and the agents are in place. We're just waiting for confirmation on transportation."

"But you're taking me?" she asked, hope a painful pressure beneath her ribcage.

"We're gonna do our best," was all he said.

"What did you mean about transportation? Do we have to switch vehicles now?"

"If we drove, absolutely. We'll switch with the agents who just arrived. But we're hoping to charter a small plane to fly us to Raleigh. Our company jets are all in use right now, getting our guys to the other witnesses, but a private plane is better for us anyhow. Lower visibility for you, less chance someone could tail us. And it would get you to your father quicker."

Taya sighed and rubbed a hand over her forehead. "I just feel like nothing's happening fast enough."

"I understand. I wish we could move faster, but we have to have systems in place first."

"I know."

When he didn't say anything else she glanced up at him, caught off guard by the way her heart lurched when she saw the way he was looking at her. There was concern in his eyes, but also a protectiveness that warmed her. Hard to believe she'd been in his arms a little while ago, holding him, kissing him back as he explored her mouth and neck. It had been even more amazing than she'd dreamed. She trusted him to do everything in his power to get her to her father, but understood it wasn't his call to make.

He reached one hand up to tap his earpiece. "Go." A pause as he listened, staring right at her. "Understood. See you downstairs." He tapped the earpiece again and spoke to her. "Just got the green light on a flight out of a small, private airport about fifteen minutes from here. One of the new agents here reported seeing a vehicle with two males drive by a few minutes ago. They're running the license plate now and keeping an eye out, but we're gonna make sure no one can see you as we leave. And leave your phone here, you can't use it anymore. I'll get you a new one. You ready?"

Taya was on her feet and reaching for her suitcase before he'd finished speaking. "Yes."

Nathan took her bag from her. "Cruz and Vance are going to follow us. We'll head out the west side entrance."

"Okay."

"Put this on." He handed her an olive drab ball cap with an American flag patch on it. Taya tugged it on and slid her chemically-lightened hair through the opening in back. She hurried down the stairs.

An unfamiliar female FBI agent with long curly brown hair was in the foyer with two male agents. Taya nodded at them but didn't say anything as Nathan ushered her out the side door. Cruz was standing by a different SUV than the one they'd arrived in, with the motor already running. Hedges and a privacy fence prevented anyone from being able to see her from the street.

"Good to go?" he asked Nathan.

"Yep. See you at the airfield." He opened her door for her, then set her suitcase into the back before sliding behind the wheel. The windows were darkly tinted, adding another measure of privacy and if she had to bet, she'd guess the glass and frame were bullet resistant.

Nathan kept the headlights and driving lights off until he'd reached the end of the street. She could see a silver minivan about a block in front of them and knew Cruz would be fairly close behind them in another vehicle.

"Any further word from your brother?" Nathan asked her.

"Not in the last hour or so, since the cardiologist was in to see Dad. No news is good news, so I'm hoping that means he's stabilized." It scared her to death, the idea of losing him.

He'd been her rock, her anchor, even before Taya's mother had died during her first grade year. If it was his time to go, then she wanted to be by his side when it happened. She wanted the chance to hug him and tell him she loved him one more time. She pulled in a shaky breath and blinked to battle the sting of tears.

"We'll get you there as soon as we can."

"I know, and I appreciate it. Thanks." It couldn't have been easy, to rearrange everything and bring in extra people for this on such short notice. She realized the importance of being the prosecution's star witness against Qureshi. Moving her was a risk, but with someone working for The Brethren hunting her, Nathan had explained they couldn't have stayed put anyway.

Nathan reached across the console for her hand, lacing his fingers through hers. Then he surprised her by raising her hand to his mouth and pressing a firm, lingering kiss to the back of it. "I'll do whatever I can, okay?"

A sudden lump in her throat, Taya nodded and squeezed his hand in reply. She was glad they were alone in the vehicle, the privacy helped calm her a little bit, soaking up Nathan's strong, steady presence. She didn't know the route to the airfield but he took what seemed like a bunch of random turns on the way there, she guessed to make sure they didn't have a tail.

When they arrived at the airfield there were more FBI agents waiting for them at the gate. They checked Nathan's ID, then Taya's, and allowed them in. Cruz was right behind them.

A small, sleek jet was waiting on the tarmac, parked near the small terminal building. More agents were waiting at the stairs set against its side. Nathan parked close by, grabbed her bag and led her to the aircraft. Two pilots were up front with a female flight attendant, who simply nodded at them as they boarded.

Taya chose a window seat near the back and sank into the plush leather. She was anxious to get going, impatient to get in the air, but it didn't escape her notice that this was no ordinary passenger jet.

"Does the FBI own this plane?" she asked Nathan as he sat in the seat beside her.

"Not exactly," he answered, stretching his long legs out in front of him. "DeLuca called in a favor to a friend over at the NSA."

"Oh." Cruz and Vance boarded, nodded at them and each took a seat on opposite sides of the plane in the middle. At first she thought it was to give them some privacy, but then she realized it likely had more to do with weight distribution for the flight.

The flight attendant closed the forward door and the pilot's voice came over the intercom, giving information about the flight. Taya had no idea how much this was costing whoever was paying for it, but she was grateful to them for making this happen. They taxied a short distance to the end of the runway then began their takeoff run.

As the aircraft picked up speed she found herself gazing out the small, oval-shaped window into the darkness at the lights on the runway skipping past, her heart thudding hard. The moment the wheels lifted off and they began their ascent, she breathed out a sigh of relief and leaned back into the seat, suddenly exhausted.

Nathan pushed up the armrest between their seats and wrapped an arm around her shoulders. Tugging her toward him, he leaned over to murmur close to her ear. "Go ahead and get some sleep if you can."

There was nothing for her to do now and worrying wasn't going to make the situation any better. Taya allowed him to urge her head down onto his shoulder. She curled into his body, resting her cheek in the hollow between his shoulder and chest. Nathan wrapped his arm around her back, his hand tucking into her waist. She felt safe nestled there, his strength surrounding her. Breathing him in, letting his comforting embrace soothe her, she closed her eyes and tried to doze.

He woke her just before they began their descent. By the time they stopped in front of the terminal building, more agents were waiting for them.

Nathan handed her a new, secure phone and put her into the backseat of another waiting vehicle. Then he, Cruz and Vance went to speak with the other agents for a few minutes. She used the new phone to text Kevin and tell him she was on her way. He responded that their father was awake. It felt like a thousand pounds had been lifted from her shoulders.

Nathan slid into the driver's seat while Cruz took the front passenger seat. "The local field office has plain-clothes agents posted at the entrance to the Emergency ward and the ICU," Nathan said to her as he drove from the airfield. "We should be there within twenty minutes."

"Great. He's apparently awake, thank God."

"Good news."

Taya nodded and stared out the window, and thankfully neither of the men tried to initiate any small talk. Nathan pulled up in front of the Emergency entrance of Duke University Hospital. Cruz got out first and opened her door for her, then walked with her through Emergency and up to the ICU. He showed his ID to the nurse at the desk and she directed them to her father's room.

"I'll wait out here with Nate when he comes up," Cruz said to her once they reached the door, his light brown eyes warm with understanding. "Take your time."

"Thank you." Lifting her chin, she took a steadying breath and pushed the door open.

Kevin rose stiffly from a chair in the corner, his gait still a little awkward with his prosthetic, a wan smile on his face. "Hey, you."

"Hi." Normally she would have hugged him but her gaze shot to her father, lying propped up in the hospital bed. Relief flooded her at the sight of him, then fear. His face looked almost gray. His thinning, nearly white hair was sticking up all over the place and he had about four days' worth of stubble on his face. An IV was plugged into his arm and they had several leads attached to his chest, an oxygen tube in his nose.

She glanced at Kevin, reached out a hand to him. "Did they knock him out?"

He took her hand, squeezed. "Yeah. They told him you were coming and his pulse spiked so they sedated him."

Taya went over to set one hip on the edge of the bed, sought her father's hands. The rough calluses on his hands reminded her of Nathan's, only her father had earned his from over fifty years of working with horses. "Hi, Dad. I'm here, safe and sound. I love you. Now you keep fighting and come back to us." She leaned forward to press a kiss to his scratchy cheek, grateful for the chance to tell him so.

Chapter Fourteen

"**S**omething's not right."

Jaleel looked over at him sharply as they walked down a sidewalk a block over from the inn. "Whaddya mean?"

Ayman shook his head. "It feels wrong." He never questioned his gut instinct. Back in Syria it had saved his life a few times. It was telling him now to get the hell out of there.

He'd watched three vehicles leave the property about twenty minutes ago. It was dark out and all the windows had been tinted so they hadn't been able to see who was inside.

They'd just done another recon pass. Yet when he and Jaleel had taken another peek at the building through the binoculars after that, hidden in some shrubs across the street, several of the curtains of the downstairs rooms had been left partially open. They'd caught a glimpse of the same woman from earlier walking past before she'd disappeared from view again.

There was no way the FBI would be so lax with such an important federal witness. They'd never let her walk in front of an open window like that. "It feels like a set up. Like they know we're here and want us to see inside. Like they're waiting for us."

He heard something moving behind them on the street, near the side entrance to the inn. Quiet footsteps on gravel.

They saw us.

Fear drove him to grab Jaleel's arm and yank him around the corner of the next house. Together they pressed up against the wooden siding, hidden from view. Holding his breath, he waited a full minute before pulling Jaleel away and darting for the alley behind the house. They raced over the asphalt, veered around the corner and ran for the car.

The moment he got inside he started the ignition and put it into gear. The car was moving before Jaleel had even closed his door.

"Do you see anyone?" Ayman demanded, darting glances in all the mirrors. He didn't see anyone behind them but that didn't mean they hadn't been spotted. His instincts were screaming at him. He had to get them out of there.

"No, nothing," Jaleel blurted, sounding shaken. "You think they saw us?"

"Yeah." He didn't know why he was so certain but he wasn't going to start doubting himself now.

Jaleel cursed and gripped the door handle. "We need to—" He stopped as a low buzzing filled the interior. Pulling out his phone, he checked the caller ID and answered. "Yes? Hold on. It's Darwish." He put the caller on speaker. "Okay, he can hear you."

"Jaleel's program just got a hit," Darwish said.

"Doesn't matter now." Ayman kept driving. Without a doubt the FBI were tailing them and he had to get out of the area. Find a new car and regroup. "I think we were spotted. We're driving back to you—"

"Are you stupid?" Darwish yelled. "You come near us now, I'll kill you both myself."

The Brethren could get to him and Jaleel. At least while they were in this vehicle, because it had a GPS chip Darwish could track. Ayman clenched his jaw. "I think they suspected someone was coming. It was a trap."

"Did you see her or not?"

Ayman hated the man's impatient tone. "We saw someone who looked like her, but we can't be sure it was."

"Well then you're lucky that Jaleel's computer program just alerted us about her father being admitted to a hospital a few hours ago. Apparently he had another heart attack."

And then it hit him. "It wasn't her we saw." He knew it in his bones.

"What?" Darwish demanded, and Jaleel stared at him.

"It was a decoy. She's really close to her father," he said, knowing that from the meticulous research he'd done on her prior to this op, "so I'm betting they took her to him. We saw three vehicles leave the property a little while ago. They must have had her in one of them, and left another agent who resembled her there. They knew someone was coming for her. It was a sting."

"Are you willing to stake your life on that?" Darwish asked him.

I've already staked my life on this operation. "Yes. Where did they take him?" It was after midnight.

"Duke University Hospital, in Raleigh."

"Then that's where we'll find her." He was more certain of that than anything at the moment.

Darwish gave a chilling laugh, but it was tinged with something else. Almost as though he admired Ayman's response. "All right. Then that's where we're headed. Be there in three hours and ready to take her out. If you're not there I'll come after you personally. And don't bother trying to skip town. You try to run, I'll go after your family."

The line went dead, the hollow sound of the dial tone matching the sensation in the center of Ayman's chest.

****

Taya followed Nathan across the hotel lobby toward the elevator. After staying with her father for the past two hours, her brother had finally convinced her to leave and get some sleep. She'd reluctantly agreed, mostly because it wasn't fair that Nathan and the others had to stand guard here if her father was stable. With her father sedated she couldn't speak to him anyway, so she'd promised Kev she'd be back first thing in the morning.

"What did you want to talk to me about in private, anyway?" she asked Nathan as they stepped inside the elevator. Vance was upstairs checking their rooms and Cruz was staying in the lobby until she was safely in her room.

"Tell you in a second," he said quietly, his gaze scanning the nearly empty lobby as the doors slid slowly closed.

Still on alert, even though she knew he must be beyond tired. When she'd exited the hospital room, he'd been standing right there leaning against the wall, waiting for her. Alone, since Vance had been by the Emergency entrance and Cruz at the ICU entrance. He'd stood guard outside the door the entire time she'd been in there with her dad and brother.

She'd smiled at him and wrapped her arms around his waist, thanked him for waiting, glad the others weren't there because she wouldn't have been affectionate with him in front of his teammates. He'd taken her chin in his hand, and his answer had made her heart squeeze.

I'd have waited for as long as you needed me to, little warrior.

They started moving. "We've got two rooms," he said, his expression serious, "and because of the potential new threat against you, you'll have to room with one of us. I wanted to give you the option of picking who you want for a roomie in private. I don't want you to feel pressured to share a room with me just because of what happened earlier. Or because of what happened in Afghanistan."

His thoughtfulness touched her. "Well I appreciate that, thank you, but I want to stay with you." In her mind there'd never been any other option for her.

Relief filled his eyes and he smiled a little. A slow, sexy smile that lit her entire body with tingles of arousal. They'd been dormant since receiving news about her father, but now they were back and stronger than ever.

She wanted more of what he could offer her. Wanted to belong to him, even if only for one night. Not because she was willing to be a one-night stand, but because their time together was short.

"Okay then," he murmured.

Had he been worried she'd pull away from him now? Or not trust him to do his job guarding her because of what had happened back at the inn?

She opened up more to him. "And the truth is, I really don't want to be alone right now." No, more than that. She didn't want to sleep alone; she wanted Nathan right there next to her. In three days she could be taking the stand and she wouldn't be seeing him until her testimony, and maybe even the entire trial, ended. Now that her father was out of immediate danger and resting, she wanted time alone with Nathan.

At that his gaze sharpened on her, his eyes darkening with a possessive hunger that sent a shiver of longing through her. "Okay."

The elevator stopped moving. A soft ding alerted her a moment before the doors slid open. Nathan stepped past her out into the hallway, checking both directions before leading her down it, his large hand firm against the small of her back, the heat of his palm burning her.

He pulled out a keycard and unlocked the door to their room. "It's already been swept but I'm going to check it again anyway." He entered the room.

Taya slipped her purse strap off her shoulder and sighed as she rolled her head from side to side. It had been a long, emotionally draining day. She was going to make sure it ended better than it had begun, and wind up in bed with Nathan.

He opened the door wide a few moments later and stepped aside for her to enter. "All clear."

She passed by him and into the room, her entire body buzzing with awareness as he shut the door behind her. The room was standard, with two queen-size beds and a small bathroom. She barely noticed any of it, too caught up with having over six feet and two-hundred-plus pounds of the sexiest man on earth standing just feet away from her. The skin along her spine buzzed with an almost electric charge, her entire body aching for his touch.

But then doubt suddenly overtook her. Compared to him she was ridiculously inexperienced at this. And she could just imagine how good he'd be in bed. While she was fairly certain he wouldn't turn her down if she threw herself at him now, she didn't want to seem pathetic and desperate, either. It was hard not to think about all the other women who called him.

Now or never, Taya. This could be your only shot with him.

She took a deep, bracing breath, and started to turn around. Before she could, two strong hands curled over the muscles at the top of her shoulders and squeezed. Taken by surprise, she smiled and let out a little groan of pleasure as her eyes slid closed. "Oh my God, that's exactly the spot."

His deep chuckle ruffled the hair at her nape as his hands kneaded her stiff muscles with firm, toe-curling pressure. "It's cuz I've got magic hands."

Oh, she had no doubt of that. Just the thought of them stroking over her naked body made her wet.

She turned to look up at him and the expression on his face stole the breath from her lungs. Hungry. Focused. Watching her closely.

Waiting. A hungry panther ready to spring.

Desire shot through her, her pulse thudding in her ears. When he reached up to pull the ball cap off her head and ran his hands through her hair, she couldn't stop the moan that spilled from her throat.

Those gorgeous, skilled hands that were equally capable of taking a life and saving one tightened in the strands, his gaze locked with hers. A heartbeat later his mouth crashed down on hers.

She'd been waiting for it, even expecting it on some level, but the heated urgency of the kiss took her off guard.

Taya gasped and grabbed hold of his broad shoulders, her fingers sinking into the hard muscle there. That coiled strength beneath her palms had carried her when she'd been too weak to go on, was protecting her even now. The sense of security combined with the feel of his mouth moving over hers, setting her blood on fire.

She pressed against the full length of him, hungry for the feel of that strength wrapped around her. He made a low sound in his throat and drove his tongue into her mouth, sending a velvet shock to the center of her abdomen and between her thighs. Her nipples were hard, achy points against the lace of her bra as they met the hard wall of his chest.

His mouth was hungry over hers, taking complete

charge of the kiss until her head spun and she couldn't breathe. Raw need roared through her, growing stronger with every throb of her heart.

Impatient to feel more of him, she slipped her hands down his chest, over his abdomen to grasp the bottom of his T-shirt and shoved it upward, hungry to explore his bare skin.

Nathan grabbed the back of it with one fist and hauled it upward, breaking the kiss only long enough to yank it over his head and throwing it aside before claiming her mouth once more. Her searching hands met heated, naked skin dusted with hair. She slid her palms over him eagerly as she twined her tongue with his, getting lost in his taste, the feel of him.

One hand controlling her head, he slid the other down to grip her hip and spun them around fast, pinning her up against the nearest wall with that long, powerful body. Both his hands gripped her hair now, his mouth still devouring hers as his hips met her pelvis. The thick, hard length of his erection pressed against her lower belly, igniting a throb between her legs.

She made a soft sound of longing and locked her hands around the back of his neck, anchored herself as she curled one leg around his. The man was a master with his mouth. He was so big and strong and he knew just how to touch her, just how to move to rocket her need into a fever pitch.

Taya shivered, needing more. Feeling like she'd die if he didn't strip her and push into her soon. Then he dropped one hand to her butt and gripped one cheek, lifting her as he bent his knees to settle more fully between her thighs.

Oh, God...

Heat exploded in her belly with every stroke of his erection against her needy core. Her lips found his jaw, teeth nipping, the frantic need tearing at her. He gave a low growl and pinned her harder to the wall, his big body caging hers, each roll of his hips sending a streak of heat through her.

"It's been so long," she moaned against his jaw, feeling like she was burning from the inside out. "So damn long. Touch me. Touch me all over." She needed him to quench this uncontrollable hunger raging inside her.

"I will, baby," he whispered against her cheek, turning her head and finding her mouth with his again.

One big hand slid from her hair, his slightly roughened fingertips trailing down the side of her neck until they skimmed over a tight nipple. Taya tore her mouth from his on a moan and arched, her hand automatically locking around his wrist to push her breast harder into his palm. The towering need made her dizzy. Then her brain caught up with her body and a trickle of uncertainty slid through her.

She stilled, heart pounding, body aching with the most intense desire she'd ever known.

Nathan stopped and raised his head to look down at her, his hand still cupping her breast. He was breathing as hard as she was, his eyes glittering with a hunger so raw it sliced her inside.

When she didn't say anything he started to remove his hand but she tightened her grip and held him there as she gazed into his eyes. "I can't be just another notch on your belt, Nathan," she whispered in an agonized voice. Not with him, it would crush her. If that's all she was to him, she would rather stop things here than continue. She'd already battled long and hard to overcome feeling cheap and used. She wouldn't do it again for any man, not even Nathan.

The anguished look on his face made her feel terrible for saying it, but she'd had to make it clear. "No," he insisted, leaning down to rest his forehead against hers and closing his eyes. She could feel the urgency in him, the way it strung his muscles tight, the fingers in her hair sliding open to cradle the back of her skull. The protective, possessive gesture made her melt and lean into his hold. "No, you're not, I swear to God you're not."

She didn't answer, but she didn't pull away from him either. Because she believed him.

And when he raised his head to look down at her again, she saw the resolve in his gaze, blended with concern and a fierce tenderness that rocked her. "Do you trust me, Taya?" he murmured.

She nodded. "You know I do." With her life. But she wanted to be able to trust him with her heart as well.

His body relaxed against her, but his expression never changed. "Then let me touch you, take care of you. I need to touch you." His eyes blazed down at her, completely molten with desire.

With a soft smile she leaned up and pressed her lips to his. This time he groaned out loud and crushed her to him, sliding his hands down to grip her hips. Turning her from the wall, he walked her over to one of the beds. After pulling down the comforter he pushed her backward onto the fitted sheet and followed, covering her with his weight.

Taya moaned in undiluted pleasure and wrapped her arms and legs around him, letting her hands explore the length of his back. Muscles bunched and shifted beneath her palms as he settled atop her and braced his forearms on either side of her head, caging her in. He took her mouth in an urgent, hungry kiss, his tongue sliding against hers.

He kissed his way over her jaw and down her throat, rolling to his side a little so he could push up the hem of her shirt. Taya helped him, lifting enough to pull it over her head. His eyes fastened on her pale blue lace bra and something close to a growl came out of his throat.

He slid his hands around her ribcage and leaned down to nuzzle the valley between her breasts as he reached beneath her to unhook her bra. She ran her hands up the deep indent of his spine to plunge her fingers into his thick hair, pulling his mouth to her chest.

Cool air rushed over her naked breasts, her nipples tightening even more, then the heat of his mouth closed around one taut peak. The last man to ever see her naked was Hassan, and her last lover nearly a year before that. With anyone else she would have been nervous and stiff but with Nathan she felt safe and…cherished.

Wanted. Needed, even.

A low sob came out of her at the feel of his lips and tongue working her sensitive flesh. She moved restlessly beneath him, the throb between her legs becoming unbearable. Nathan cupped her other breast as he sucked at her, his free hand smoothing down her stomach to the button of her jeans.

Desperate for more, she released his hair and undid her jeans for him. He grabbed the unfastened waistband and tugged, peeled the denim over her hips and down her legs, where she kicked them off with an impatient flick of her feet.

His big hand trailed up her inner thigh, spreading electric tingles over her skin and making her even wetter for him. He turned his head, captured her other nipple in his mouth as he cupped her slick sex with his palm.

Taya shuddered, her soft cry mixing with his deep groan of approval. "You're so wet, baby," he murmured, adding pressure with his palm.

"Nathan," she moaned, twisting in his hold, the need becoming painful. She craved this, craved the release he could give her.

"I've got you," he murmured against her breast, his hands sure on her body.

The words froze her for an instant. She raised her

head and stared down at him. Releasing her nipple with a knowing flick of his tongue that made her back arch, Nathan looked up at her. His eyes were made up of flecks of gray and blue with a tawny ring around the pupils. For an instant the present merged with the past, the line separating them blurred.

I've got you, Taya.

The hands giving her pleasure right now had been pressed hard to the side of her neck when he'd said that to her last, in Afghanistan.

He hadn't let her down then, and he wouldn't now. Whatever happened after this, she knew at least tonight he'd do everything in his power to give her what she wanted.

A needy sound came from her throat when he drew his fingers through her damp folds. His eyes smoldered in the lamplight as he watched her response, and Taya was too far-gone with pleasure and need to feel shy.

He didn't tease or make her wait, just pushed two fingers inside her. Her back bowed and she clutched his head, panting at the exquisite stretching sensation, being filled by a man who cared about her after all this time. Apparently satisfied by her reaction, he lowered his head to suck one tender nipple, his tongue flicking against it as he withdrew his fingers from her core and slid them up to circle her aching clit.

"Ah!" She was drowning in need, clinging to him, wanting him closer.

Nathan slid his free arm beneath her back, firmly anchoring her to the bed. He caressed the swollen bud at the top of her sex, his body so hot and hard against her side, then pushed his fingers inside her again. This time he curled them upward, finding the hidden bundle of nerves inside her then rubbing his thumb against her clit at the same time.

Taya whimpered and squeezed her eyes shut, the

muscles in her thighs and abdomen pulled tight. Thick, syrupy pleasure spread inside her with every movement of his hand, his talented mouth. It coiled low in her belly and expanded outward with each skilled caress. She rolled her hips against his hand, her yearning increasing at the way he pinned her down with his weight and strength.

The orgasm rose inside her, looming like a giant wave and she reached for that crest, needing the release with every cell in her body. Those maddening fingers pushed inside her then withdrew before plunging back inside in a steady, unhurried rhythm that drove her mad. He increased the pressure of his thumb slightly, rubbing her clit in tiny circles as his teeth scraped her nipple and his tongue soothed the slight sting.

Ecstasy exploded inside her, release shattering her in powerful waves. She heard herself cry out his name and shuddered, letting it roll through her for long, endless seconds.

Gradually it faded, leaving behind a blissful lassitude that made every muscle go lax. Nathan kissed his way up her chest, up her throat to her chin, lingered on her mouth for a long moment before he pressed his lips to each of her closed eyelids.

Taya was still catching her breath as he withdrew his hand from between her legs, then collapsed back against the mattress with a groan. She rolled toward him, let out a deep sigh of contentment when he gathered her into his arms and held her tight against his chest. He chuckled low in his throat and squeezed, one hand running through her hair.

The denim of his jeans felt rough against her inner thigh as she draped one leg over his. She could feel how hard he still was, knew he had to be hurting. But when she reached down for the button fastening his jeans, he grabbed her hand and made a negative sound.

Surprised, she leaned her head back to look at him.

"Why not?"

His thumb stroked over the inside of her wrist, igniting tiny tingles across the fragile skin. "Because you're not like the others. And I'm not that guy anymore."

Her heart turned over at the serious look in his eyes. "You don't have to prove anything to me, Nathan. I want to touch you too."

He shook his head. "But I've got something to prove to myself."

Taya stared into his eyes for a long moment before deciding he was telling the truth. This was important to him and it made her care for him even more. She leaned up to press her lips to his. "Thank you." But she still hoped he'd change his mind before they left the room in the morning.

She felt his smile form beneath her lips. "Was my pleasure, sweetheart. Happy to do that any time you want."

She wanted to do the same for him before they left this room. "You'll sleep beside me tonight?"

Another low chuckle, his fingers sliding through the length of her hair. "Not budging from your side for a second, little warrior." Reaching down to grab the covers, he tugged them over them and leaned to the side to switch off the lamp on the nightstand, plunging the room into darkness.

Taya snuggled up against him, her head on his shoulder. She felt utterly, blissfully relaxed for the first time in recent memory. With his arms wrapped securely around her and the steady thud of his heartbeat beneath her cheek, she closed her eyes and sank headfirst into oblivion.

Chapter Fifteen

Ayman sat in the front passenger seat of a rental vehicle Darwish had gotten them last night using fake IDs. He rubbed at his eyes and smothered a yawn before shifting his attention back to one of the exits at the rear of the hotel.

After arriving in Raleigh and meeting up with Darwish just a couple hours ago, they'd gone to the hospital and quickly discovered that the security there was way too tight. There was no chance they'd be able to get inside and up to the ICU unnoticed, and with that many trained bodyguards watching the target, trying an attack there would have been useless. And suicidal.

While he was willing to die for their cause if necessary, he wanted his death to be worthwhile and not wasted.

They'd had to wait until the very last bodyguard had left, a built Hispanic guy who moved with military precision, half an hour after the target and two other bodyguards had. Thankfully Darwish had managed to follow the Hispanic guard to this hotel.

Ayman hadn't asked how he'd been able to do it without being detected and Darwish hadn't volunteered any details. The specialized training Darwish had received during six months at a military camp in Mauritania was coming in handy and Ayman continued to learn as much as possible from his more experienced mentor.

The driver's side door opened and Darwish slid behind the wheel, a black 9 mm pistol in his grip, his once full beard trimmed into a short goatee. "We're in."

Ayman blinked. Already? "You found her? She's here?"

He sank farther down into the seat and cast a surreptitious look around. "I paid off an employee to find me the whore's room number, and for some extra cash he told me they'd just placed a room service order a few minutes ago, so it's perfect. Although he won't be using my money anytime soon."

His sly smile left no doubt that the man was dead. Ayman tried to ignore the way his conscience pricked at him. People had to die in this operation; there was no way to avoid it and he'd known that from the outset. Killing the target to prevent her from testifying and helping in the effort to free Qureshi was worth far more than the lives of a few innocent infidels.

"Jaleel's getting changed into a uniform now," Darwish continued and Ayman didn't ask where they'd gotten it. "He'll go up to the room first with the room service order."

"What? Why Jaleel? He's not trained for this."

"Because we need someone else to verify whether the whore's inside the room, and my other operatives are busy. You and I can't do this. We need to be ready to attack later, after Jaleel leaves and her security lets their guard down a little bit. We can't do it during the room service delivery, it'll be too obvious."

He shook his head, continued. "We'll each wait in the opposite stairwell at the end of the hall until he's inside and can verify that it's her. He'll alert us by radio when he leaves the room, let us know what kind of security is with her. If I decide there's a good opportunity, we attack the room as planned and take her out. If we get clear after that, we meet back here."

He said it all without so much as a hint of inflection in his voice, his restless gaze scanning the rear loading area for any threats. He was better trained and more experienced in ops and combat than either him or Jaleel, but Darwish was also far more valuable to The Brethren than either of them. They'd put him in charge of this op for a reason—and Ayman knew it was because they had far bigger plans for him in the coming weeks.

Darwish was to play a critical role on the main attack planned for the trial, so if he wasn't certain about being able to assassinate the Kostas woman here, he'd withdraw and wait. If they couldn't kill her today, they'd let her come to them and take her out at the trial.

"He's got a uniform for you too, waiting in the supply closet just inside those doors." Darwish indicated the steel doors that led into a loading area off the kitchen. "The rifle's not an option now—too hard to disguise. You'll have to do it with your pistol. Now get going." He shoved Ayman's shoulder.

Ayman set his jaw, pushing aside the resentment as he mentally prepared for what lay ahead. Everything hinged on Jaleel's recon, then on Darwish's decision afterward.

This was all happening way faster than he'd anticipated.

He didn't like rushing this, even though they'd gone over the plan several times and studied the layout of the hotel last night and he knew where all the emergency exits were located. Security was down in the lobby, and unless they'd posted extra men on the target's floor, only the bodyguards would be up there. The men watching over the whore were far better trained than him, but he and Darwish would have the element of surprise.

Still, a cold knot of fear formed in his belly, his mind trying to overrule his heart. He ignored it, reminded himself that he was brave enough to do what needed to be done.

With no option now but to carry out the plan, Ayman gathered himself and exited the vehicle. Thankfully there was no one else around and he'd pulled the ball cap down over his ears and forehead to help conceal his face from any security cameras. The car's engine whined as Darwish put it into reverse and backed around the corner out of sight. Would Darwish wait for him if they aborted and had to evacuate? Fleeing on foot would leave him too exposed.

He kept his gaze straight ahead as he crossed the parking area, staring directly at the metal doors before him, his heart slamming hard against his chest wall. It was open a crack.

Pushing it inward, he saw that the small entry room was deserted except for stacks of pallets loaded with food, and stepped inside. In front of him was the door to the kitchen, and to his right lay another, he assumed for the supply closet.

He tensed as it cracked open, automatically reaching for the weapon stashed in the back of his waistband. Jaleel's voice floated out toward him. "Come on," his friend whispered impatiently.

Ayman hurried inside the small space. Jaleel shut the door and switched on the dim flashlight he carried, illuminating the body lying on the floor, naked but for his underwear. The man's eyes were still half open, his lips parted in a silent cry. But there was no blood. Why wasn't there any blood?

"Is he dead?" Ayman whispered, trying not to stare. Dead bodies didn't bother him—he'd seen more than his share back in Syria. But he'd never personally taken a life before and knowing this man had died as part of this operation suddenly made this situation real.

No second thoughts. I'm ready.

"Yeah. Syringe to the neck. Here, quick, put this on." Jaleel thrust a fistful of garments at him. "I've gotta take the room service order upstairs in a few minutes. Hurry."

Ayman's hands shook a little as he shrugged out of his clothes and put on the hotel uniform: gray pants that were too short and a burgundy jacket that hung on his frame. The nametag on it read Raul. Ayman assumed Darwish had killed him as well, with another syringe, likely filled with morphine or cyanide.

He slid his weapon into the back of the waistband and wiped a damp palm over his freshly-shaven jaw. It felt weird and sacrilegious to be without the beard he'd been growing for the past four months, but it would hopefully help him avoid suspicion and change his appearance enough to fool anyone looking for him.

"Which room is it?" he whispered to Jaleel.

"Six-oh-three. We don't know if she's still in it or how many guards there are. I'll find out when I take the food in." His friend's voice was tense, slightly higher in pitch than normal. This was outside of Jaleel's area of expertise, and that increased Ayman's anxiety.

Jaleel's nervousness spread to him like a virus, spiking his heart rate. "How long will you need?" He wasn't scared. He just had to shut off his brain and act. Once it was done, it would be a relief. Then his part in this operation would be over and he could start a new life elsewhere.

But knowing Darwish was armed and waiting made him nervous. He didn't trust the other man not to turn on them if it saved his own skin. Ayman was prepared to take out whoever he had to in order to protect himself.

"Won't take me long," Jaleel said, sounding steadier now. "Once I'm at the door it should only take a minute or two, tops. I'll wait for you down in the stairwell afterward, in case you need backup."

"Okay. But if anything goes wrong, just get out of there. I'll cover you." Jaleel was armed, but he wasn't nearly the shot Ayman and Darwish were. And he had no experience with the kind of violence Ayman had witnessed time and time again back in Syria.

Ayman clapped his friend on the shoulder, smiled to lend him courage. "You can do this. May Allah be with you."

"And with you." With a nod, Jaleel exited the supply closet.

Ayman waited a full minute before following, and headed to the west-side stairwell that led to the guest floors. He'd already memorized the layout of everything, so he could choose the best option when it came time to escape. He jogged up to the sixth floor and stole a peek through the hallway to make sure he could access it without a problem. Thankfully it was empty.

On his way down he froze at the sound of footsteps above him on the concrete stairs. More than one person. Seconds later a young mother with a toddler in tow and a baby on her hip came into view. She smiled when she saw him, and Ayman made himself unfreeze and smile back.

"Good morning," she called out.

"Good morning." He even smiled at the kids, stepping aside to let her pass him on the narrow landing, careful to keep his back to the railing to hide the slight bulge beneath the back of his jacket.

"Oh."

Gripping the railing with one hand, Ayman looked back at the woman, who had stopped a few steps below

183

him. She wasn't looking at him in a suspicious way, merely curious. He didn't want to hurt her but he couldn't afford to have her delay or report him. And he didn't like that she'd seen his face up close. *Walk away*, he told her silently. *Walk away NOW*.

"One of the faucets in our bathroom ran all night. Could you have someone take a look? Room three-nineteen."

He relaxed. "Absolutely. Have a nice day."

She smiled again before turning away. "You too."

Ayman released his grip on the cold metal railing and began his swift ascent to the sixth floor, preparing himself for what lay ahead. He'd come too far to fail now. Everything he'd ever wanted—money, the respect of his peers, his freedom—was almost within his grasp now.

All he had to do was commit a murder first.

****

After placing the rushed room service order, Nathan got off the bed and crossed to the bathroom door, knocking once. "I ordered us breakfast. Food'll be here in a few minutes," he said to Taya. The shower was still running, had been for the last five minutes.

"Can you cancel it?" she called back. "I'll grab something at the hospital later."

"You need to eat first. It'll only take a few minutes and then we'll go see your dad." She hadn't eaten much at dinner last night and needed to keep her strength up. The faster they ate and got going, the better, and with her father now awake and able to talk, he knew she wanted to see him as soon as possible.

"All right," she answered, not sounding too happy about it.

Nate glanced at his watch. He'd already talked with Cruz and Vance this morning, who'd opted to take turns running to the lobby for a bite to eat rather than get room service. He'd spoken to the head of hotel security personally last night when they'd checked in.

Placing a guard outside Taya's door would only draw unwanted attention and possibly flag her presence, so instead they'd opted to have two hotel security guards come up and check the floor at scheduled intervals. Also, someone was monitoring the video cameras on this floor.

Tuck was due in town shortly and would meet them at the hospital. After her visit this morning, they'd move Taya to a new location, whatever safe house the Bureau could secure for them, then get her back to D.C. and another safe house in time for the start of the trial two days from now.

The shower continued to run. Standing before the closed door, he was having trouble thinking about much of anything besides Taya naked beneath the flow of water. Need and desire curled inside him at the image that conjured, of rivulets cascading over every delectable inch of her skin, tracing all her curves. Now that he'd seen her completely naked and run his hands over her gorgeous body, slid his fingers into her heat and brought her to orgasm, it was impossible to stop thinking about it.

He'd crossed a line last night that he shouldn't have crossed while on this job, but he didn't regret it. Last night with Taya had been the most emotionally satisfying sexual experience he could ever remember having, and he'd barely scratched the surface of what he wanted to do to her.

Even suffering from an arousal so acute it had kept him from sleeping most of the night, he'd refused to act on it. She could never be a one-night stand to him and he wanted no confusion about that. She'd also been through so much emotional upheaval over the past few days, he'd just wanted to take care of her, have the pleasure be all about her. He'd happily have taken care of her multiple times throughout the night but she'd slept right through and it was probably for the best.

It had also been the most peaceful night he'd spent in months. Having her snuggled against him so warm and soft and trusting last night had soothed him on the deepest level. Being able to hold her all night had made the torture he suffered completely worthwhile. It only made him want her more.

Getting her off with just his fingers had been gratifying, and he'd thoroughly enjoyed the experience of making her come, but he wanted way more. He wanted his tongue between her legs next time, to taste and tease, then feel her clench around his cock as he buried himself inside her and watched her eyes go hazy with pleasure while he took her on the climb to ecstasy.

She'd begged him so sweetly for release, just the memory of it made him hard. He couldn't wait to make her his completely, burn the feel of his body and touch into her memory.

And not just because he knew intuitively the sex would be the best he'd ever had. He wanted a real relationship with her once this was all over. Wanted to take her on dates. To dinner. Dancing. Movies, whatever. Hold her and kiss her and seduce her in public until she was all hot and bothered for him, then take her home and make love to her in his bed, a place that he'd begun to dread being in.

But he wanted Taya there now, wanted her scent all over the sheets and her hair fanning out across one of his pillows. To erase what he'd done before her and replace it with something pure and good.

I can't just be another notch on your belt, Nathan.

God, those words had knifed him right in the heart, even though he'd understood why she'd felt the need to say them. He wanted the chance to prove to her just how much he cared, show her how different she was compared to all the other women he'd been with. He knew how special the connection between them was, and he was pretty sure she did to. He'd fight for the right to nurture it, but hoped he wouldn't have to.

The shower stopped running. Nate shifted and rolled his shoulders to alleviate the tightness there. He went back to the bed, was just about to turn on the TV when a tentative knock came at the door.

"Room service."

Nate tossed aside the remote at the soft male voice and rose.

"It's here?" Taya asked through the door.

"Yeah, but stay put while I bring it in," he said, receiving a quiet "okay" before he crossed to the door. As a precaution he reached back one hand for the weapon in his waistband and checked the peephole.

A fair-skinned, clean-shaven guy in his early twenties stood there wearing a hotel uniform, a silver-domed tray on the cart before him. His eyes were dark brown, thickly lashed. He resembled one of the men DeLuca had sent pictures and partial files of to Nate and the others last night, upon arrival at the hospital. But missing the dark beard they'd all had, it was impossible for Nate to be certain.

"Show me your ID," he said to him.

The guy's eyebrows jumped a fraction before drawing together. "Sir?"

"Your ID. Let me see it."

He seemed taken aback by the request for a moment, then glanced down at his waist and fumbled around in his pocket. He pulled out a card and held it up at peephole level. The credentials looked legit but Nate couldn't get a good look at the photo ID and that made him uneasy. "Step back across the hall and stay where I can see you."

The waiter blinked at him, his eyebrows drawing together in confusion. "I...across the hall?"

"Now."

Slowly the man did as he was told and backed away to the opposite wall, glancing uncertainly around him. Nate watched his hands, which were empty. He couldn't see a bulge beneath the jacket that indicated a hidden weapon, but he could have one tucked behind him or under the dome.

Sliding the security chain over, Nate undid the deadbolt and unlocked the door. He pulled it open a few inches and stopped. Again the guy blinked at him, his hands now twitching restlessly at his sides.

Nate reached out to grasp the handle of the serving tray and the man visibly swallowed. Nate held his stare for a moment, then lifted the lid and took a quick glance. Nothing there but two servings of pancakes, sliced berries, a pitcher of syrup, some butter and a bowl of whipped cream.

He set it back down and settled his gaze on the waiter, who seemed frozen there across the hall. Could be surprise or nerves because Nate wasn't exactly being friendly…or it could mean something more dangerous.

He didn't take his eyes off the waiter. "I'll take it from here. Just charge it to the room."

The guy licked his lips. "But it's my job to bring it in for you…"

"Not today." He stared into his eyes. Nobody was getting inside that room with Taya in it.

Even from where he stood Nate could see the sheen of sweat that popped out on the younger man's upper lip and brow. "Sir, really, I'd—"

"No, we're done." He took a step forward into the open doorway, the motion deliberately menacing, and caught the way the guy's gaze flashed down to the hand Nate had behind his back.

The move set off alarm bells in his head.

His hand tightened a fraction more around the

pistol's grip, the muscles in his arm tensing as he prepared to draw. But then the server pivoted without a word and strode away at a rapid pace, heading toward the elevator.

Something was definitely off though and Nate wasn't going to let it go.

Staring after him, Nate tapped his earpiece. There was something underneath the back of his jacket, but he couldn't tell whether it was a weapon or not. "Cruz," he murmured, "there's a server passing by your room. Follow him. I'm gonna stay in here and call security. I want him questioned."

"What's up?"

"Just follow him."

A second later Cruz opened his door, two rooms down and across the hall, and stepped out, his gaze immediately locking on the server. Halfway down the hall, the guy glanced back over his shoulder, saw both him and Nate watching him…then turned and bolted.

Shit. Nate tore out of his room, letting the door slam shut behind him as Cruz raced ahead of him. "Stop right there!" his teammate shouted.

The waiter put on a burst of speed.

Running full out, Nate spoke over his earpiece. "Vance, watch my room," he ordered, not wanting to say Taya's name in case anyone else was close by and listening, "and alert security." If this fucker was part of a plot to get her, there'd likely be others at the hotel. Protectiveness surged through him in a torrential rush.

"I'm on it." A door opened behind him and Nate knew without looking that it was his other teammate, already moving into position outside Taya's door. He wouldn't let her out until they'd secured the place.

Ahead of him, the surprisingly quick bastard had reached the metal door leading to a stairwell. Nate lengthened his stride, pushing his legs to move faster. The waiter plunged through the stairwell door and disappeared from view. Nate raced after him, Cruz right behind him, fury and adrenaline blasting through his body.

No way, asshole. You're mine.

Chapter Sixteen

Nate halted when he reached the door, his pistol gripped in both hands. He put his back to the wall opposite the door handle and waited for Cruz to mirror him on the other side, his weapon also at the ready.

He reached one hand up to tap his earpiece. "We're moving down the east stairwell," he said so Vance would know their position.

"Got it. Security's been alerted."

Good.

Waiting in position, Nate focused on the area that opening the door would reveal, and nodded at Cruz. His teammate gripped the handle and pushed the door open, then stepped back to hug the wall.

Nate crept slowly forward, his gaze pinned to the space revealed to the left of the open doorway as Cruz covered the other side, their combined angles forming an X pattern. He held his pistol in front of him, wishing he had an M4 or MP5 instead. Clearing a stairwell with a pistol wasn't tactically ideal.

The stairwell below him was empty but he could hear

running footsteps moving away from them. No telling if someone else was waiting down there, preparing to take a shot. Or if the server might turn and attack if he felt trapped or desperate. Nate had every intention of stopping the bastard before that happened, and every intention of getting back to Taya in one piece.

"Clear," he murmured, just loud enough for Cruz to hear him.

"Clear," his teammate responded. Together they moved down the first set of stairs, clearing each section as they moved. It took precious time that allowed the tango to gain more of a lead, but better that than getting shot by being careless or sloppy.

Vance's voice came through his earpiece. "Security's on the way up, and they're sealing off the exits near the east stairwell. Local field office is sending us more agents, en route now."

"Copy." It would take the field agents some time to get here. Hopefully hotel security would stay the hell out of their way until they'd cleared the entire stairwell. He and Cruz moved as fast as possible, smoothly working together as a unit.

Somewhere below them came the hollow, metallic clang of a door hitting the concrete wall. "He's near the kitchens," Nate said to Vance.

"Copy that."

They reached the last flight of stairs and took up position on opposite sides of the door, as they had upstairs. Nate was just about to nod for Cruz to throw it open when two gunshots cracked through the stillness. Nate stilled. "Shots fired outside the kitchen area." He looked at Cruz, nodded.

His teammate threw the door wide. Two more shots exploded. Small plumes of dust burst free where the rounds buried themselves into the concrete wall next to them.

Nate set his jaw. Their tango had just changed the rules of engagement. Nate and Cruz played to win.

Game on, motherfucker. With Cruz covering him, he burst around the corner with his weapon up, just in time to see a dark-haired man race through the exit and out of sight.

****

Ayman tore down the west side stairs, his boots thudding on the concrete steps. His heart was in his freaking throat, nearly choking him as he ran, pistol in hand. Jaleel had fucking blown it by taking off like that, making it obvious he'd been up to something. Now they were all at risk. He had to get out, meet up with the others and get the hell out of here.

He skidded around the last turn and raced down the final set of steps. Just as he hit the bottom, two gunshots rang out. Muffled, but unmistakable. Not in the stairwell, but somewhere close by.

Ayman stopped, his heart thundering in his ears as he listened.

Pop, pop. Pop, pop. In rapid succession.

The place had to be crawling with security personnel by now. He wasn't waiting to find out who'd fired.

Shoving through the metal safety door, he burst into the loading area off the kitchen. Other uniformed employees were in the narrow entryway, transporting boxes of foodstuffs. They shouted when Ayman plowed through them, knocking the boxes out of their arms and sending them reeling.

Vegetables and fruits rained to the floor. His right foot landed on one. He slipped, barely caught himself against the wall before pushing up and aiming straight for the exit.

Someone blocked the doorway. A big man in a hotel

uniform. Weapon in his hand.

Ayman raised his weapon and fired. The man grunted and fell to his knees, clutching his shoulder. Cries and shouts rose up behind him as he raced past the man and outside.

He squinted against the sudden glare of sunlight and blindly careened around the corner toward where Darwish was supposed to have left the vehicle. He'd only taken two steps when he rammed into something solid. The impact knocked him down.

He rolled to his side and brought his weapon up to fire, at the last moment recognizing Darwish towering over him, pistol in hand. Darwish reached down and clamped a strong hand around Ayman's wrist. "Come on," he snapped, hauling him upward.

Ayman scrambled to his feet and ran after him to the car, parked near the entrance to the alley. Security personnel were already converging on the area. A man shouted at them to stop.

"Go!" Darwish shoved him in the direction of the passenger side.

They both veered around opposite sides of the vehicle, ripped the doors open. Shots slammed into the car. Two punched through the rear windshield. Ayman ducked and whirled in his seat, ready to return fire. The engine roared to life. Darwish hit the gas and they peeled away from the curb, tires squealing. More shots sounded behind them, one pinging off the trunk.

"What about Jaleel?" Ayman shouted, casting a desperate glance toward the exit for him. Guards and employees were scrambling into position and he could hear the wail of sirens approaching.

"He's not coming," Darwish snapped in a cold voice, speeding away from the hotel.

Ayman's head jerked around to stare at him. "You killed him." Even to his own ears his voice was hollow with disbelief.

Darwish's harsh features were tense with fury and frustration. "He'd served his purpose and became a liability when he ran and gave us away. If they'd captured him he would have talked. I did what I had to do."

Ayman sucked in a breath and ran a hand through his hair in agitation. Jaleel. It had been Ayman's job to protect him. He knew Darwish was right, knew he'd done it to protect them, but Allah help him, to shoot Jaleel down in cold blood like that… Was he a liability now too?

"He brought it on himself with his cowardice and now we're the ones paying the price for his actions," Darwish spat.

Ayman didn't respond. He already knew the contingency plan. They'd ditch the vehicle a few blocks over where more members were waiting to pick them up. They'd keep switching vehicles until they reached the Virginia state line, where another vehicle was waiting for them at a designated spot. From there they'd go dark, to a safe house provided by the founders of The Brethren, and wait to be contacted.

Ayman pressed his lips together as Darwish swerved around slower-moving traffic and screeched around the corner, the blare of horns ricocheting in his head like bullets. His freedom seemed so very far away all of a sudden. They faced days of being on the run now, going into hiding and praying they'd evade capture so they could both take part in the big upcoming attack at the trial. Only then could he try to escape the country.

Battling the grief and guilt trying to take hold inside him, he focused on what had to be done now. He'd known the risks, known that Jaleel was expendable to The Brethren. Now his roommate was gone, killed by one of their own. His suffering was over. Ayman's was coming.

He closed his eyes. First he prayed for Jaleel. Then he prayed for the rest of them.

Allah forgive us.

****

"Tango down." Nate rushed forward, his attention focused beyond the man lying on the floor of the back entrance, to the sidewalk beyond. The man he'd seen just as he'd turned the corner was gone but he'd heard more shots outside.

"Two tangos escaped on foot to a car. They took off to the south. Locals are in pursuit now," Vance reported.

"Anyone else?" Nate demanded as he approached the wounded man. He was lying on his back, two bullet wounds to the chest. He'd pulled the two halves of the uniform jacket apart. Still breathing, but not well. Blood bubbled up from the holes, telling Nate he'd been shot through the lungs. Lethal wounds.

"Negative. Entire building's on lockdown now. Taya's with me, she's fine."

Some of the tension bled out of his muscles. "Thanks. One tango down, two shots to the chest. Get some EMTs in here ASAP. I'll do what I can." This asshole was bleeding out because of one of his own, but Nate wasn't letting him die without a fight. They needed intel and they needed it now.

With Cruz covering him, Nate dropped down to search him for weapons and found a pistol in the back of his waistband. Nate tossed it aside before ripping off his own shirt and kneeling beside the wounded man.

Wide, dark brown eyes focused on him, glazed with pain, hope and desperation. Nate had seen that same look many times before in men's eyes. He wadded up his shirt and pressed it to the guy's chest, ignoring the incoherent cry of pain and the way the man thrashed weakly.

Placing two fingers on his carotid artery, Nate leaned over him. "What's your name?" Pulse was rapid,

196

irregular.

The eyes focused on him once more, glassy now, his breathing raspy, wet. He made a gurgling sound. One hand reached up to curl weakly around Nate's forearm. Blood gushed out of his mouth and he choked.

Nate rolled him to his side and swept the guy's mouth, but knew he was running out of time. "Who sent you?" This man, or one of his accomplices that had just shot him and fled, would have killed Taya given the chance. The only reason Nate was even attempting to prolong his miserable life was to get intel from him.

"Hel...help meeee," he wheezed out, already growing weaker.

I am fucking helping you, Nate thought in irritation, adding pressure to the wounds. Without advanced equipment there was little he could do but try to slow the bleeding. The guy wouldn't last much longer and he needed to get whatever information he could out of him before it was too late. It might make the difference in catching the guys responsible, and it might stop another attack.

"Who?" he demanded, a growl this time. "Ambulance is on its way but you need to talk to me right now. Understand? Now who sent you?"

The man's mouth opened and closed, his body convulsing as more blood came from his mouth, foamy from being mixed with air in his shattered lungs. He stilled, his body twitching. Cruz knelt down on the man's other side. One of the hotel security guards rushed over with a first aid kit and ripped it open. Nate glimpsed a portable defibrillator in it.

"Who?" Nate barked. The pulse beneath his fingers was thready, growing weaker by the second.

The man jerked at his shout. "B... Breth..."

"The Brethren?"

A slight nod, then a low, anguished moan came from

him and his eyes closed. One more gurgling breath and his chest stopped moving.

Dammit. Mouth compressed into a tight line, Nate rolled him to his back and started compressions. Without his med kit there was sweet fuck-all he could do to restore the guy's airway and his heart wasn't going to hold out for long now. When he stopped compressions to check for a pulse, as if on cue, it was gone.

"Give me the AED," he said to Cruz.

His teammate handed over the automated external defibrillator and Nate activated it, put it in place on the man's chest. "Clear." He took his hands off the bloody chest and shocked him. The man's torso lifted slightly with the force of the current coursing through his body.

Nate's eyes shot to the heart rate monitor. A slight blip, nothing more, and still no pulse. He set the paddles again. "Clear." *Come on, come on, dammit. I need more out of you.* Like how many men there were, what they'd been planning to do here, what other plans were in the works. Realistically he knew he'd never get all that from a dying man, but he was determined to try.

Still a flat line.

He shocked him twice more, and still nothing.

Gone.

Nate sat back on his heels, his entire body tight with helpless frustration. "Fuck. *Fuck*."

"At least you got something out of him," Cruz said as he stood and safetied his weapon.

But not enough. They'd already suspected The Brethren were behind this latest threat against Taya; the dead tango had merely confirmed it.

Nate expelled a harsh breath and pushed to his feet, rubbing his chin against his bare shoulder. The iron-tinged scent of fresh blood filled his nostrils, conjuring up flashes of memories. O'Neil bleeding out into the dirt. Taya's upper body soaked in her own blood.

He looked down at himself. He had blood spatters all over his chest and arms and his hands were soaked with it. The security guard handed him a towel. "Any word on the other tangos?" Nate asked him.

The man shook his head. "Not yet. One of our guys was shot in the shoulder. Can you take a look at him until the ambulance gets here?"

Should only be a few minutes and he needed to talk to the cops anyhow before he could go back upstairs. Once he did, he was getting Taya the hell away from here. "Yeah."

Chapter Seventeen

When Nathan finally walked through the hotel room door Taya sucked in a breath and shot to her feet as the blood drained out of her face. He was shirtless, his torso streaked with blood spatters, his forearms and hands stained with it.

"It's not mine," he said to her immediately.

She swallowed, willing her heart back down her throat. "Are you okay?"

"I'm fine." He glanced over at Vance, who was on the phone with DeLuca, then back to her. He seemed tense, agitated.

"Whose blood is it?" she asked.

"He hasn't been officially identified yet." Meaning, he wasn't allowed to tell her until everything was verified. "But he tried to deliver the room service earlier."

Holy shit. Taya put a hand to her throat, sat back down on the edge of the bed. They'd both nearly been attacked. Nathan had put himself in harm's way by going after the guy. "Were there others?"

"Yeah, but they took off. Cops and some of our agents are going after them now. Won't be long until they're captured."

He sounded so certain that Taya believed him. "So the threat's still ongoing?" She knew it on an intellectual level, but she needed to hear it from him.

His hazel eyes were grave as he nodded. "Yeah."

But how the hell had they found her, here in North Carolina? "They followed us here last night?"

"Must have, though we were all careful about watching for a tail."

Which meant that the men who'd come here were well trained, not to mention motivated. To risk attacking her here while under armed guard, they obviously weren't afraid to die. It chilled her to the bone. "Vance showed me the files of the men DeLuca sent you yesterday."

Nathan's face changed subtly, taking on an unreadable expression. "Do you recognize any of them?"

"No, but Darwish Abbas, the file said he was trained in a militant camp in east Africa. Is he the one who..." She let her sentence trail off, gesturing at the blood staining Nathan's body.

"No. He could be involved, though. We've got agents looking at the hotel's security footage right now. The guy who died was shot by one of his own men. We think it's the computer programmer."

"Jaleel?" She remembered his face, the dark eyes and smooth, light-toned skin. Both his and Ayman's families had emigrated from Syria a few years ago.

He nodded. "Waiting for official identification. Without his beard, at first I wasn't completely sure. But yeah, I know it's him."

Taya rubbed her hands over her upper arms to ward off a sudden chill. They'd tracked her from the east coast of Virginia to here. How was that possible? Was someone still leaking intel to them? Someone from the Department of Justice, or maybe even the FBI?

Vance got off the phone and spoke to Nathan. "Just

got confirmation from the boss. Dead tango's the hacker. Video footage shows Darwish and another guy fleeing out the back exit."

"Has to be Ayman Tuma," Nathan said.

Vance nodded. "Chances are pretty high, yeah. They found two hotel employees in a supply closet just off the kitchen. Looks like they were injected with something in their jugulars. Maybe insulin or a mix of something and fentanyl."

A wave of cold swept through her as she processed all that and realized how close she'd come to being attacked again. Except this time, her attackers would have killed her outright rather than kidnap her. If not for Nathan and the others, she'd be dead right now. Her skin turned clammy at the thought, nausea rolling in her belly.

Nathan's gaze shot to her, a mixture of anger and concern there. "I'm gonna clean up quick, then get you outta here," he said, heading for the bathroom. "Get your stuff together."

She was already packed and ready, but didn't bother saying so as he walked past her. Instead she looked at Vance. "Do I still get to go to the hospital?"

He slid his phone into his pocket and folded his arms across his chest. The man was huge, even bigger than Nathan, the muscles in his upper arms looking like they might split the seams of his T-shirt sleeves. "We're still planning for it, but if we do it'll have to be quick. In and out within fifteen, twenty minutes, tops, and then from there we get you out of town. I know with your dad still in the ICU that's gonna be tough on you, but we've got no choice now."

"I understand." She just hoped she got the chance to see her dad in person, talk to him before they took her back to…wherever they had in mind. Where they'd take her now, though, she didn't know. And if those other two men and the men commanding them were still hunting her, where would she be safe?

Suddenly she felt small and helpless, things she hated and had worked damn hard to leave behind since returning to the States.

Vance tilted his head slightly. "You met Tuck yet?"

She shook her head. "No."

"He's our team leader. And he's also engaged to agent Morales, who I'm sure you remember. She's kinda hard to forget."

The matter-of-fact FBI agent with the scar on her cheek who she'd met at the hotel in D.C. "I remember her."

"He's already at the hospital with a couple regular agents, working with security there to get everything locked down before we head over. If he doesn't feel good about it, we don't go. It's his call." He searched her eyes. "Going back there's definitely a calculated risk though."

He didn't sound or look worried as he said it, and she understood he was merely underscoring the point for her sake. They were the best in the business, willing and able to protect her, but heading to the hospital now while her would-be attackers were still at large put them all at risk.

"I don't want to put anyone else in harm's way for my sake, but I need to see my father." She'd do whatever it took to make that happen, even if that decision made her seem selfish. They were taking her out of town within the next few hours and the trial was starting soon. She wouldn't get another opportunity to see her father for at least a week or more, and there was a chance his heart wouldn't hold out much longer.

She couldn't leave without seeing him, talking to him one last time. "He and my brother, they're all I've got left," she said in a tight voice. She wasn't looking for sympathy, only to plead her case and explain her motivation.

Vance nodded, his eyes warm. "I get it. But I don't

think that's quite true." His gaze went meaningfully to the closed bathroom door and back.

Taya lowered her eyes as warmth pulsed through her. She didn't know how to answer. Did both he and Cruz suspect something was going on between her and Nathan? Would it get Nathan in trouble? She shifted position, her face flushing. "I don't…"

Vance held up a hand, his teeth flashing white briefly against his dark skin as he grinned at her. "Hey, no need to explain anything. Not my biz."

His phone rang. He muttered an apology and pulled it out. "Yo. You on your way up?"

The bathroom door opened a moment later and Nathan walked out with a cloud of steam billowing behind him. He was still shirtless, all those gorgeous muscles exposed to her interested gaze, all traces of blood gone. He wore clean jeans, his wet hair two shades darker than when it was dry.

Crossing to his duffel, he tugged a new T-shirt on and gave her a quick, assessing look before turning to Vance. "What's the story?"

"Cruz is done downstairs. He's pulling a vehicle around the east side exit for you. Tuck's already at the hospital, just gave the green light. I'll follow you guys over." He grabbed Taya's suitcase and headed for the door.

When they were alone Nathan shoved his shaving kit into his bag and focused on her. "You ready?" When she nodded he tucked a pistol into the back of his waistband then set a hand on the small of her back, the imprint of his hand sinking through the material of her shirt. She could feel his tension though, and knew it was because of what had happened earlier, that he was angry about her nearly being attacked.

"Wait," she said.

He stopped, looked down at her questioningly.

Without a word Taya stepped in front of him and slid her arms around his back.

Resting her cheek against his solid chest she murmured, "I'm glad you're safe." When he'd shot out of the room like that without any warning to give chase she'd been scared, and the whole time he'd been gone she'd worried he might not come back. She of all people knew how fleeting life could be, especially to someone in his line of work. He was smart and an amazing operator, but he was still human. And that meant he wasn't bulletproof.

Seeming surprised by the gesture, Nathan wrapped his arms around her and hugged her tight. His lips brushed over the sensitive spot where her neck and shoulder joined, sending electric tingles racing over her skin. "No one's ever going to hurt you again, Taya. Not on my watch."

There was no defense in the world that could protect her heart from him when he said things like that.

Angling her head up, she cupped the back of his head and lifted up to give him a soft, lingering kiss. Just being near him made her feel safe, stronger. He reminded her of how hard she'd fought to live, how hard she'd battled to take back control over her life. "You're making it really hard for me not to fall for you," she murmured against his lips.

One side of his mouth kicked up as he lifted his head, his eyes glowing with a possessive light that thrilled her. "Good," was all he said. Then he set a hand on her waist and led her to the door.

Security guards, uniformed police officers and FBI agents stood in the hall, by the elevator and down in the lobby. They escorted her and Nathan to the exit where Cruz was waiting in an SUV, more police cruisers stationed along the narrow street. Nathan put her into the backseat before getting into the front beside Cruz and they drove to the hospital in near silence with Vance tailing them.

More security was posted at the rear entrance to the Emergency ward. Nathan and Cruz walked her up to the ICU. A well-built man with dark blond hair was waiting for them with her brother. He pushed away from the wall near her father's room and nodded at them. "Special Agent Brad Tucker," he said to her, holding out his hand.

"Nice to meet you," she responded, accepting the handshake. She glanced behind him at Kevin. "Is he still awake?"

"Yes and he's been waiting impatiently for you to get here," her brother said in a dry voice.

Taya didn't tell him why they'd been delayed, already knowing from his calm demeanor that Tuck hadn't said anything to him about the thwarted attack. But he'd hear it soon enough through the media, and then maybe it wasn't such a bad thing that the FBI was moving her out of state again. Kevin would go ballistic when he found out what had happened at the hotel.

"We can give you fifteen minutes, but no more," Tuck said to her. "Plane's already waiting for us at the airport."

"I understand. Thanks." She shot Kev, then Nathan a little smile before entering her father's room. He was indeed waiting for her, propped up into a semi-reclining position, his head turned toward the door. The first thing she saw was his smile beneath the oxygen mask he wore. Weak though it was, it made her eyes fill with tears.

"There's my sunshine," he rasped out, voice nearly inaudible. And when he reached out an arm, beckoning her into his embrace, she damn near lost it.

Burying her face in his sturdy shoulder, Taya held on tight. "You promised not to leave me," she whispered. "Remember? You *promised*."

He patted the middle of her back and grunted. "And I'm still here, aren't I?"

She squeezed him. Stubborn, wonderful man. "Love you, Dad."

He fingered her hair, a scowl creasing his brow. "What the hell did you do to your hair?"

She gave a watery laugh at the disapproval in his voice. "Just changed the color and took a straightening iron to it. It's only until after I testify. Don't worry, it'll still be just like Mom's when this is all over. A little wild, impossible to tame."

The scowl faded, replaced by a fond smile. "She was one of a kind."

She sure was, a pure force of nature, taken too soon by a drunk driver speeding down the wrong side of the road at night with no headlights on. "And you were the only man who could tame her."

His smile grew, spreading across his face until his cheeks creased. "Yeah. For a little while, anyway."

****

"So, you heard about the latest fuck-up?"

Nate pulled his gaze from the sight of Taya hugging her father on the other side of the small rectangular window set into the hospital room door, and focused on Tuck. "No, what's up?" Taya's brother had left to grab some food and Cruz had taken up position at the ICU entrance, leaving him and Tuck to guard the door.

"Locals and our guys lost track of the other two tangos."

His brows crashed together. "Seriously?" How the hell could that be, with all the law enforcement personnel and Feds hunting them with satellite feeds? "They had less than a minute's lead time."

Tuck grunted. "They were well prepared, apparently. They had other vehicles stashed and ready, and they've got people helping cover their tracks. Gonna take a while to pull on all the threads, figure out where they might be heading, and who else is involved. Now that their hacker's dead, the investigators have a starting point at least. Best we've got at the moment."

Well that sucked. Nate set his hands on his hips, shook his head, pissed off all over again that they'd dare come after Taya. Fucking ballsy, to try and pull that off in broad daylight with so few operatives. Made them all the more dangerous and unpredictable. "You get official confirmation on the tangos yet?"

"Yep. Celida called to tell me it's definitely the remaining two in the files I sent you. Bureau's hoping they'll lead us to whoever took the other witnesses."

Yeah, but first they had to capture Darwish and Ayman, then hope they'd break under interrogation. Based on what he'd seen of their performance so far, Nate didn't see that as being quick or easy. These guys were motivated and though technically their training paled in comparison to what Nate and his teammates had, they were still alive and leading authorities on a merry chase across the North Carolina countryside right now. Even if they caught the men, the upcoming trial gave investigators a short timeline to work with to try and break up this cell.

His eyes shifted back to the window. Taya was still embracing her father. He could see her lips moving, and the smile on the old man's face. She was like a freaking ray of sunshine, lighting up every room she walked into with her calm, loving energy. Even after spending such a short amount of time with her, Nate couldn't imagine being deprived of that warmth now. She'd thawed the icy core inside him, made him want more time with her.

"There's more."

Nate's gaze snapped to Tuck. "What?"

Tuck searched his eyes, and Nate knew it was bad news. "We're all being pulled from personal security to prep for a stand-in at the trial."

Nate's heart sank, dragging his stomach with it. "When?"

"Tomorrow at oh-four-hundred."

No. The thought of being pulled away from Taya now, when she needed him most, was like a punch to the gut. "Who's taking over her security?"

"WITSEC."

Nate bit back the automatic refusal in his throat, blew out a breath and rubbed a hand over his face instead. Tuck kept on talking. "I know, man, but according to Celida they've cleaned house over there. The leak there's been sealed up tight and it's not our call anyway. We've been personally ordered to D.C. by the Director. I know this isn't your first choice—"

Nate gave a bitter laugh. "No, not even fucking close." He sighed, decided he'd better come clean. "Okay, look, we're…involved."

Tuck kept his expression carefully blank. "Involved."

He could feel himself flushing. He knew how unprofessional it was to have a relationship with a federal witness under his protection, but he couldn't help how he felt about Taya. "It's not casual." Not by any means.

Now Tuck's eyebrows rose as the significance of that registered. "I know she's important to you."

A not-so-subtle way of probing the subject but Nate wasn't going to deny it. "Yeah, she is. I'm gonna talk to Matt about it." He needed to disclose the nature of his relationship to Taya to his commander.

Tuck nodded. "That's a good call, Doc."

"Gotta be done. And I'm also gonna talk to someone when this is all over." He cleared his throat, fought past his embarrassment of admitting this out loud to Tuck. "Find real help and get myself squared away." He was looking forward to the conversation with DeLuca about as much as he would a punch in the face, but there was no avoiding it and he didn't want Vance and Cruz put in an awkward position if their commander asked them about it.

"Wow, she *really* means a lot to you," Tuck said with a smile.

"Yeah." He'd fucking die for her, if it came down to that. No one else would be even half as motivated to keep her safe as him. Now he not only had to step back, abandon her when there were armed terrorists actively hunting her at this very moment, but entrust her safety to a total stranger and a program that had recently been corrupted. *Shit.* "You believe they've dealt with the situation over at the DOJ?" He wanted details.

"From what Celida told me, they arrested the guy responsible, brought in all the people he's worked with and grilled them, looked into their contacts and checked timelines. So far only the one marshal's been incriminated and everyone else checks out. Apparently the guy had a bad gambling habit and was willing to take a bribe from The Brethren to pay off the shitload of debt he'd accumulated. He'd been leaking what looked like innocuous information. Nothing too juicy, just enough for them to read between the lines and figure out Taya's location."

"Motherfucker," Nate muttered, hands balling into fists.

Tuck angled his head. "You want me to tell her?"

Nate shook his head. "No. She should hear it from me." Hell, he could just imagine the look on her face when he told her.

Tuck nodded. "Guys said you did good today."

He made a face. He'd done his job, nothing more. God knew he'd have taken on any threat to protect Taya. "Wish I'd been able to get more out of the bastard before he went to his seventy-two virgin dating service in the sky."

Tuck cracked a grin at that. "Something's better than nothing."

Nate didn't respond, his gaze shifting back to the window in the door. Taya was walking toward him. She opened the door, gave him a little smile. Combined with her slightly puffy eyes and reddened nose, the joy radiating from her made him want to cup her face between his hands and kiss her.

"My dad wants to meet you," she said to him.

For a moment Nate hesitated, unsure whether this was a good idea. Meeting her father at this stage of their relationship and under these circumstances was a little unnerving, but there was no way the man could know anything was going on between him and Taya. She must have told her father about him beforehand. After she'd first returned to the States. "Okay."

Following her into the room, he'd be damned if he didn't feel a little nervous. All the women he'd dated, all the women he'd slept with, he'd never once been asked to meet their fathers. It hadn't even remotely been a possibility. And since Nate planned on showing Taya he was serious about her, he couldn't fuck up this first impression.

Ted Kostas was propped up in his bed, his steel gray gaze so like his daughter's locked on Nate like a heat-seeking missile. Nate crossed to the side of the bed and held out his hand. "Mr. Kostas. I'm—"

"I know who you are." The man gripped his hand, his hold surprisingly strong for someone recovering from a second near fatal heart attack. Nate read the intensity in the other man's eyes, a fear bordering on desperation. "You saved my little girl's life."

In Afghanistan, he meant, confirming Nate's theory. He resisted the urge to look away, maintained his grip on the other man's hand. "I just did what I was trained to do."

The answer was automatic. It probably sounded cold, even though he didn't mean it to. Taya's rescue had been both the best and worst thing that had ever happened to him. His hell and salvation, all wrapped up into one.

The older man's grip tightened. "You keep her safe through all of this." A father's plea.

Even though Nate couldn't remember his father and had never had any kind of father-figure relationship until he joined the military, he could see how hard it was for this man, lying helpless in this hospital bed while depending on total strangers to guard someone who meant the most to him in the entire world.

Nate knew exactly how he felt.

Man, he hated lying right to the guy's face, but what was he supposed to do, tell him WITSEC was about to take over Taya's security, a day after he'd nearly died? He might go into cardiac arrest again, right in front of his daughter.

"I will," Nate told him, looking him dead in the eye as he returned the pressure. Inside, he hated what was going to happen in the morning.

Taya's father gave a satisfied nod and released Nate's hand. He seemed to slump then, as though the short encounter had exhausted him, and let out a weary sigh. Nate stepped back and looked at Taya, who gave him a soft, warm smile that turned his heart over. How the hell was he supposed to walk away from her in a few hours?

"I'll wait outside," he told her before stepping out into the hall. There was an ache in his chest, a heaviness that wouldn't go away.

He'd give her another couple minutes to visit and say goodbye. Not as much time as she deserved with her father, but as much as he could offer before taking her to the airport.

They had one last night together before she'd be taken away from him. And he was already dreading the moment when he told her what would happen in the morning.

Chapter Eighteen

Ayman winced as he shifted on the vanity in the tiny, cluttered bathroom, angling his body to get a better look at the damage in the mirror. He used a damp facecloth to wash the cuts on his chest, courtesy of broken glass and one bullet graze. A fraction of an inch in any direction, and it would have gone straight into his chest.

Two were deep enough that they kept seeping blood, so he stuck bandages on them and cleaned up the mess he'd made in the sink. His entire right ribcage was one massive bruise from slamming repeatedly against the passenger side door every time Darwish had taken a sharp left turn. They'd barely evaded police in Raleigh, had nearly been spotted when the second driver had ferried them into Virginia in the back of a cube van.

Twice more they'd been dropped off at a waiting point and picked up by new drivers, each from The Brethren's network. Each time Ayman had been prepared for the worst, for one of them to turn on them or turn them in or for the police to discover them. He'd made up his mind to fight to the end, ready to take on whoever he had to with the pistol and rifle at his disposal.

Even if it meant killing Darwish to survive.

"Ayman. Hurry up," Darwish said impatiently from the kitchen of the house their latest driver was renting.

"Just give me a minute," he snapped, the stress and pain already eating at him. He didn't know their exact location, except that they were somewhere in southern Virginia. A rural area with lots of trees around and plenty of space between properties.

When he was dressed once more he found Darwish at the kitchen table, a plate of rice and meat before him. "Eat," he said, shoveling in a mouthful as he indicated another serving on the table. "We have to leave soon. Next driver will be here in a few minutes."

Not bothering with a response, Ayman took the seat across from him and ate what was on the plate he'd been given. He barely tasted the food, hungry though he was, too keyed up to do more than chew and swallow. His throat was dry. It took two swallows to get the first bite down. When it hit the bottom of his stomach, for a moment he feared it would come right back up.

Darwish eyed him. "You need to stop thinking about him. He was dead weight and we're better off this way."

Shooting him a glare, Ayman forced himself to take another bite. He was thinking about Jaleel, yes, but he was also thinking about the man who'd run after Jaleel. For that Fed or whoever he was to react the way he had, the man must have been more than suspicious. Ayman would bet the FBI knew far more about their plans than they realized.

Just then their host, Hamid, walked into the kitchen. Ayman didn't know the middle-aged man, but even he could tell something was wrong.

Darwish lowered his fork and frowned at the man. "What?"

Hamid looked back and forth between them. "I just

spoke with Mahmoud," he said, referring to the leader of The Brethren. Ayman set his fork down, his appetite gone. "The FBI is onto us."

Darwish's gaze sharpened, his brows lowering in a menacing expression. "What do you mean?"

Hamid licked his lips, darted a glance at Ayman that set off a warning buzz in his brain. "Someone reported you and Jaleel to them, told them you were involved with The Brethren. Your father."

Ayman felt Darwish's gaze cut to him, felt the lethal stare burning into him, and a cold sweat broke out along his spine. "It doesn't matter, he knows nothing. Unless one of you or Mahmoud has betrayed us, then we go ahead with our plan."

"I would *never* betray us," Hamid said in an insulted voice. "How dare you even suggest such a thing?"

"How dare you defend your traitorous father after this," Darwish growled, rising from his chair and leaning forward, the threat implicit in his hard stare. Ayman braced himself, curled his hand around the handle of his fork, ready to use it as a weapon. He'd ram it into Darwish's jugular and twist it, rip him wide open if he so much as twitched.

Darwish must have sensed his intent because his gaze flickered down to the fork, then back up. His posture eased. He straightened slowly, never looking away, an almost taunting light in his eyes.

"Stop," Hamid ordered, waiting until Ayman looked back at him before continuing. "Mahmoud has decreed that your father pay for his sins."

Ayman felt himself blanch. "Leave him out of this. We no longer have contact. He is dead to me as I am to him. If you go after him, the Feds will be watching now that he's turned on me. Don't be stupid."

Hamid shook his head. "I was ordered to tell you that he will pay. And if you abandon your duty now, your entire family will pay as well."

Fury and helplessness surged through him. His nostrils flared, his breathing growing shallow as the rage built. "They have nothing to do with this. Nothing to do with me. Leave them alone."

A car engine sounded outside. Hamid rushed to the window, drew the drapes aside a fraction to see out back. "It's him. You have to go." He made a shooing motion at them with his hands, his nervousness clear. "Go, before you get us all caught."

Ayman stood slowly, feeling far older than his nineteen years, every muscle protesting as he got to his feet. The wounds in his chest throbbed, but it was nothing compared to the deep, desolate ache beneath his ribs. Was it worth it? Was the path he'd chosen worth these sacrifices? He might have just sentenced his family to death. His parents, his sisters…

His conviction wavered and for a moment he considered running, but then realized it was impossible. He ruthlessly shut his mind to the regret bombarding him. Darwish and Hamid would watch him even more closely now. Even if he wanted to go to the Feds, he'd never be able to make so much as a phone call in private now. He was well and truly trapped.

"Move," Darwish snarled at him, the malice in his eyes so cold it burned.

Ayman followed him out the back door on leaden feet, exhaustion pulling at him. He climbed into the back of the waiting van, tried not to flinch when the rear doors slammed shut, sealing him inside the coffin-like interior with Darwish. The man he was committed to working with to carry out the coming attack.

The man who would now gladly kill him as he had Jaleel, the moment this operation was over.

****

Taya was quiet on the drive from the airport in Virginia to the safe house, lost in her own thoughts.

"We'll make sure we find a way for you to contact your brother, check in and see how your dad's doing," Nathan said to her as he drove along the highway.

"Thanks." She couldn't shake the melancholy mood. "It's just hard, leaving him like that." Knowing it might be the last time.

"He's through the worst now. He'll just need to rest up and take it easy this time as he recovers."

"They're not going to send him home right away this time. Kev's trying to see if they can put him in a rehab facility for a couple weeks."

"Probably a good idea."

With her dad's stubbornness, yes. "I'm glad he got to meet you. He's been curious about you ever since I got back from Afghanistan."

Nathan glanced over at her. "Hope I made him feel a little better about all this."

"You did." And her, too. Watching him treat her father with such respect and care had filled her heart with warmth. She was curious though. He knew so much about her and there were still things she didn't know about him. Not the details, anyway. "What about your family? You never talk about them."

"My team's my family."

"No contact at all with your biological family though?"

He shook his head, changed lanes as he followed the vehicle Tuck was driving. Cruz and Vance were tailing them. The sun was high but the tinted windows helped make her feel more secure.

"My dad took off when I was a few months old, so I don't even remember him. Apparently he was a low-level dealer. My mom and half-sister... They've got problems.

Big problems." When she stayed silent he seemed to weigh his words before continuing. "My childhood wasn't pretty, Taya. I grew up in a ratty old trailer park in a poor area of town. There were lots of drugs, booze, different guys staying over every week. I wasn't abused, exactly, but there was a fair amount of neglect, emotional and otherwise."

It made Taya's heart ache to imagine him growing up that way, not feeling loved and nurtured by those who were supposed to love him unconditionally. She'd been very lucky to have that, never doubting her parents' love.

He gave a slight shrug, but she sensed the tension in him as he continued. "My mom's an expert at playing the system, milking every penny out of all the government programs out there, and my half-sister's turned out exactly the same way. The truth is, they're both addicts and couldn't hold down a job anyway. They drink, get high and cash their welfare checks. I wasn't going to be like that. Leaving was the best decision I ever made."

Taya could see his past embarrassed him, even though it shouldn't. "They're behavior isn't a reflection on you."

"Not anymore, no, but when I lived there it sure as hell was. I hated it. Hated being looked at and treated like the worst kind of white trash." His jaw flexed. "That kind of poverty stains a person's soul. It's a hopeless, apathetic kind of poverty, made worse because the people living it just don't give a shit." He shook his head. "Even when you leave the stain's still there. It just fades over time, is all."

"Just like grief and trauma," she murmured, understanding more than he realized.

He shot her a sideways glance, clearly surprised, then nodded. "Yeah. Just like those."

At *those*, she was an expert. And so was he. One more thing they had in common. As well as the will to overcome those very same obstacles.

She reached across the console for his hand, laced her fingers through his. His hand was so big and strong compared to hers but he always treated her with such care. "I'm glad you got out. And I'm glad you've got good people around you now."

He seemed to relax at that, and a small smile curved his mouth. "My teammates are the best."

Taya smiled back. "I bet they all say the same thing about you."

"Doubt it. But I hope they think so. I'm kinda still earning my stripes with the squad," he said, a sardonic edge to his voice.

She suspected he was wrong about that. He probably still felt the need to prove himself, even though he'd earned his spot by making the team in the first place. "They're lucky to have you."

He glanced over at her, surprise clear in his eyes before he focused back on the road. "I'm lucky to have them."

Tuck turned into a tidy, residential neighborhood. Nathan followed him to a two-story brick house in a middle-class subdivision and pulled into the garage. "Guess this is us," he murmured. When the garage door was lowered Nathan came around to open her door for her.

In the modern kitchen with cherry cabinets and black granite counters they met Tuck, Cruz and Vance, sitting around the island as they went over the security plan. The layout of the house and neighborhood. Entry and exit points. Various exfil plans. Taya stayed quiet, memorizing most of what they decided.

"So that's basically it for now," Tuck said, then shared a pointed look with Nathan that made Taya's heart constrict. They were keeping something from her. Something big.

"What is it?" she asked.

In unison, Tuck and the others stood. "We'll let you two talk for a while," he said, and led the way out of the kitchen, Cruz and Vance following him.

When they'd gone she focused on Nathan. He was standing at the far end of the island, both hands on the granite top, his face serious. He held her gaze and she saw the torment in his eyes. "There's been a change in plans for tomorrow," he said.

She braced herself. "Okay," she said slowly.

He straightened with a sigh and shoved both hands into his front jeans pockets. The set of his shoulders was rigid, his jaw tense. "The entire team's been called in for extra security at the trial."

Entire team. Dread expanded inside her. "Including you."

He nodded, his expression full of regret. "Yes."

He was leaving her. She pushed that painful thought aside and focused on the more important issue. "So who's my new security detail going to be?"

"WITSEC."

She stiffened. "What?"

"I know," he said quickly, pulling his hands out of his pockets and gripping the edge of the counter, "but they've taken care of the problem over there already. They arrested the guy at fault then cleaned house, re-vetting every single marshal involved with the case. Some are on administrative leave until the trial's over, just as a precaution. Only their most trusted marshals are working on this case now. They're damn good at what they do, and they'll keep you safe."

He said it with confidence, but she still wasn't convinced. "Is he in jail?"

"Yes, and he's not getting out any time soon. They're using the intel he gave during his interrogation to locate The Brethren members and break up the cell responsible for all this. Celida's heavily involved with it. Believe me, she'd say something if she didn't consider WITSEC safe anymore."

She still wasn't convinced. Considering everything that had happened to her, she had a serious mistrust of the government where her personal welfare was concerned. In fact, the only reason she felt they were stepping in now was solely to protect her testimony, not because they particularly cared about her as a human being. "I still don't trust them. And I'm not a prisoner, I have a choice in this. Nobody's going to force me to go into WITSEC without my consent."

"No, of course not," he said with a shake of his head. "But when I leave here I want to know you're as safe as possible, and the fact is, the best protection the government can offer at this point is still WITSEC."

God, she felt sick all of a sudden. Taya stood, one hand pressed to her middle as she tried to force down the panic clawing inside her. Someone in WITSEC had leaked details about Chloe and she'd paid the price. How was Taya supposed to entrust her safety to them?

"Hey." Nathan stepped up behind her. He set his hands on her hips, eased her back against his body and wrapped his arms around her waist. Warm, hard muscles enveloped her. His chin rested on her shoulder, the stubble scraping her cheek gently as he spoke, his breath warm on her skin. "I swear to you, it's gonna be all right. I wouldn't let them take over if I didn't think it was absolutely safe."

She made a disparaging sound, standing rigid in his arms. "You have even less say in this than I do."

"No." His arms contracted, drawing her closer, so close she could feel his heartbeat against her back. "I would've raised hell, done whatever I had to do to make other arrangements if I thought you'd be at risk with them. You'll be in good hands, baby."

Hearing that endearment from him would normally

have warmed her from the inside out. She was too cold inside for it to penetrate. The fear kept rising inside her, too sharp, flooding her brain. "I'd rather be in yours."

Nathan expelled a long breath and pressed his face against her hair, his distress clear. "God, me too. Believe me, I wish I didn't have to go, but if you're dead set against WITSEC then I'll call my commander and step down from this one—"

"*No*. No way." Taya was aghast that he'd even consider such a thing. Leave the team for her? Risk his career, leave the guys who meant so much to him, because of her? She was deeply touched that he'd make that sacrifice for her, but she'd never allow it. "I would never let you do that."

"I'd do it though, to keep you safe." His murmur stirred the hair at her temple.

She shook her head. "Thank you, but no." She needed to move, to burn off this frenetic energy rising inside her. She pushed his hands off her middle and pulled from his embrace, immediately feeling colder as she paced away from him. "When?"

"Dawn."

The word landed on her ears like a death knell. She rubbed a hand over her forehead, made herself turn to face him. His eyes were tormented, but that didn't make her feel any better. She realized he had no control over this. Neither of them did. It was her call whether or not to join WITSEC, but given the circumstances and the short timeline involved, she already knew what her decision had to be.

It was hard though, to take this step. All the control she'd battled to regain had been stripped from her yet again. All because of one sadistic, evil man.

I'm going to bring you down, Qureshi, she vowed. *I'm going to bury you in that courtroom.* "Okay, I'll do it."

He let out a relieved breath. "Thank you."

She nodded, one last question foremost in her mind. She wanted the truth. "Am I going to see you again?"

At that his expression turned incredulous. "*Yes*. God, Taya." He closed the distance between them in two strides, pulled her back into his arms. His hold was fierce, protective. The grip of a man desperate for her to believe in him. "I care about you. More than I've ever cared about another woman. You think I want to let you go?"

Then don't. She slid her arms around his waist, hugged him back, unable to keep from touching him. Her heart was already in his hands, whether he realized it or not. She just didn't have the courage to tell him yet. "I care about you too. So much."

He slid one hand into her hair, pressed her head harder into his shoulder, his big hand cradling the back of her skull. "We're going to see each other again. As soon as the trial's done."

For the entire trial to wrap up it could take weeks, maybe longer, depending on how things went. Would he still want her as much by then? What if their connection was this intense because of the current circumstances, and it faded while they were apart? Would he move on without her? Go back to the lineup of available women he had to choose from? Absence made the heart grow fonder.

But it could also make it wander.

She'd been on the receiving end of that one once already. She didn't want to go through that again with Nathan.

"Say something," he whispered fervently, squeezing her tighter.

"Okay," she said, only because she didn't know what else to say and didn't feel like arguing when they only had a few hours left together. Either he'd contact her after the trial or he wouldn't, that was as out of her control as him leaving. Suddenly it felt like her entire life was out of her control.

She pulled free of his arms when someone discreetly cleared their throat from behind them. Cruz stood in the kitchen doorway, his expression apologetic. "Sorry, but Tuck wants to brief us on some new intel that just came in. About tomorrow," he said to Nathan, probably meaning whatever training they'd be doing to get ready for the trial assignment.

"Yeah, I'm coming," Nathan muttered. He spared her a long, poignant look before turning and following his teammate into the next room, where Taya knew better than to follow.

Chapter Nineteen

It was almost midnight by the time the meeting with Tuck and the others began to wind down, ending with a conference call to DeLuca and a debrief. Things were moving fast now.

The FBI was tracking dozens of tips throughout southeastern Virginia, including two possible sightings of Ayman and Darwish. Still no sign of the missing witnesses, and no one in the FBI had a solid theory about why The Brethren hadn't splashed pictures of their dead bodies all over social media, to brag about their exploits.

Nate's gaze kept straying to the staircase as Tuck wrapped things up. After eating a quick takeout dinner with them, Taya had gone upstairs at about nine. He'd heard the pipes running half an hour ago and assumed she'd taken a shower or bath. After all she'd been through the past few days and his announcement about leaving her in the morning he figured she might want time alone, but that's the last thing he wanted to give her.

He was going crazy sitting down here with the minutes ticking away, aching to be up there with her instead, spending their remaining few hours together. The look on her face when he'd told her he was leaving was burned into his brain. Sorrow and resignation.

"We keeping you from something?" Tuck drawled, a hint of amusement in his voice.

Nate swung his gaze back to him. Shit, he'd totally spaced there for a minute, right in front of his team leader. While he was on unofficial probation. "No."

Tuck shared a knowing look with Cruz and Vance before looking back at him, and grinned. "You sure? Cuz I'm pretty sure you didn't hear a word I just said."

Nate could feel the tips of his ears turning red as the others stared at him.

Tuck closed the folder in front of him, signaling an end to the meeting. "Cruz and I'll take first shift while Vance watches the street. You'd better talk to Taya some more about the change in security, see if you can ease her mind about it."

Nate threw him a suspicious look. If he didn't know better, Tuck had just given him the green light for alone time with their witness. But that couldn't be right. "Yeah, okay."

Tuck raised a dark blond eyebrow, amusement glinting in his dark brown eyes. "Unless you'd rather take first watch?"

Okay, he wasn't stupid. And he sure as hell wasn't going to pass up the opportunity Tuck was giving him. "No, it's... I'll talk to her," he finished, feeling awkward and humbled at the same time.

Tuck nodded and stood. "See you in four hours," he said without looking at him, and headed for the living room.

Nate didn't have to be told twice. He jogged up the stairs, anticipation building inside him with every step. Having a few hours alone with Taya with two other guys in the house wasn't ideal, but it was the best he could ask for and he wasn't going to pass up the opportunity to spend these last few hours with her.

Her door was closed but a strip of light came from beneath it. He knocked softly.

"Come in."

Turning the knob slowly, he opened the door a crack. The covers rustled as Taya sat up with the blankets pooling around her hips. "Hey," she whispered without a trace of grogginess.

"Hey." He stepped inside and closed the door, noted the book and pen in her hands. "Can't sleep?"

She shook her head, watching him in the soft glow of the lamplight. "Just doing some journaling."

He'd seen the book before, sticking out of her purse or sitting on her nightstand. "What are you writing about?"

"Just thoughts, things that have happened lately. I don't write the way I used to now. My psychiatrist started me on something called cognitive processing therapy when I first got home. You asked me once how I could move on, and this was a big part of it. You start by writing your traumatic experience in the present tense, in as much detail as you can. Just let yourself bleed all over the pages until it's out there. Then you read it aloud, either alone or to someone else."

She tucked a lock of shiny golden brown hair behind one ear. He missed seeing her curls, thought about the way they tangled around his fingers when he touched them. "You do that a half dozen times or so, maybe more, until it's as authentic as you can make it. Then you do it again, but you write it in the past tense."

Nate had seen a documentary on something similar a few months back, when he'd first begun to slip.

"By writing it and reading it aloud when it's in the past tense, eventually your brain gets the message and helps file the experience in the past, where it belongs."

She gave a half-smile. "I know that probably sounds hokey, but it worked for me. One day the images stopped being quite so vivid. That's when I was able to start the process of moving forward again." She set the book aside on the nightstand. "Have you ever thought about trying something like that?"

He eyed the book, torn between wanting to know what she'd been through during her captivity and her forced marriage, and afraid of what he might learn. "Nah, not much of a writer."

She studied him, those big gray eyes delving deep inside him. "I bet you are."

"I think you'd be disappointed."

Her mouth curved in a seductive smile. "Pretty sure you could never disappoint me." From the way she said it there was little doubt she meant sexually, and he was totally on board with that. He'd love nothing better than to spend the rest of their time making her come over and over again, burying his tongue or fingers inside her while covering her mouth with his free hand to muffle her cries.

So that when she was alone in her bed in her new safe house, she'd think of him and what he'd done to her. Maybe stroke herself while thinking about it.

Hot. He was hard just thinking about it.

Taya sat up straighter and shifted on the bed. The sleep shirt and shorts she wore exposed the length of her bare legs, emphasized the curve of her breasts and the indent of her waist. "How long until you leave?" she asked.

"Just over four hours." He closed the distance between them, lowering his weight beside her onto the edge of the mattress, caught her warm cinnamon-vanilla scent. He leaned in to press his face into the curve of her neck, breathe her in.

Her breath caught. He lifted his head to see her pupils had dilated and her nipples were hard points beneath her shirt. "Where are the others?"

"Tuck and Cruz are downstairs and Vance is taking first watch outside." He lifted a hand to trail a fingertip down the side of her face. "I think they're trying to give us some privacy."

With a soft smile she leaned into his touch, but he could see the emotions warring in her eyes. The knowledge that their time together was running out. "I'll take it."

Nate's heart squeezed. "You're gonna be okay, Taya."

She nodded. "Yeah. I'll miss you though."

Ah, damn, he was going to miss her too. "Come here." He wrapped his arms around her and pulled her into his lap. She curled into him and held on, her cheek pressed to the side of his neck.

Each of her soft exhalations sent sparks dancing across his skin. She was soft and warm and trusting in his arms and he couldn't let her go without having one last taste to tide him over until they saw each other again. He had this one last chance to bind her to him, reinforce the connection between them. He was going to make it memorable.

Cupping her chin, he turned her face up to his and kissed her. Taya twisted toward him, sealing their mouths together, her tongue gliding between his lips. With a low sound of need Nate took over, rolling her onto her back beneath him. She wriggled impatiently, stripped off her shirt while he tugged her shorts over her hips and down her legs.

Before he could enjoy all her naked skin, she was pulling his shirt off.

She hummed in her throat and bent to kiss and nibble at his chest, driving him crazy as he shucked his jeans and underwear. Naked, he knelt before her on the mattress, swallowing a groan when her soft, cool fingers closed around his rigid cock. She lifted up on her knees to kiss him again. Her tongue slid along his as she fisted him, dragged her palm over the length of his erection. Fire streaked up his spine.

Nate growled and closed his hand over hers, guiding her motion. Slowing her down, wanting to draw this out. He was so primed he couldn't take much more of her hands on him, and he sure as hell didn't want any of the guys to overhear them up here.

When the sensation became too much he broke the kiss and gently pulled her hand away from his aching cock. She made a sound of protest but he smothered it with another deep kiss, his hands gliding up her ribs to cup the full, luscious mounds of her breasts. Her back arched as he played with her nipples, rubbing and lightly pinching the dusky brown peaks.

He could feel her urgency in the bite of her fingers in his shoulders, the rigid set of her muscles as he lowered his head and sucked and teased each tight tip before kissing a path down the center of her body. He paused to dip his tongue into her navel, fingers still working her stiffened nipples. Then he lowered his mouth to the trimmed hair between her thighs and kissed just above where her clit peeked out.

Taya whimpered and parted her thighs, exposing the slick, flushed folds to his starved gaze. She was unbelievably sexy, so responsive to his every touch. Her inner thigh muscles trembled as he pressed his lips to her, letting her feel the warmth of his mouth for a moment before licking her nice and slow. Her quick intake of air cut through the room.

"Mmm," he murmured, closing his lips around her clit to suck gently.

She moaned and lifted her hips, one hand plunging into his hair. Her fist contracted around the strands, the sharp sting on his scalp an accelerant on the flames raging inside him.

"So soft, baby." He continued to taste and tease her, getting lost in the experience, pushing his tongue inside her then licking slow circles around her clit with the flat of his tongue. He could feel the tension building in her, wanted to push her over the edge with his mouth.

The hand in his hair suddenly tightened, her thighs tensing around his head. "Stop. Want you in me this time," she panted.

He hadn't planned to go that far but he wouldn't deny either of them this chance if that's what she wanted. And God knew, he wanted inside her in the worst way.

Reaching back to take a condom from his wallet, he rolled it on and sat back on his heels to grip her hips. She lay spread out before him like an erotic offering. Her cheeks were flushed, eyes glowing with desire, breasts rising and falling with each shallow, rapid breath. The pulse in her throat fluttered fast and hard.

With one hand he positioned the head of his cock against her entrance, watching her face. He eased forward an inch or two, just enough to feel her close around the head, then stopped.

Taya made an inarticulate sound of protest but he stilled her restless movement with his hand on her hip, keeping her right where he wanted her. He slipped his free hand between them to caress the sides of her swollen clit, circle it. Her eyes closed and her lips parted on a breathless cry, the sensual torment clear on her face.

Sensation splintered along his nerve endings. He was panting, trembling with the force of the pleasure streaking through him. He couldn't remember ever being this turned on before. Wanted her just as desperate as him.

Holding her steady, he pushed forward, slowly burying himself to the hilt in her warmth. They both groaned at the sensation of him filling her.

Nate's head fell forward, his eyes squeezing shut as

her pussy clamped around him. His heart was pounding out of control at the feel of her heat surrounding him. Her arms and legs gathered him close, pulling him down into the cradle of her body. He went willingly, letting her absorb his weight, savoring the sensation of being fully embedded inside her. Taya locked him to her and buried her face in the side of his neck.

But something was off. She was too still, her breath hitching, holding him so tight he felt her muscles quiver.

A flood victim had hung onto him like that once. During a hurricane relief operation years ago the little girl had wrapped her arms around his neck and her legs around his waist, clinging to him with all the strength in her body while he held her tight to him and hoisted her from her roof into the helo's hold.

Taya clung that way to him now, as though he was the only thing keeping her from drowning.

Then her shoulders jerked and she gave a ragged gasp against his neck.

Nate pressed his cheek to her temple. *Ah, baby, don't...*

His first impulse was to pull out and quiet her, to tell her *shhh, don't cry, everything's okay*. But clearly everything wasn't okay and when he tried to ease back she shook her head.

Nate closed his eyes. She'd held him in silence the other night, acknowledged and accepted his pain. He'd give her the same now, while they were connected as intimately as two people could be. The most intense connection he'd ever experienced in his life.

Slipping his arms beneath her, he banded them tight around her back and rested his full weight against her, being her anchor, giving her a safe place to hide while the storm of emotion rolled through her.

She battled it like the little warrior he called her and held on, forcing back the sobs until she calmed enough to take several slow, deep breaths, her face remaining tight to his neck. He was still hard inside her, as deep and close as he could possibly get. A fierce yet tender protectiveness flooded him. Gradually she calmed, the desperate edge to her hold easing.

Nate kissed her neck, her jaw before lifting his head but she wouldn't let him look at her. She cupped his face between her hands and leaned up to kiss him, her mouth open and hungry against his. He tasted the salt of her tears on his tongue.

Taya sighed into his mouth, her tongue twining with his in a languid, sexy caress, her hips undulating. Bracing his weight on one arm, he eased his hips back, the slow drag of her slick sex around his cock sending pleasure rocketing up his spine.

His left hand trailed down her ribs, tracing the curve of her waist and hips before sliding inward to lie between them once more. Resting his thumb over her clit he applied a gentle pressure and surged forward, driving his cock deep. He swallowed her fractured cry. Her hand went to his nape, dug deep into the muscles there, her heels coming to rest on his ass as she pulled him deeper.

A raw groan tore from his chest as he moved inside her. God, it felt amazing. Fucking spectacular. And when he lifted his head to stare into her eyes, the tenderness and longing reflected there made his heart swell until he thought it might burst.

Needing to savor being on the edge for as long as he could, he continued his slow, lazy thrusts, his thumb working her slick clit. He ignored the desire roaring through him, focused on her pleasure, needing her to crave him.

"Oh my God," she choked out, throwing her head back, eyes closed as an expression of pure bliss stole over her features. "Don't ever stop."

Nate gripped a fistful of the sheet with his free hand

and kept driving into her, his thrusts growing more and more forceful as the pleasure spread through his body like slow, hot honey.

Taya's breathing turned shallow, tiny mewls of pleasure rising from her throat. She trembled and wriggled in his hold but he held her still with the hand on her hip, using the angle to ensure his cock stroked across her sweet spot with every thrust.

"*Nathan.*" She grabbed his face, turned her lips to his in a desperate kiss as she came apart for him.

He muffled her shattered cries of release with his kiss and savored every tiny quiver of her body, triumph roaring through him. When she sighed and relaxed slightly he plunged his tongue deep into her mouth as he drove his cock to the hilt and stayed locked there, letting the orgasm overtake him.

He shuddered with the force of it, groaning helplessly into her mouth as she held him tight. He didn't know how long they stayed that way, kissing deep and slow as the pulses faded, too hungry to let each other go.

Finally he eased off her, released his grip on her hip and gently rubbed at the marks his fingers had left on her light-bronze skin. The most primitive part of him loved seeing those marks, wished they were permanent to remind her of him and what they'd just shared.

She flinched slightly as he withdrew so he paused to trail kisses over her chin, along her jaw. "Be right back." He eased from the bed and went to the bathroom where he flushed the condom down the toilet so no one could find it in the garbage, washed his hands and returned to the bed.

Taya was on her side, facing him, the covers drawn up to barely cover the generous curves of her breasts. She looked relaxed, at peace. He slid in next to her, automatically lifted an arm so she could snuggle into his body. She fit against him so perfectly, her head resting on his shoulder.

A quiet peacefulness stole through him, dimming the sharp sense of loss. His arms contracted around her, the pressure fierce. "I'm coming to find you once the trial's over," he murmured against the top of her head.

She kissed his chest. "You'd better."

"We're not done," he told her. "Not by a long shot."

She hummed in agreement and caressed his chest with her fingertips. Nate stroked the length of her spine, savoring the silky texture of her skin. God, he missed her already and she was still lying naked in his arms. "Just a few more days and this'll all be over."

"Don't make me wait too long, okay?"

"I won't." He leaned his head back, tipped her chin up with one hand until she met his eyes. If there was even a tiny part of her that doubted his intentions, he wanted that cleared up now. "I've never felt like this about anyone before."

Her eyes softened and she smiled that serene smile that soothed him deep inside. "Me neither."

God, he could drown in this woman and die a happy man. He admired her so damn much. "You're strong, baby. So much stronger than you even realize. You've got this."

"Have I got you, though?"

Normally the question would have freaked him out. Hearing it from her made him feel insanely possessive. "Yeah, you've got me, baby." He was falling so hard and so fast, and it didn't even faze him.

"Then I can handle everything else on my own," she whispered, and pulled his mouth down to hers.

Chapter Twenty

When Taya wheeled her suitcase into the hall at dawn, her new security team was waiting for her downstairs, along with Cruz, Vance and Tuck. Nathan looked up at her from where he was standing in the foyer with the U.S. Marshals from WITSEC. The moment their gazes locked she felt a wave of warmth wash over her, memories of last night bombarding her.

They'd slept tangled together for a while before she'd woken and begun exploring him with her hands and mouth. He'd already been hard when she'd wrapped her hand around his cock and scooted down to take him between her lips.

It'd been a long, long time since she'd done that with a lover but Nathan hadn't seemed to have any complaints about her technique. She'd relished pleasuring him that way, savored the feel of his hands wrapped in her hair, the deep sounds of enjoyment coming from his throat, those sculpted muscles in his abdomen and thighs rigid beneath her exploring fingers.

Stroke yourself while you suck me, baby.

The deep, rumbled command echoed in her head now as he looked at her, making her shiver with the memory. It had been so incredibly hot to comply, to just give over to sensation and enjoy. When he'd finally swelled against her tongue and groaned in agony, he'd tugged her head away and grabbed her, rolling her to her hands and knees on the bed.

Bent over in front of him, she'd fisted the covers, burying her face into the pillow as he drove into her from behind, one powerful arm locked around her waist, his hand stroking slow and sweet between her spread thighs. He'd stroked her most sensitive spots, inside and out, turning her into a mindless, helpless mass of need with each thrust, each caress. And that deep, seductive voice rasping against her ear, telling her what a good girl she was, how he couldn't wait to slide his cock inside her...

Combined with the scrape of his teeth and glide of his tongue against the place on her neck that lit her up like a Christmas tree, she hadn't stood a chance.

So good, Taya. Wanna feel you come around my cock.

The orgasm he'd given her had been the most intense yet, heightened all the more by the feel of his big body covering her from behind and his deep, rough groans of release muffled against the crook of her neck.

And now she was leaving him, when every atom in her body demanded she stay with him.

Nathan jogged up the stairs to take her suitcase from her, guided her back down with a hand on her lower back. "Taya, you remember Rick Duncan," he said, indicating the U.S. Marshal in the foyer who'd been assigned to her before.

"Yes, hi." She nodded at him, unable to shake the lingering nerves dancing in her belly.

"Good to see you again," he said, then shifted and indicated two other men standing by the front door. "This is Agent Kelly and Agent Wilson. We'll be taking over your security, along with several others, including the drivers waiting outside. I know you must be concerned about the former agent we had in the program, but I want to personally assure you that he's long gone and is being prosecuted for what he did. No one else was involved with him in the leak. I've personally handpicked all the agents on this assignment and no one except them and my direct superior know anything about what's happening from now on. You're getting the best team we've got."

Okay, that made her feel slightly better, and she did trust Duncan, based on his previous performance. "Thank you, I appreciate it."

He nodded. "We've got you something to eat in one of the trucks. You ready to go?"

She glanced at Nathan, fighting the tide of sadness swamping her. She'd known for hours that they'd have to say goodbye, but it was even harder than she'd imagined. Her throat tightened.

He stepped in front of her, cupped her face in one hand in full view of Duncan and the others. His touch was tender, but there was no mistaking the proprietary intent behind the gesture. He was marking her as his and wanted the others to know it. "You take good care of her," he said to the other man as he gazed down at her, his eyes alight with possessiveness.

"We will," Duncan answered, looking surprised by Nathan's overt display.

Taya gripped Nathan's solid wrist with one hand, her other slipping down to curl around his waist. "You be careful," she whispered, unable to hide the roughness in her voice. She was strong and she would do this on her own, but she was going to miss him like hell while she did.

"I will be," he promised. His thumb stroked across her cheek gently. "You take care of yourself and I'll see you soon." He'd promised to contact her if possible while they were apart, but that depended on their schedules.

Taya nodded, allowing herself to cling to him for one more moment before dropping her hands and stepping back. "Bye." Heart heavy, she followed Duncan out the front door, the others behind her.

When the SUV she was riding in pulled out of the driveway she looked back. Nathan stood on the front step, hands in his pockets, his gaze locked on where she sat behind the darkly tinted window.

****

Ayman woke at the tense whisper close beside him. "Get up."

His eyes snapped open in the darkness. He was in an unfamiliar room, a lumpy mattress beneath him, and he ached all over.

"*Now*. We have to move."

His heart rate doubled at the urgency in Darwish's gravelly voice. "What's going on? What time is it?" he whispered back, rolling out of the bed, each muscle protesting the movement. Felt like someone had beaten him with a hammer.

"Time to go. Have to get to our pickup point."

Still groggy, Ayman shoved his feet into his boots, laced them up and grabbed his jacket and backpack from beside the bed. Their host was waiting at the side door, his face hidden in shadow. "You'd best hurry," he said in a grim voice. "They won't wait for you."

Today was pivotal. All the final preparations would be made, including finalizing the intel and plan for the whore's demise.

Ayman slipped out the door behind Darwish, pistol in hand. The sounds of the waking forest surrounded him, birds beginning to stir and call out as the sky began to lighten to the east. It was dark amongst the tall trees though.

Dark enough that accidents could happen.

His fingers tightened around the grip of his weapon, his gaze trained on Darwish. After yesterday he trusted the man even less, knew he had to watch his back with him. The Brethren still needed him for the big op, but that didn't mean Darwish felt the same way.

Their boots were quiet over the forest floor as they wound their way through the thick growth of oaks and maples. They kept a fast pace and soon sweat began to break out over Ayman's body. The cool morning air felt good against his skin, his muscles limbering up as he moved. About ten minutes later they approached the parking lot next to the entrance to the walking trails. Darwish slowed, his movements cautious as he circled the area.

Ayman automatically took the other side, pausing behind some thick bushes to peer at the vehicles parked in the lot. Two of them. A small sedan that sat empty, and a white delivery van, the driver's silhouette visible through the windshield.

He read the license plate, relaxed a little when it matched the one they'd been given the night before. Glancing over at Darwish, he waved and nodded.

Together they approached the van. The door locks popped open. Ayman kept his weapon at the ready, not willing to take any risks. Opening the side door on the driver's side, he scanned the driver then the interior, index finger resting on the trigger guard. The man was the one they'd been told to expect.

"You have any trouble getting here?" he asked, using the prearranged challenge.

"No, traffic was good," the driver responded calmly, glancing in the rearview mirror at him and Darwish on the other side.

Correct response. He and Darwish slid inside and shut the doors.

"Anyone follow you?" Darwish asked, scanning out the windows.

"Not that I noticed." The driver backed out of the spot and headed for the lot exit. "Everything's in place. Meeting's on schedule."

Just hours from now, Ayman knew.

"Good," Darwish grunted. "Finally we get to act."

Anticipation curled inside Ayman. Soon he'd get his final assignment. He already knew the most important parts of the attack, but not who was responsible for what. The Brethren had been planning this for months down to the last detail, and the impact was going to be huge.

He had too much at stake to fail. Once they saw he was still committed and stalwart with the coming attack, they'd trust him and hopefully leave his family alone. There hadn't been an opportunity to warn them yet. He'd speak to Mahmoud tonight about it, but actions were stronger than words and he would prove himself to them.

No. He would prove himself to the *world* when he took part in the attack that would free their revered leader and shake the United States to its core.

****

Nate was in the team room cleaning his M4 late that afternoon when Blackwell popped his head around the corner, his ice blue eyes finding Nate's. "Briefing in five," his teammate said.

He paused in the act of reassembling the firing mechanism and eyed the other man. They'd just finished up a long meeting about security protocol for the trial about an hour ago. "Something up?"

"Looks like. DeLuca and Tuck are having a meeting with Celida and her partner right now."

Must be something urgent then. Nate shoved to his feet and followed Blackwell out into the hallway. "Other guys know anything?"

"Nope."

Typical Blackwell. Straight to the point, no bullshit, kinda like Bauer, only not as grim or quiet. Nate didn't hang out with him much outside of work, at least not these days. Blackwell was former SF and married to an official with the Defense Intelligence Agency. Nate had never met her. Based on a couple things he'd heard from some of the other guys on the team, apparently things weren't going too well on the home front for Blackwell, which probably explained why his wife never showed up at team social functions.

The door at the end of the hallway opened and the rest of the team walked in carrying bags from a burger joint just off base. Bauer was in the lead, his face set in his characteristically grim expression that said he was in work mode. "What's up, Doc?" he said to Nate, sipping at the soda in his hand.

That Bugs Bunny thing never got old for the guys, but he far preferred it to Dr. Feelgood. "Dunno. Investigators are here though, so it could be another intel briefing, or it might be more." *Please don't let it have anything bad to do with Taya.* He hadn't been able to contact her yet. She'd be settled in to her new safe house by now, awaiting the start of the trial tomorrow. She was scheduled to be the first witness called, as early as tomorrow afternoon.

Bauer nodded and headed straight for the briefing room, pushing the door open for the others. Cruz, Vance and Evers filed in behind him, all stuffing their faces as they went. Nate had passed on going out to grab a bite to eat, saying he wasn't hungry. Mostly he'd just wanted some time to himself without the guys around.

He'd been doing a lot of thinking about Taya. They'd

only spent a short amount of time together, relatively speaking, but it blew any other experience he'd had with a woman out of the water. The sex was fucking amazing, but that was only part of why he was falling so fast and so hard for her.

Something had shifted inside him, and he felt…lighter inside somehow. He knew he had a long way to go before he got past the survivor guilt and dealt with the issues he'd dragged along from his childhood, but already he could see an improvement in his thoughts and mood. The self-destructive cycle he'd been in had been broken, at least for now. He intended for it to stay that way.

"Here man, gotcha something." Evers handed him a bag. "Extra bacon."

They all knew he was pretty much a bacon whore. Nate took it with a smile. "Thanks."

DeLuca and Tuck were up at the front of the room with Celida and Agent Travers. "You guys go ahead and eat while we do this," DeLuca said as Nate and the others sat.

Nate dug into his bag and made short work of the burger while the briefing started, his attention glued to his commander.

"Credible tip came in about twenty minutes ago. The two tangos who escaped the hotel in Raleigh are rumored to be at a high level meeting with top commanders of The Brethren."

Nate lowered his burger, forced the mammoth bite he'd taken down his suddenly tight throat. He wanted those fuckers. Wanted them bad.

"Recent satellite footage confirms that vehicles have been arriving close to the target house throughout the day. The way the roofline's set up, we haven't been able to get a head count or even any shots of who's entering the house." He nodded at Celida, who pulled up images on a large screen mounted on the wall behind her.

"Target's forty minutes away by car," she said. "If we're right, most of the key Brethren leadership will be there as well, including Mahmoud Abbas."

The guy rumored to be at the helm of all this.

"We've got a standing warrant for him from a federal judge," Travers added. "Just waiting for word from one of our agents near the target location, but in the meantime you guys can plan how you want to execute the search warrant. It'll be a search and seize operation. They'll have bodyguards and sentries at the minimum, and as the trial begins tomorrow, it confirms recent chatter that they're planning something big for tomorrow."

Not if we get to them first, Nate thought, his attention riveted to the image on screen.

Something dripped onto his palm. He glanced down at the forgotten burger, saw a blob of sauce had landed there. He crumpled the burger up in its paper wrapper and wiped his hands with the napkins in the bag, never taking his eyes off the screen. God, he hoped all the tangos were in there.

"Let's plan it out," DeLuca said once the two agents were finished speaking. "Tuck?"

Their team leader stepped forward and used a laser pointer on the satellite image of the target house as he went through the basic plan. Entry and exit points, order of entry, who would do what, contingency plans.

They came up with variations to be used in particular circumstances. It was a residential neighborhood so they'd have to ensure they sealed off a tight perimeter to reduce the chance of any collateral damage.

"Any questions?" DeLuca finally asked.

No one said anything, but in the silence Agent Travers's phone rang. He turned away to answer it, spoke for a second then faced them with a smile and a thumbs up.

Green light.

Fuck, yeah. The hair on Nate's arms stood up.

"Let's saddle up," DeLuca commanded. "You've got ten minutes to suit up and grab your gear."

Nate jumped out of his seat and rushed for the door. He was the first one through it, each stride taking him one step closer to ending the threat against Taya.

Chapter Twenty-One

"Cruzie, hold up a second."

Special Agent Ethan Cruz paused partway to the door of the briefing room at DeLuca's words. "Uh, sure," he said, surprised. Agents Morales and Travers had just left, along with all his teammates, except Vance, who was holding the door for him.

Vance glanced back at him from the doorway. "Later, man." He stepped into the hallway and let the door shut behind him, leaving Ethan alone with Tuck and DeLuca.

He walked back to the seat he'd just vacated and lowered his weight into it, facing his commander and team leader. "What's up?"

DeLuca stood in front of his desk, leaning his weight against it casually, his arms crossed over his chest. Tuck stood off to the side, his arms also folded. "Wanted your opinion on Schroder," DeLuca said.

Ethan concealed his surprise. They wanted to talk about this now, when they were about to execute a search warrant? "My opinion about what, exactly?"

"Where his head's at. You've been with him for the better part of a week now. How's he doing?"

"Good. He's solid." That was about the best thing he could say about another operator, and he'd said as much in his report after the incident at the hotel in Raleigh.

DeLuca nodded, eyes grave. "That's good. Any concerns about him being on this op?"

He understood why DeLuca had asked. If someone's head wasn't totally in the game, things could go sideways in a heartbeat. Then people started dying. But he also sensed DeLuca's concern had something to do with Schroder's feelings for Taya.

"No, none," he answered without hesitation.

"What about him and the girl?"

Ethan shrugged. "WITSEC's handling her security now. Whatever's going on between Doc and Taya, it's pretty serious for him. Actually, I'd say he's more in the game now than he's been for the past couple months. More himself." Schroder was a solid operator who always did his best and all but bent over backward to please the guys on the team. The past few months, everyone had noticed the downward spiral Schroder had been on.

From what Ethan had seen though, ever since Taya had shown up, Schroder seemed like a different guy. Yeah, he was doing his job in guarding her, but there was more between them than that. Even in his downtime Schroder hadn't been on the phone lining up booty calls or talking to one of the many women waiting in the wings for him.

That alone told Ethan Taya meant something to Schroder, and it had to somehow be related to their history in Afghanistan. Whatever was going on between them, it was serious, and Ethan thought the change looked pretty damn good on his teammate. Hell, she seemed like a quality individual, and considering what she'd been through she was freaking tough. He was happy for the guy.

DeLuca exchanged a look with Tuck, who nodded his confirmation. "I'm real glad to hear that," his commander said, looking relieved, then pushed away from his desk. "Now let's rock and roll."

But ninety minutes later Cruz stepped out onto the front stoop of the target house with Schroder and headed back to their vehicle, disappointed and frustrated as hell. The op had been a total bust.

Schroder removed his helmet with a discouraged sigh and ran a hand through his hair. "Couldn't have missed them by much."

"No." The satellite they'd been using to monitor the target house had moved out of range about twenty minutes ago, leaving only a few local FBI agents and some cops to watch the house as best they could. They'd reported several vehicles coming and going from the residence as the HRT was en route, but it'd been impossible for them to tell who was in the vehicles.

"They must've left in a helluva hurry though," Ethan added. The suspects had left dishes with half eaten meals on them strewn on the tables in the kitchen and living room, more on the counter and in the sink. The coffee pot was still on and two-thirds full. Forensics people were in their now, gathering evidence for DNA testing, to try to determine who'd been at the meeting.

Something had obviously spooked the suspects.

"There's no way they could've known we were coming, unless they spotted one of our agents watching the place," Schroder said, his eyes burning with frustration.

Possible, but not likely, and Ethan searched for something to ease Schroder's mind. "We've still got time. One solid tip, and we'll nail them."

Schroder shot him a hard look as they headed down

the front steps. "We're on a short timeline."

Ethan decided it best to shut his mouth. The guy was worried as fuck about Taya already, and given the amount of chatter they'd heard about and the kinds of attacks they were prepping for at the trial, he couldn't blame him. The threat against her was still very real.

They waited by the vehicles as the others left the house. Blackwell, Vance, Bauer, Evers and finally Tuck. "Next time, boys," their team leader said.

Everyone was looking at Schroder. They all felt for him. Every last one of them wanted to take this cell down and protect Taya and the surviving witnesses.

Evers clapped a hand on Schroder's shoulder. "It'll be all right, man," he said.

"We'll get 'em," Bauer added.

Tuck, Evers and Bauer knew exactly what Schroder was feeling right now. Each of them had experienced having the woman they cared about in mortal danger. Aside from a show of solidarity, however, there was nothing they could do to make this any better. Ethan moved aside for Schroder, who nodded his thanks and stowed his gear, not saying a word.

"Let's get back to base," Tuck said, heading around the rear of one SUV to stow his tactical gear. "We've got a lot to cover by morning."

****

Taya rolled to her side when her new phone rang on the small table beside her bed. When she saw Nathan's number she smiled, excitement leaping inside her. She'd been struggling to keep her anxiety under control, wondering where he was and what he was doing, so hearing his voice was exactly what she needed. "Hello?"

"Hey, gorgeous. How're things?" Just the sound of his voice soothed her.

"Okay. I spent most of the day reviewing notes about the kinds of questions the prosecution is going to ask me, and what the defense is likely to counter with."

Her new security team had taken her straight from the airport to the new safe house, where she'd spent the past few hours reviewing notes she's made about the trial and re-reading sections of her journal. Her captivity was as vivid in her mind as the day she'd arrived back in the States, and she planned to use those memories to paint as accurate a picture as possible for the judge and jurors. "I'm definitely taking the stand tomorrow afternoon. Likely right after lunch." She was both excited and nervous about it.

"You ready for it?"

"As I'll ever be. What about you, how was your day?"

"Fine, except I miss you like hell."

Aww. "I miss you too." She eased back against her pillow and looked at the bouquet on the nightstand. "I got your flowers. They're beautiful, thank you." A gorgeous riot of Gerber daisies and lilies in a rainbow of reds, pinks, yellows and oranges.

"Welcome. Bet Duncan loved sending one of his guys out to pick them up for me." She could hear the smile in his voice, imagined the devilish twinkle in his eyes.

"Oh, he did. Said it's probably the first time in the history of WITSEC that a U.S. Marshal delivered flowers to one of their witnesses."

A low chuckle. "Well, this was a special circumstance, so they helped me out."

"I loved the card you sent with them the best though." *Proud of you. Give 'em hell tomorrow.* He'd signed it Nathan rather than Nate, which had made her smile.

"I had no idea you were romantic," she continued. "All these interesting things I'm learning about you." She hadn't been able to wipe the silly smile off her face after one of the security team members had knocked on her door and handed them to her with a goofy smile and a, "special delivery".

"Baby, you haven't seen anything yet. When the trial's done you're gonna get all the romance you can handle, and then some."

"Really?" Now that was something for a girl to look forward to, and it sure as hell did the trick in taking her mind off her worries. "Well I'm all intrigued, because it's been forever since I was romanced. What do you have in mind? Candlelit dinners? Going to the movies? Long walks? Lazy afternoon picnics?"

"Not gonna give away my hand this early on, but I'll take those into consideration."

"And what's the key to your heart, by the way? I mean, other than the thing I did to you this morning."

"What thing is that? Refresh my memory," he said, a teasing note in his voice.

She smiled, enjoying the light banter. It felt good to let her worry about tomorrow go and focus on what she had to look forward to when this was all done. Being with him again, seeing her family, getting back to her life. A life that would hopefully include Nathan in a romantic capacity. "Waking you up with my mouth."

He gave a low groan. "I loved every second of it. But think simpler."

Simpler than sex? For a guy like him? "Food, then. I bet you're a sucker for a home-cooked meal. Am I right?"

He chuckled. "That works too, but it's still not the key."

"Then what?"

"You."

She blinked, her heart squeezing at the conviction behind his answer. "Me?"

"Yeah, just you. And maybe bacon," he added, a

smile in his voice.

He was so freaking adorable. "So you're saying if I made and served you a BLT, you'd be putty in my hands?" Seemed hard to imagine, but okay.

A masculine rumble filled her ears. "God, yeah."

She couldn't help the sappy smile that spread across her face. "Wow, you *are* easy. And I can definitely arrange that."

"I can hardly wait. Will you serve it to me naked? Or maybe wearing just a frilly little apron and heels?"

She smothered a laugh, but a clear image of her doing just that popped into her head, serving him the sandwich in that sexy outfit while watching his eyes go all heated. "Depends on how good you are."

"Oh, baby, I'll be *so* good to you, you have no idea."

The man completely melted her and turned her on at the same time. It scared her, to fall so hard and fast when they'd only spent a short amount of time together, but she knew the most important things about him. His sense of honor and dedication to those he cared about, his work ethic. His loyalty and bravery. She believed in him, that he truly cared about her, and she believed they had a shot at something more together. They'd both earned the right to find happiness with each other.

"What are you wearing right now?"

She gave a sly smile at the change in subject. "Your shirt." She'd asked for one of his T-shirts this morning and he'd given her an old pararescue one from his duffel. It was pale gray and super soft from many washings. On the middle of the chest it bore an angel set against the backdrop of a parachute, her arms wrapped around the globe above a scroll that read *That Others May Live*.

Nathan and his fellow PJs had lived by that motto. O'Neil had given his life upholding it. She'd never forget that.

A pause as that registered. "*Just* my shirt?"

"Yeah." She lifted her arm to bury her nose in the sleeve, breathed in. "Mmm, and it still smells like you." Clean and spicy, a hint of male musk.

"Holy hell, that's hot. You naked in my favorite shirt. Text me a picture?"

"Maybe. I'm taking good care of it though."

"I bet you are. Hell, now I'm jealous of my own shirt," he said with a laugh. "So, you ready for tomorrow?"

She sobered. "Ready as I can be. Mostly I'm worried about the security situation and seeing Qureshi face-to-face in the courtroom."

"I can't go into too much detail, but believe me when I tell you that whole area's gonna be locked down so tight, they're gonna need to coat you with cooking spray just to pass through security tomorrow."

The image made her smile, as did his attempt to lighten the mood. "Will you guys be there?"

"We'll be at a staging area, on standby. But near enough, yeah, just in case. That make you feel better?"

"A little." She liked knowing he'd be nearby if anything happened.

"Just stay close to Duncan and the rest of your security team. They're not gonna mess around. They'll get you straight in there and stay in the courtroom with you. You'll be well covered."

"Thanks. I'm gonna bury Qureshi on that stand tomorrow." She'd see him in hell before she'd allow him to walk free after what he'd done to her and the others.

Like the time he'd had two of the captured women stripped and beaten with sticks for daring to meet his gaze. He'd had the beatings done in front of all the others, to serve as a warning. One of the women had suffered broken ribs and they'd both been bruised and bloody by the time the punishment ended.

"That's my girl." His voice rang with such pride that

it warmed her inside. Then masculine voices sounded in the background. "Sorry, baby, I gotta go."

"Are you still at work?" she asked, surprised. It was almost midnight. She'd assumed he'd been at home when he'd called.

"Yeah, meetings and stuff."

She knew they were prepping for tomorrow; she just hoped it wasn't because of an imminent attack. He wouldn't want to worry her more than she already was, and he couldn't talk to her about operations and other classified things anyway. "Thanks for calling. Be safe and I can't wait to see you."

"Hang tight, sweetheart. I'll be with you in spirit tomorrow and watching over you from close by."

Her throat tightened. His words gave her additional strength to take into the courtroom with her. "Thanks, and stay safe. Bye."

"Bye."

She disconnected, feeling acutely alone. Lying back against her pillow, she blew out a deep breath and stared up at the ceiling. The security situation was beyond her control. She had to keep her eye on the prize now, focus on the importance of her role tomorrow.

Qureshi was going to pay for what he'd done, with his life if she had anything to say about it.

****

Ayman finished cleaning his weapons and loaded them into the large duffel open at his feet where he sat cross-legged on the bedroom floor. Across the room, two other new additions to the team did the same. It had been a long but productive day. The meeting he'd been part of earlier had been eye-opening, to say the least.

There he'd met most of the founding Brethren in person, as well as others fighting for them, and learned the full extent of tomorrow's operation. He'd expected a multi-faceted and well thought out plan, but nothing of this complexity or precision. Nearly two million dollars were being funneled into this effort, including weapons, vehicles, manpower.

After reviewing everything as a group and discussing assignments, they'd been halfway through a meal together when one of the lookouts had radioed in, suspicious about the increase in traffic around the perimeter. Their leader, Mahmoud, had called an end to the meeting and ordered everyone out. Ayman had heard later that a crack FBI SWAT team had showed up not twenty minutes after the last man had left.

Now he and his teammates were all anxiously awaiting the morning, when they'd begin their assignments three hours from now.

The attack—or rather, attacks—would be fast, bloody and carefully choreographed. Designed to inflict maximum fear and maximum carnage.

They even had a few surprises in store that no one would be expecting. No amount of security could stop the wave after wave of men they were sending in.

Ayman's lips curved into a pleased half-smile. He was extremely impressed by The Brethren's preparations, and honored to be a part of such a large and historic attack.

His group was tasked with killing as many security agents as possible before targeting the whore inside the courthouse. Seven other teams would carry out simultaneous, coordinated attacks to help them gain entry. Some of them would die, but every one of them was prepared to make that sacrifice, and with the sheer number of attackers involved, at least a few would get through.

The biggest push, of course, would be concentrated on freeing Qureshi. Once the chaos started they should have ample time to get in, take advantage of the confusion and get him out. A private plane would be waiting at a nearby airfield, ready to take him back to Pakistan and then he'd make his way to the tribal region with the help of his most loyal followers over there.

If Ayman survived the attack, he'd be heading south for a chance at freedom across the border. If he didn't…then it was Allah's will.

He darted a glance toward the living room of the borrowed house. Darwish was stretched out on the couch, flipping through channels with the TV remote. He paused and sat up suddenly. "Look at this," he called out in Arabic, turning up the volume.

Ayman got up with the others and entered the next room. The moment his gaze fell on the TV, his stomach dropped.

His father was on screen talking to the news anchor, dressed in his janitor uniform, his face drawn with worry. It must have been recorded previously because from the angle of the sun it appeared to be midday. The headline at the bottom of the screen read *The FBI is asking for help in locating 19 year old Ayman Tuma, from the D.C. Metro area. Anyone with information is asked to call 911.*

Ayman couldn't look away, could barely breathe as the camera rolled, his heart bashing against his ribcage.

"What would you like to say to your son right now if you knew he was listening?" the anchor prompted.

His father's throat bobbed as he swallowed and looked into the camera, his face haggard. "I would tell him to come home," he said in heavily accented English. "Please, just come home and turn yourself in. We are so worried." His gaze dropped, his shoulders sagging. "So worried," he repeated in a lost voice.

Ayman ruthlessly blocked the pain and guilt tearing at him. He would *not* allow himself to feel such things now. The only way to protect his family and be free of The Brethren was to take part in the coming attack. He started to turn away.

"Don't you dare leave."

He froze at Darwish's cold voice, turned back to meet that icy gaze head on. Darwish shut off the TV and swung to face him with an accusing glare. "He's going to ruin everything—the attack's scheduled only hours from now!"

"No, he won't," Ayman insisted, trying to ignore the terror forking inside him. "The police and FBI have been searching for me—us—for days now, and they haven't caught us yet. Mahmoud gave me his word that no one would touch my family, no matter what they've done. You all heard him." He looked at the other two men for confirmation and they both nodded. He allowed himself to relax a fraction. As long as he carried out the attack, his family was safe from The Brethren.

The digital tones of a phone alarm suddenly filled the room, severing the quiet.

The first phase of the operation would be underway any minute now.

Ayman glanced at the man closest to him, who silenced his phone. The eldest of the group, at thirty-two Tarif was even more experienced than Darwish, having seen combat in Syria and Iraq as part of a secret militia group. He was far more religious than the rest of them, motivated by the need to serve Allah. Ayman was driven by the offer to get paid a sizeable amount of money to attack the country he blamed for his family's—his people's—woes.

"Time to pray," he said. Tarif had also shaved his beard into a tidy goatee in a bid to decrease suspicion in the morning. Those dark eyes watched each of them in turn as they unrolled their prayer mats and knelt upon them.

When everyone was in place he began the evening prayer, calling on Allah to protect them. "We are not afraid to die, only that we will fail in our duty to you," he went on, eyes closed. "We pray that you grant us the courage to do what must be done, and the protection of your benevolence."

Listening to the words, Ayman mentally suppressed a shiver of unease. Over the past few hours he'd made peace with the fact that he would likely die tomorrow. That didn't mean he'd given up hope. God willing, the American whore would die by his hand, then he'd make his escape.

Whatever happened, he'd inflict as much death and suffering on his enemy as possible. If he was to die today, then he would go out fighting, resolute in his decision that had started him on this path. That was his only comfort, and it would have to be enough to sustain him through the long and difficult hours ahead.

Chapter Twenty-Two

In the back of the armored SUV, Taya released a slow, deep breath and tugged at the hem of her pencil skirt. Her palms were damp as she smoothed the gray fabric into place. The closer they got to the courthouse, the higher her anxiety spiked. Thoughts raced in her mind. The security threat hanging over this trial, taking the stand, giving the best answers to the questions posed to her.

Facing Qureshi again after all this time.

Up front in the passenger seat, Duncan swiveled around to speak to her. "We're going to circle around and approach from a different route, just like we talked about."

Taya nodded. She knew the plan because they'd gone over it several times before leaving the safe house. One vehicle was in front of them and another behind, to provide extra security.

On arrival out front they would rush her to where the exterior perimeter was set up, get her as close as possible to the security checkpoint where more agents from the Department of Justice and the FBI were stationed. Some in uniform, many more in plain clothes. Sniffer dog teams and sniper teams were also in place, scattered in various positions around the area. Once she got out with Duncan, he and two other marshals would rush her through to the inner perimeter and from there straight inside the courthouse.

"Everybody's ready and in place," Duncan continued. "You good to go?"

"Yes." Her heart was thudding hard as the driver took the final turn and brought them in front of the courthouse. An imposing long, two-story building constructed of gray limestone with Corinthian columns spanning the façade. A huge crowd had gathered outside the exterior perimeter. Media crews and civilians carrying signs.

Qureshi was in there.

It had been five years since she'd last seen him. The thought of meeting that cold, dark gaze head on was both vindicating and terrifying. She straightened her spine. He was the one in chains now. There was a certain poetic justice to that.

The driver slowed as they reached the edge of the crowd lining the area where the security forces had pushed back the onlookers. "Here we go," Duncan murmured.

Taya shifted in her seat to face the door, fingers on the latch of her seatbelt. The second they stopped and Duncan gave the signal, she had to move fast.

The driver stopped in front of a pair of FBI agents armed with rifles. Duncan burst out of the vehicle and opened Taya's door as she released her seatbelt. He grabbed her arm and pulled her out. Immediately two other marshals from the tail vehicle surrounded her, acting as a living shield, ushering her straight through the security gate with a wave of their ID. The moment they cleared the metal gates the three vehicles took off. Taya didn't look back.

A sudden flurry of movement erupted on both sides of her. Media crews, hungry for a juicy story, began to converge toward the gate. Agents and cops blocking the way held them back. The crowd's noise seemed to grow louder, until she could hear some of the shouts distinctly over the mingled voices.

"Burn in hell, Qureshi!"

That one she agreed with.

"Bring the girls back home!"

Even though she'd been prepared for this day, that one hit home. It made her think of all the other women who'd been married off to Qureshi's soldiers and then left behind when Hassan took Taya and fled. Guilt clawed at her insides but she shook it off.

There was nothing she could have done for the others back then, and she'd been doing her best to help them ever since. Lobbying government officials about their rescues. Speaking to audiences all over Europe and North America about their plight and the evils of human trafficking.

And once she stepped through those tall doors ahead of her at the top of the third flight of steps, she would seek justice for those she hadn't been able to save.

Several reporters were straining against the metal barriers as she walked past, sticking out their microphones toward her. "Taya, tell us how you're feeling right now, about to confront Qureshi after all this time."

"How does it feel to confront the man responsible for what you went through?"

They recognized her, even with her wearing sunglasses and her hair being styled so differently. That, and she was the only one arriving with a human shield.

Taya kept her head held high, studiously ignoring the reporters and the crowd. She lengthened her strides to keep up with her guards, her high heels clicking on the pavement as they rushed her toward the second perimeter. Far fewer people lined the security barriers here; a few media crews surrounded by more cops and FBI agents. She tuned them all out, kept her gaze fastened to the entrance to the courthouse where more guards waited.

They reached the inner perimeter fence. Duncan and the others flashed their badges. The guards had been expecting them, but still checked their ID before allowing them inside. She'd just stepped through the opening in the metal railing when a commotion broke out behind them.

Duncan's head whipped around. His arm tightened across Taya's back. Startled, she glanced over her shoulder to see a knot of people moving just beyond the first barrier. People shouted, several tripping in their haste to get out of the way. Security was converging on someone just out of view.

A warning tingle slithered up Taya's spine.

"Move," Duncan commanded, his voice terse.

She whipped back around, started jogging, intuitively knowing she had to get away from that first gate.

"Taya!"

The frantic edge in the female voice sent a bolt of alarm through her. She faltered, her body reacting automatically to the woman's fear and desperation. The way she called her name was personal. The voice sounded familiar.

"*Taya!*" The scream made the hairs on her nape stand on end.

Despite herself, she looked back.

Twenty yards away, a woman was being surrounded by security personnel. She bowed under the strength of the arms grabbing her, pushing her downward. Her knees hit the pavement.

But her eyes stayed locked on Taya.

Light blue eyes stared back at her, huge and wide in

a pale face, beseeching her not to look away.

It had been five years since they'd last seen each other but Taya sucked in a shocked breath as recognition slammed through her. *No...*

"Chloe," she breathed, and automatically tried to pull from Duncan's grip.

He was still dragging her, overriding her need to help her friend. She dug in her heels, tried to wrench her arm away. Her friend wasn't dead. She was right there, Taya had to help her. "Chloe!"

"Taya," Chloe cried out in a choked voice, her face filled with abject terror. "*Help* me!"

A warning buzz built at the base of her spine. Something was terribly wrong.

Ice flooded Taya's veins. Her eyes shot to her friend's torso, hidden by a bulky jacket. A jacket far too heavy for the warm spring day.

The hair on her arms stood on end. *Oh my God, no.*

Duncan cursed and grabbed her around the waist. "Bomb!"

The whole world seemed to still.

He threw her to the ground as people screamed behind her. Her elbows, ribs and hips hit with a bone-jarring thud, her chin cracking against the pavement. Then Duncan's weight landed atop her, knocking the remaining air from her lungs. She could hear the panic in the crowd behind them, hear people shouting and yelling.

Fighting to draw in air, she struggled to free herself from Duncan's grip. Trapped. She was trapped and her friend was in terrible danger.

Duncan cursed and pinned her down, his muscles straining with the effort of keeping her still. Taya bucked and twisted, shouting at him to let her go, to help Chloe.

Need to help her. Have to—

An explosion rent the air. A wall of heat and noise blasted over her, searing the exposed skin on her face, arms and legs, the pressure compressing her chest and eardrums.

Duncan grunted and held her tighter, his grip bruising. In the vacuum of silence that followed all she could hear was the roaring of blood in her ears while her heart tried to pound its way out of her chest.

Chloe!

The instant Duncan's weight shifted, Taya struggled up onto her battered forearms and knees, then swung her head around to look behind them.

Carnage met her stupefied gaze.

Chloe was gone and so were all the security personnel, the bystanders who'd been close to her. All reduced to nothing more than slippery red and pink gore that covered the ground for dozens of yards in every direction, flames licking at what was left of their clothing and body parts.

Beyond the inner blast zone, people were writhing on the ground in pools of blood, some missing arms and legs.

Taya's stomach lurched, the horror of it penetrating her brain.

Strong arms hauled her upright and she realized belatedly that Duncan was screaming at her. She looked up into his face, blinked as his mouth moved, not understanding a word. Her arms came up to grab onto his shoulders as he lifted her and began to run. The panicked crowd was fleeing now, running for their lives.

Taya flinched when a second, larger explosion detonated to her left. Her gaze shot to the huge orange ball of fire that burst into the sky at the far end of the courthouse. Seconds later, another explosion erupted on her right.

A siege.

She was shaking, trembling all over, her heart rising into her throat. Levering upward on Duncan's back, she cast a glance over her shoulder. Duncan was running full out toward the courthouse doors, the other two marshals flanking him. Guards on either side of the door had their weapons up, aimed at something beyond her and her security team, and opened fire.

Taya jerked and shut her eyes as bullets tore past her, every muscle in her body locked tight. More screams, more gunfire, the rounds whizzing all around them like a swarm of angry hornets.

Gritting her teeth she gripped the back of Duncan's shirt and held on as he raced for the safety of the building that was now their only hope for survival.

****

When the crowd assembled fled in panic in the aftermath of the second suicide bomber's device, Ayman seized his chance.

Pulling the automatic rifle from inside his trench coat, he and the others converged on the epicenter of the destruction.

He surged forward, shoving through the terrified mass of bodies running toward him. The heat of the fire singed his face as he ran. Darwish ran beside him and two others behind, Tarif carrying a body draped over his broad shoulders.

Ayman's heartbeat thundered in his ears, adrenaline and euphoria coursing through his bloodstream, heightened by the amphetamine they'd all taken prior to arriving at the courthouse. The explosions had been timed perfectly, and he loved the irony of using the kidnapped witnesses as suicide bombers.

The security forces would be attempting to lock down the building, but they'd never make it. All the personnel guarding the entrances were either dead or preoccupied with securing the perimeter, aiding the wounded or taking out the teams of shooters who were now moving into position. The smoke from the fires only helped conceal Ayman and the others from the snipers positioned on the surrounding rooftops.

The large truck bomb at the east side of the building had done its work. People lay dead or dying, survivors fleeing the area, adding to the chaos. Ayman's path to the exterior door was clear, the doors wide open, imploded from the powerful force of the explosion. He charged ahead, leaping over a pile of debris, climbed up a mound of fallen bricks, rifle to his shoulder.

Two Feds appeared in the blackened doorway, wearing marked windbreakers. Ayman fired, hitting them both in the chest before they'd even stepped into the daylight. They fell, twitching where they lay, their weapons lying useless on the ground.

In his peripheral vision he saw more security converging on them. He wheeled and fired to the right as Darwish did the same on his left, clearing a path to the building. He sprayed a burst of rounds into the black rectangle of the open doorway. Someone inside fired back. Bullets whizzed past him.

The screams of the wounded and fleeing people trapped inside only spurred him onward. A gleeful laugh bubbled up in his throat. This was the most intense rush he'd ever experienced. He felt powerful, invincible as he tore over the open ground toward his target.

Other teams of attackers were converging on the building from different directions. Four other death squads, more than sixty trained men here to take out as many law enforcement and civilians as possible. The additional attackers fueled the chaos, aiding Ayman and his team in their primary mission.

He plunged through the doorway into the dimly lit hallway, the acrid smell of smoke and burned flesh stinging his nostrils. Screams and distant gunfire echoed along the hallway. Another group of shooters appeared at the end of the hall. Security forces inside were shooting at them. Ayman saw some of his brothers fall, but there were so many of them, security was overwhelmed and outgunned.

Someone popped around the corner ahead of him. He fired once, dropped the man where he stood and kept running. His blood raced through his veins, a sense of euphoria blotting out everything else.

His target was here. She'd tried to fool them by altering her appearance, but it hadn't been enough. Not nearly enough. Ayman had spotted her the moment she'd stepped out of that SUV with her security team.

Time to kill the American whore for the part she'd played in bringing this mockery of justice to fruition. That was the role he'd been given for this attack.

Up ahead at the end of the long hallway he could hear the sounds of other, smaller explosions, probably from grenades like the ones he carried. More raw screams of terror punctuating the silence that followed. It was all going exactly as planned so far.

Ayman kept running, Darwish and the others close behind him, Tarif dropping back due to the heavy load he carried. The teams currently breaching the interior into the courtrooms knew what to do: seize Qureshi and protect him at all costs until they could get him out—just another few minutes. Ayman and Darwish had a different task to complete. One they both relished.

His boots thudded against the marble floor, the sound echoing off the walls. The hallway was deserted now, everyone fleeing for what they thought was the safety of the inner chambers.

A fatal mistake, as they would soon find out.

Darwish shouted a warning. Ayman veered sharply to the right and hugged the wall a split second before the loud hiss whizzed past him. Seconds later the rocket propelled grenade Darwish had fired detonated at the solid mahogany doors up ahead.

It exploded, the reverberations flowing through his body, pulsing in his ears. He grunted at the force of the concussion in his chest, kept running. More explosions pounded through the building, out of sight. The lights flickered once, then went out.

Through the burning doors ahead of him, Ayman could see the people scrambling for safety in the courtroom he'd been ordered to take. Raising his weapon, he fired two bursts through the open doorway.

Screams. The people in the threshold melted back inside.

He fired again, clearing the way for himself, high on the knowledge that he was making Americans suffer the way his people were suffering back home.

Plunging through the doorway, he sprayed a burst of rounds in a half circle, screaming in English at the top of his lungs. "Get down! Don't any of you move! Anyone moves, I shoot!" He immediately moved into the shadows at the periphery of the room as Darwish did the same on the other side. Labored breathing and frightened whimpers sounded in the sudden silence.

His hostages couldn't see him, but he could see them.

And when those emergency lights came on, he was hunting one person in particular.

Chapter Twenty-Three

Nate was in the team room of the warehouse serving as their staging area when the first muffled boom rumbled through the floor. He and his six other teammates all froze, their gazes shooting to the window set high into the south wall.

"Shit," Cruz muttered, heading toward the window. Nate shot to his feet and followed, his heart seizing for an instant when he saw the column of smoke boiling up into the clear sky.

"Was that at the courthouse?" he asked. Had to be, but it was hard to tell from this distance.

"Yeah, think so," Cruz muttered, craning his neck to see out the window. A few inches taller, Nate had a better view. All he could see was that tower of black smoke and hoped to hell that Taya was nowhere near the place yet. She was due at the courthouse around this time though.

As he turned around to race for his gear, another explosion boomed in the distance, the floor undulating a heartbeat later.

Fuck. Nate's gaze shot back to the window. This

time he couldn't see the second plume of smoke, but that explosion had been way bigger than the first one, or closer. His hands curled into fists, apprehension winding tighter inside him. There was no way to reach Taya or her security team—he didn't have the proper channels anymore.

"Let's go," Tuck called out.

Nate grabbed his medic ruck from the ground. His team lined up at the door, exited with caution to make sure their perimeter was clear and raced around the side of the warehouse to the abandoned parking lot out front where the bird was supposed to land. Armed FBI agents stood guard around the perimeter.

Nate immediately looked south, eyed the towers of smoke billowing in the distance.

Taya was there, maybe trapped by flames or gunfire. He refused to accept that she might be dead. It made him fucking sick to his stomach to think of her going through that kind of hell again.

Tuck's expression was grim as he held his phone to his ear. Before anyone answered, the handheld radio in his web gear chirped. "This is Tuck," he said into it.

"Two explosions confirmed at the courthouse." Nate recognized DeLuca's voice immediately. "Gold Team's mobilizing now, along with two of our regular SWAT teams. Stand by—"

A third boom shook the ground. Vance swore beside him. Nate dragged a hand through his hair, going nuts with the thought of Taya being anywhere near those bombs.

"Fuck. Me," Evers muttered, staring in the direction of the last explosion.

"Make that three," DeLuca said. "Second one's reported to be a truck bomb. Heavy casualties and damage to the east side of the courthouse reported. Attack's ongoing. Unknown number of gunmen on site, rushing the building. Sniper teams have picked some of them off, but not enough and the smoke's providing good camouflage."

"Yeah, copy that." From across the room Tuck met Nate's gaze squarely, nodded when he saw that Nate had grabbed his ruck full of medical supplies. "Any word on the current location of the witnesses and their security teams?"

Nate held his breath as he awaited the answer.

"Taya arrived a few minutes ago," DeLuca confirmed.

For a moment Nate couldn't breathe. He held Tuck's stare as the blood drained out of his face, felt the others all watching him. He refused to accept that she might be gone. Couldn't even go there.

"You'll coordinate with Grant," DeLuca continued to Tuck, referring to Gold Team's leader. "Right now plan Charlie looks like our best bet. Keep this channel clear."

"Roger." Tuck switched frequencies and contacted Grant. Nate caught snippets of the exchange as he strapped on his gear, his heart racing. Plan Charlie was to counteract a mass hostage taking at the courthouse. It called for a dual assault of the building, with Gold Team arriving in vehicles to assault at ground level, and Blue Team—Nate's team—arriving via helo to begin the assault from the roof.

His mouth was dry, his throat tight by the time Tuck ended the radio transmission. "Okay, listen up," he called out, his voice booming through the cavernous warehouse. "We're going with plan Charlie. Helo's inbound, ETA thirteen minutes. Federal agents and cops inside the courthouse are trying to lock it down but they're under heavy fire. They're holding their own for now but can't for much longer."

Nate was fucking ready *now*. He wanted to move *now*. Get to Taya, pull her the hell out of there.

A solid hand landed on his shoulder. He looked up into Bauer's grim face. "We'll get her out, man," the big guy said, his gaze steady, determined.

Nate nodded and counted the seconds as they ticked past, dying a little with each passing minute. Sporadic updates came in from Grant, DeLuca and Celida, all reporting from near the courthouse. The carnage was bad, at least dozens killed and hundreds wounded. The gunmen had stormed the building, were in control of it and had taken nearly a hundred more people hostage inside the courtrooms.

Finally, he made out the distinctive sound of a Black Hawk's rotors thumping in the distance. Moments later, against the clear blue sky the Black Hawk soared into view. It circled the area once before touching down in the center of the lot.

Nate waited for the crew chief to wave them in, then ran for the helo at a crouch, the powerful rotor wash beating against his utilities. He hopped in and took a seat between Cruz and Evers, Vance on the far end, and set his medic ruck at his feet. The others fanned out on the helo's other side.

Tuck was up front, yelling to the pilots over the noise of the engines and thud of the rotors. He turned back toward the hold, sat across the deck from Nate. The pilots increased power, the pitch of the engines changing.

Come on, come on, Nate urged in frustration, his muscles drawn as tight as cables. Nothing was fucking happening fast enough.

Finally the bird eased forward, gaining speed, then lifted off the ground. They soared upward, leaving the warehouse and the industrial area behind. Everyone was quiet on the short flight there. Nate's gaze remained riveted out the helo door, staring at those three pillars of smoke boiling into the air. The pilots circled the area around the courthouse before heading for the rooftop.

Nate's heart was in his throat as he and the others got their first look at the damage on the ground. It was total, utter chaos. Emergency crews weren't even on scene yet, held back a block away due to the heavy firefight still going on. The helo banked and dipped toward the roof. Nate watched a group of Feds outside the building engage some militants already inside. One of the agents fell and was quickly dragged away by the others. More smoke boiled from the windows and doors along the front and ends of the courthouse.

Taya's trapped in there.

And the gunmen would kill her if they found her.

His chest felt tight, his muscles rigid. He sternly reminded himself about how tough she was, how smart and resourceful. She wouldn't crumble. She'd fight right up until her last breath to survive.

Hang in there, baby, please, just another few minutes. I'm coming.

A solid hand landed on his shoulder. Cruz. He nodded at Nate. "We've got this, man."

Yeah, they did. And those terrorist assholes were going to meet their maker very soon.

Giving Cruz an appreciative nod, Nate glanced at their team leader. Tuck was busy staring out the open door, scanning the area below, probably trying to assess how bad the fires were inside and how far they might have spread. If he judged it to be too dangerous, they'd switch gears and assist Gold Team from the ground on the opposite side of the courthouse, rather than assault from the roof.

Nate could see Tuck's lips moving as he spoke over the radio to someone, likely either DeLuca or Grant. Then he slid the radio back into his web gear and gave the thumbs up.

Rooftop landing was a go.

Nate shifted on the seat, body primed for action. His

hands tightened around his weapon as he imagined the moment they reached the ground floor. Anticipation and urgency hummed through him, increasing his heart rate.

He pushed thoughts of Taya out of his mind, saving it for later. He couldn't afford to think about her right now. His teammates were counting on him to have his head on straight. Their lives—and Taya's—depended on it and he wouldn't let them down.

The door gunner kept his weapon trained on possible threats below as they neared the target. Moments later the pilots lowered the helo into a hover above the rooftop. The crew chief deployed the fast rope and turned to face them, signaled it was go time.

Nate stood with his teammates, put on his ruck and waited his turn to slide down the rope. Tuck was the first one down. Then Blackwell, Bauer. Vance, Evers. All of them fanned out in a defensive half circle, weapons to their shoulders.

The crew chief gave him the signal to go. Nate gripped the thick rope between his gloved hands and swung out of the helo. Wrapping his feet around it, he controlled the speed of his descent with pressure from his feet and hands. The second his boots hit the ground he turned to steady the rope for Cruz, who'd already begun his descent. When he was on the ground everyone else got up and raced after Tuck, who led the way across the rooftop to the access door.

****

Pressed against the far wall of the darkened courtroom by Duncan's big frame, Taya stayed absolutely still, her heart pounding against her ribs. All around her people were crouched in the darkness, the sour smell of fear sharp in her nostrils. Some cried or whimpered, others were silent, huddling in the room they were trapped in together.

A gunman had stormed in a few minutes ago and opened fire. In the confusion Duncan had tackled her to the floor while the other two marshals returned fire. From the cries and sobs she knew people had been hit, but then the gunman had left, continuing down the hall to the next room. She had no idea whether the marshals had hit him or not.

Her pulse drummed in her ears in the eerie stillness. The screams from down the hall had died down now, but she could hear automatic fire popping somewhere in the background. The fire alarms were still going off, the shrill sound adding to the sense of panic she battled to keep at bay. Duncan and the other two marshals were armed, but she wasn't sure about anyone else. Those gunmen were still in the building, some right next door, and no one knew whether they planned to come back. If they did, Taya and the others needed all the firepower they could muster.

Suddenly lights flashed on overhead. Everyone gasped and cringed, but no shots rang out. Duncan eased off her and drew his weapon, the other two marshals already moving with purpose toward the door near the front of the courtroom. Across the room, a woman covered her mouth and started sobbing.

Following her gaze, Taya saw five bodies lying in a pile near the open doorway. Three more bodies lay in spreading pools of blood near them. Some survivors were bent over the wounded, at least a dozen that she could see.

"Let's go," Duncan ordered, grabbing her wrist. Taya kicked off her high heels and scrambled to her feet. Her impulse was to help the wounded but she understood that she needed to get out. Her presence put the survivors at further risk and the shooters might come back at any moment.

Her legs wobbled as she followed Duncan, weaving

in and out of the people crouched on the floor. Some looked at them in confusion, others begged them to help. She shut them out, kept putting one foot in front of the other.

Taya was supposed to have been seated in the room down the hall, the one where all the screams had come from. She shuddered.

"You've got to get out, *now*," Duncan said to everyone. "Don't sit here like a target, get up and move!"

A flurry of motion met his words. Some people huddled deeper into themselves, others got up and ran, trampling slower moving victims in their panic.

Someone crashed into Taya. She stumbled, grabbed hold of Duncan, who spun and clamped an arm around her waist to catch her before she hit the floor. He dragged her with him toward the front of the room and she saw the other marshals pause near the pile of bodies. A flash of bright orange caught her attention.

"Qureshi," one of them said.

Taya's mind cleared instantly, the fog of shock and fear evaporating like mist on a hot summer day. Her gaze zeroed in on the body dressed in the orange prison suit. The man was lying on his back, his head turned away from her, prayer cap knocked askew and his dark beard matted with blood.

She didn't take her eyes off him as she hurried alongside Duncan. She wanted to see Qureshi with her own eyes. Wanted to know he was dead.

Pulling away from Duncan's hold she stepped toward the body. Stared into that still face.

The fierce satisfaction rising inside her dimmed, then disappeared altogether.

"That's not Qureshi."

Duncan and the others paused and looked at her sharply. "Are you sure?" he asked, his sweat-beaded brow furrowed.

She nodded. "Positive." She'd never forget his face. Never.

Screams erupted from out in the hallway. Taya started. Duncan lunged for her, grabbed her upper arm and yanked her toward the door. "Go, go!"

Running footsteps pounded over the marble outside the courtroom. Taya bolted for the exit.

More screams, followed by the roar of gunfire. A sharp, hot pain kissed the back of her right calf. She dove to the ground, saw Duncan on his belly, grabbing for her. Rolling, she caught sight of the two men standing in the doorway, AK-47s brandished.

Ayman and Darwish. She recognized them from the pictures in the file Vance had shown her.

Her heart stuttered, terror paralyzing her as Ayman's gaze landed on her and locked there. A strange, hideous smile spread across his face and the muzzle of his rifle swung toward her. Duncan and the other two marshals aimed their own weapons at him.

The lights went out, plunging them all into complete blackness once more as the roar of gunfire echoed around her.

Chapter Twenty-Four

They were in. No booby-traps on the door leading from the rooftop. But that didn't mean there weren't other nasty surprises waiting for them below.

Weapon up, Nate stayed right on Vance's ass as they crept down the stairway from the roof. Tuck was up front, Bauer directly behind him. They were headed to the main floor where they'd begin clearing the building one room at a time, beginning at the eastern end while Gold Team did the same from the west. By the time they met up at the middle, they'd have the remaining tangos contained in the center courtroom, with nowhere to go.

And then pray the militants didn't plan on blowing the entire building up when they realized they were trapped. Agents had been able to listen in to some radio communications between the militants, confirming they planned to free Qureshi and take out as many others as possible, including anyone in that courtroom.

Which meant Taya.

Tuck paused at the base of the stairwell when the rattle of automatic fire rang out from down the hall outside the door. Nate's hands remained steady on his weapon as he stayed in place with his team, his breathing even.

When the firing stopped Tuck and Bauer moved to opposite sides of the door, readying to clear the hallway when it opened. At Tuck's nod, Evers stepped up and hit the release bar, opening the door a crack while the others covered him. Nate stayed in position, muscles tense, gaze locked on the slice of hallway revealed by the open door.

No shooting. No grenades.

"Clear," Tuck murmured, his voice crystal clear in Nate's earpiece.

Tuck and Bauer piled in the doorway, covering every angle before Tuck gave the signal that the hallway was clear. "Grant, report," he said quietly to the Gold Team leader. A moment later Tuck looked back at them, nodded to confirm that the other team was in place and moving forward from the opposite end of the courthouse.

Tuck slipped out into the hall, Bauer right behind him. Evers was next, then Blackwell. Just as Cruz stepped into the hallway, the emergency lights went out. Without pause Nate and the others reached up to pull the NVGs down on their helmet mounts, then activated them. The slight ambient light in the hallway lit up everything in a green glow.

Let's go hunting, boys, Nate thought as Tuck stepped out into the hall.

Automatic fire burst from the courtroom to the left. The team froze in position against the right wall of the hallway, but no one stormed out of the room. The bastards were in there shooting at helpless civilians.

Tuck waved them forward. As a unit they crept toward the besieged courtroom. The soles of Nate's boots were silent against the marble floor as they worked their way to the far doors.

He was more than ready to take the tangos down and get one step closer to finding Taya.

****

Flat on her belly on the courtroom floor, Taya swallowed a scream as the shots erupted around her, the muzzle flashes lighting up the darkness. Bullets smacked into the wall and floor beside her, peppering her with hot bites of marble.

A hand closed around her forearm. Duncan grunted and yanked her hard, rolling her beneath, then behind him. Taya flattened herself against the cold floor tiles and held her breath, afraid to move.

One of the marshals beside her cursed and hit the ground, falling half on top of her. She winced as his weight landed on her, felt the spray of blood and a wave of terror coursed through her. Even in the darkness the shooters could see their general location, probably from the light of the muzzle flashes.

"Go," the man ordered her weakly, shoving her in the direction of the doorway.

Taya turned her head to gauge the distance but couldn't see it in the dark. She remembered it wasn't that far away, maybe fifteen yards. She could make it. Kick the door open and slide around the safety of the sheltering wall outside.

More shots rang out, the pitch different this time, higher than the AK-47s used by the shooters. The marshals were returning fire, even though they couldn't see their targets clearly.

She set her palms flat on the floor, eased upward and pushed her body forward a few inches.

Behind her, Duncan screamed and fell. Taya froze, automatically turning back toward him. She reached out, her hand landing on his chest. It came away wet and sticky.

"No," he argued, pushing her hand away as he reloaded his weapon and fired again. "Go. *Go*."

She was torn between the desire to flee and the need to stay put and help him. Before she could move he jerked again, his growl of agony reverberating beneath her hand. Blood spurted over her arm.

Oh, Jesus. He'd been hit bad.

She couldn't leave him. He'd acted as a human shield, was sacrificing himself even now to provide cover for her.

Flattening herself against his back, she groped around for a weapon, found the pistol lying in his hand. His grip was lax. He was already so weak that he didn't even protest when she pulled it from his grasp. She knew how to handle a weapon. Had learned to shoot as a little girl, but when she'd come back home from Afghanistan she'd had her brother work with her for weeks until she felt confident in her ability to hit what she aimed at every time.

And she was damn well going to hit her target now.

Curling her hands around the pistol, its grip slick with Duncan's blood, she raised her arms slightly, using him to steady herself and aimed toward the shooters. Her finger curved around the trigger, a sense of hope filling her at the solid feel of the weapon in her hands. She fired four rounds in the direction of the muzzle flashes, two at each man. The volume of return fire slowed suddenly and she swore she heard one of them cry out.

Hope it hurts, you piece of shit. Here's another.

She aimed higher, squeezed the trigger again and again, just the way Kevin had showed her. If she was going to die in this room, she would do it while fighting for her life.

****

Ayman grunted and stumbled back a pace as a bullet slammed into his outer thigh, but he didn't go down. The intense burn faded beneath the rush of the adrenaline and amphetamines in his blood, his heart racing with it.

He'd been certain they'd killed the whore and her security team but someone was still over in the corner shooting at them. He shifted his stance, the pain in his leg barely registering as he turned the muzzle of his weapon farther to the right. Just as his finger applied pressure to the trigger he heard Darwish cry out. His teammate swung out a hand blindly and grabbed for him, hitting Ayman right in his wound.

This time even the drugs couldn't dull the pain. Ayman cried out, lost his balance as Darwish crumpled to the floor and knocked him down. He scrambled to his feet, kicked out at Darwish, his foot connecting with something hard. Maybe his head. More shots cracked through the air, streaking past his head. Darwish shouted in pain, calling out to Allah, his voice gurgling.

Ayman ignored the fear curling inside him, struggled to his feet. Another round hit him in the chest, then another, in rapid succession. The Kevlar he wore made it feel like someone had kicked him in the chest but he didn't fall.

Over the radio attached to his shoulder he could hear someone shouting directions in Arabic. He'd long since stopped listening to the transmissions as one commander after another reported heavy losses and urged the rest of them to keep fighting.

Ayman would fight to the death to save himself and his family.

He swung his weapon up, fired blindly in the direction of where those shots had come from. Another bullet sank into his leg, deep into his calf. He wobbled, stayed upright, a scream of rage and agony erupting from him. Pain swirled, a red mist obscuring his thoughts. It built relentlessly, swirling up to combat the drugs, taking over his body. Fear and panic began to sink into him like fangs, stripping away his resolve.

The Brethren had done this to him. Sent him and the others here like lambs to the slaughter, knowing they would never make it out.

His breathing came harder, faster, his heart pumping a desperate rhythm. He was staring death in the eye now, and he didn't dare blink.

And he was taking that shooter out before he drew his last breath.

Ayman saw the muzzle flash from the pistol, felt another round slam into the armor protecting his chest. He grunted, adjusted his aim at the shooter. His finger curved harder around the trigger and the noise of the shots suddenly turned muted in his ears, as though everything was happening under water. The roaring of his own blood drowned out everything else.

Then Darwish cried out to him in a garbled voice. "Behind you!"

Ayman whirled, and suddenly everything was happening in slow motion. His hands tightened reflexively around his rifle as two men appeared in the doorway, their silhouettes starkly black against the faint light streaming from down the hallway. They wore helmets and had rifles set to their shoulders.

They were coming to kill him.

Baring his teeth, he turned to face his executioners and squeezed the trigger.

****

Someone was returning fire inside the courtroom.

Nate kept his focus on the blown-open doors ahead

of them, the change in pitch of the weapon registering. A pistol. At least one person was in there fighting back.

At the head of the line, Tuck used hand signals to coordinate the attack. He reported two tangos.

Nate slowed his breathing, put his mind into neutral and let his training take over. When Tuck and Bauer fanned out to either side of the door to get a better look inside the room, Nate and the others followed suit, piling up behind them.

Tuck confirmed the situation with more signals. Two tangos.

The hallway behind them was empty, the area in front cleared by Gold Team, who were moving toward them to assist. Nobody else seemed to know they were there.

One of the shooters began firing again.

Tuck gave the signal and stepped into the room, covering the far right side while Bauer covered the left. Nate was next through the door. Everything slowed down, as it always did under fire.

A man's voice called out in what sounded like Arabic.

In the space of a heartbeat Nate took in the scene before him. One shooter was down. Another stood facing them, an AK in his hands. Beyond him, he clearly saw a woman lying half draped over a man's body, a pistol gripped in her hands.

Beside him, Cruz fired at the shooter on the ground.

In the split second it took Nate to transfer his attention back to the remaining shooter, the man was swinging the barrel of his weapon at him. Nate didn't hesitate. He fired two rounds, hitting him in the chest.

But he didn't go down. Only stumbled back a half step. The muzzle of his weapon dipped.

Nate aimed at the center of his forehead and fired again, hitting him cleanly between the eyes. He crumpled on the spot, his weapon clattering to the floor.

Nate crept forward, weapon trained on the two bodies on the floor. Cruz mirrored his movements. They both bent, checked for pulses. "Tango two down," Nate reported.

"Tango one down," Cruz echoed.

In the sudden silence Nate stood, held his ground and swept the room for further threats. The other team members fanned out, checking the room.

"Clear," Tuck said.

"Clear," Vance said a moment later.

"Gold Team's confirmed, all tangos down," Tuck reported. "Doc and Cruz, start helping the wounded. The rest of us will lock the building down."

"Roger that."

Now that the threat was over and the building clear, Nate's heart began to pound. He grabbed a tactical flashlight from his web gear, shined it in the direction of the woman he'd seen earlier. She flinched and held up a blood-soaked arm to shield her eyes, but not before Nate saw her face.

Taya. She was still alive, had been returning fire while using Duncan as a shooting platform.

She broke his heart with her bravery in the worst of circumstances.

Swallowing a cry of relief, he lowered the flashlight and ran to her.

Chapter Twenty-Five

"Taya."

At the sound of that wonderful, familiar voice she looked up into Nathan's worried face. Relief crashed through her, making her body turn limp.

He went to one knee in front of her, on the opposite side of Duncan, and took her face in his gloved hands, his eyes scanning her anxiously. "Baby, are you hurt?"

"I can't stop the b-bleeding," she whispered, hating the way her jaw shook. She had no idea how long she'd had her hands clamped to Duncan's stomach. They'd gone numb, the muscles in her arms like jelly. She had her full body weight pressed on him but still the blood continued to leak out from beneath her stiff fingers. Her hands were coated with it, the warm, iron scent of it making her stomach roll.

Nathan slung his rifle across his chest and knelt next to Duncan, immediately sliding his fingers to the pulse in the other man's neck. A second later he glanced behind him. "Blackwell, gimme a hand here."

He got on the radio, his voice totally calm while he transmitted Duncan's condition and requested immediate medevac for him. "Keep doing what you're doing," he told her, and shrugged out of his ruck. He rummaged through it, came up with gloves and some bandages she recognized as pressure dressings.

Taya locked her jaw and held on, glancing down at Duncan's face. The man was pale from blood loss and had stopped responding to her a few minutes ago.

One of Nathan's teammates came over, she assumed Blackwell. Nathan handed him a pair of surgical gloves then gently took hold of her wrists. The warmth of his fingers wrapped around her made tears sting her eyes. "Taya, look at me."

The calm, steady sound of his voice pushed through the numbness invading her. She met his eyes, stared deep into them and blinked back tears. She couldn't fall apart. Not now. "I didn't know what else to do."

His expression softened with tenderness. "You did great, sweetheart. But are you hurt?"

"N-No." A bullet graze, some scrapes, bruises and nicks didn't matter. It could have been so much worse. Would have, if not for Duncan. He'd taken the rounds meant for her. He was dying because of her.

Taya bit down on the inside of her cheek. She wanted Nathan's arms around her so badly but needed him to work on Duncan more.

He nodded once. "Blackwell and I'll take it from here. You go with Cruzie out to see the paramedics, let them look you over. I'll be there as soon as I can, okay?"

She managed a nod, realized belatedly that Cruz was already next to her. He slid an arm around her waist and helped her to her feet. Her legs wobbled but she locked her knees and cast another look at Nathan. He was already prepping an IV, getting ready to slip it into Duncan's arm.

"He s-saved me," she whispered, unable to fight the shakes rolling through her.

Nathan looked up at her, his hazel gaze steady. "And I'm gonna do my best to save him. Go with Cruz now, baby."

"Come on," Cruz urged, gently pulling her away.

"Qureshi," she blurted, then pointed behind her at the body in the orange jumpsuit. "That's not Qureshi."

"Qureshi's been captured," Nathan told her.

She stared at him, wanting to believe him. Needing to believe that all this horror hadn't been for nothing, that all these innocent people hadn't suffered and died in vain.

"Gold Team got him," Cruz added. "He's on his way to a deep, dark federal holding cell right now, until he stands trial."

Oh, God, she still had to come back here, relive this whole thing when she testified against him. Exhaustion hit her like a sledgehammer, making it an effort just to stay on her feet.

"Cruz," Nathan said in a warning tone.

"Yeah, we're going. Come on, come with me," he said to her.

Taya went with him, her limbs feeling wooden and jerky, as though someone else was controlling them. She'd been in shock like this before and hated it, resented the weakness that sapped her remaining strength.

Cruz angled his body between her and the rear door of the courtroom, but he needn't have bothered. She'd already seen all the dead and wounded, had memorized the sight of Ayman and Darwish's dead bodies, the puddles of blood staining the marble floor.

Outside the sights and smells only got worse. Her eyes automatically scanned the area, searching for more threats.

The stench of burned metal stung her nose, the sight of people bleeding from shrapnel and bullet wounds, some bodies covered with tarps and sheets, others still lying out in the open, broke her heart. Police and other security agents swarmed the area. Beyond the twisted ruins of the inner security gate, emergency vehicles flooded the area, the constant blaring of sirens and the flashing strobe lights making her dizzy.

"Whoa," Cruz said, tightening his grip when her legs gave out. He bent to slide one arm beneath her legs but she protested and pushed against his shoulder until he straightened.

She needed to walk out of here on her own two feet. Prove to herself that she had the strength to do it. "Did you g-get all of them?" she asked him.

"All of them," he confirmed. "They're either down or captured."

She nodded, relief bleeding through her. "That's good."

"Yeah." His arm remained around her in a solid hold she appreciated all the way out to one of the waiting ambulances.

Again she protested. "I'm fine."

"You're bleeding. Your right leg and shoulder."

Now that some of the numbness had retreated she was aware of the sharp sting in her right calf and the warm trickle of blood down her right shoulder blade. She stubbornly shook her head. "Others need help more than me." She didn't want to take the paramedics away from someone else who needed them more.

"Yeah, but you're a star federal witness and Nate's asked me personally to look after you. We'll get you triaged, then I'll take a look at you, patch you up before we get you out of here."

"Where am I going?"

"Nate's place. A team of agents is going to take you there for the night until WITSEC can send another team for you."

290

Oh God, she couldn't wait to see Nathan. Going to his place was such a welcome relief that she let out a shuddering breath. Cruz walked her to the closest ambulance and sat her down on a blanket. He checked her over, took her pulse and cleaned her up with some alcohol wipes one of the paramedics handed him. His touch was gentle, professional as he bandaged up her shoulder blade.

She flinched when he probed at the deeper slice on the back of her calf, the alcohol burning like fire in the wound.

"Sorry," Cruz murmured. "Gotta get this clean."

"It's okay," she whispered. The pain continued to increase as the minutes passed, every cut, scrape and bruise making themselves known but Taya didn't utter a sound. She watched as a woman on a stretcher was loaded into the ambulance, the stump of her right shoulder covered in blood-soaked bandages.

Taya shuddered and looked away, bit her lip as Cruz finished putting on the bandages and wrapped a blanket around her shoulders. Even with the thick material draped around her she couldn't warm up. She was cold all the way to her bones, frozen inside. Was Duncan going to make it? When would she see Nathan again?

When he was done Cruz got on the radio and requested agent support. Two FBI agents appeared at his side a few minutes later. He explained the situation and gently helped her to her feet. The female agent slipped her arm around Taya and began to lead her away.

Taya stopped and grabbed Cruz's forearm, bringing his light brown gaze back to her. "You'll take care of Nathan for me?" She was worried about him. Going through this attack today, nearly losing her, might amplify the symptoms of his PTSD.

His lips quirked, his eyes warming. "As long as you're safe, he'll be okay. But yeah, I'll watch out for him. On this team all of us watch out for each other. It's what we do."

That made Taya smile. "You guys are like family to him, you know."

Cruz nodded. "We're all just brothers from other mothers. Some of us better looking than the rest." A dimple appeared in his cheek as he grinned. "Agents Rosedale and Timmins will take you to Nate's now, and watch the place overnight. Not sure when Nate'll be home though, so don't wait up. Get some sleep if you can."

"Okay." She'd wait up though. She'd wait as long as it took for him to come home, and she doubted she'd be able to sleep anyway.

The agents drove her to Nathan's upscale apartment, checked it for her then left her alone while they kept watch outside.

Taya wandered around the place, taking in the layout. He kept it tidy. The dark, masculine furniture suited him and she could smell the faint scent of his cologne in the air. On the mantel were pictures of him during his days in the Air Force, including one of him and O'Neil. A few others were of him and some of his current teammates.

She wandered into his bedroom, saw the neatly made king-size bed and couldn't wait to nestle in it. She knew he'd taken other women there before her, but she didn't care. What mattered was now, and he wasn't the same person he'd been even a week ago. Already she'd seen him trying to change. There was no doubt in her mind that she meant something important to him, just as he did to her.

After scrubbing the residual blood off her in the shower and washing her hair, she toweled it dry, grabbed a T-shirt from Nathan's closet and curled up beneath the comforter on his big bed. She wasn't planning to sleep but the adrenaline crash had left her exhausted so she allowed herself to close her eyes and rest.

Her eyes snapped open at the sound of a key scraping in the lock. It was full dark outside and she was surprised to see it was two-fifteen in the morning when she looked at the bedside clock. The lock turned.

Nathan.

Her heart leapt and she sat up, wincing as her cuts and bruises protested the movement. On bare feet she hurried to the front door.

Nathan stepped through it and flipped on the foyer light. His face lit up when he saw her standing there, taking away the exhaustion etched into his features.

With a glad cry Taya rushed for him. He caught her in his arms with a rough sound and lifted her off her feet, his face buried in her hair. The muscles in his arms shook as he held her tight to him, seeming to take as much comfort from the embrace as she did.

"Let me look at you," he murmured, easing her head away from his shoulder to tip her face up. His eyes roved over her, his fingertips tracing over the marks on her chin. With a low sound he kissed the tip of her nose, her lips, her chin, his arms tight around her.

Taya caught his face between her hands and pressed her mouth to his, sinking into him, letting this moment fill her senses. He was home and they were both safe.

Nathan murmured in approval and slid one hand into her hair to cup the back of her head. Without breaking the kiss he slid his hands down to her butt and lifted her, then walked her into his bedroom with her legs wrapped around his waist. He lowered her carefully onto the mattress and reached over to flip on the bedside lamp.

She touched his shoulder. "How's Duncan?"

"Out of surgery and in ICU. The next twelve hours are critical, but he's got a good chance of pulling through."

Taya said a prayer for him. "And is it over?"

"All over. Captured eight and the rest of the attackers

at the courthouse are dead. Some of them were wearing federal marshal or FBI uniforms."

No wonder they'd been able to breach security in the confusion after the bombings.

"FBI and DHS are working to mop up the rest of the cell, find all the other members linked to it." She let out a breath of relief and he cupped the side of her face, his hazel eyes scrutinizing her. "Cruz told me you took some shrapnel."

"I'm okay, really, it's nothing. He took care of it before the other agents brought me here."

Apparently unsatisfied by her response, he carefully peeled his shirt off her and set about inspecting every inch of her naked body. His hands glided in a soothing, possessive caress up the front of her legs, torso and arms, his lips trailing kisses in their wake, touching every single mark he found. He kissed the abrasions on her hipbones, then rolled her to her stomach and peeled off the tape holding the bandages to her calf and shoulder blade.

Taya relaxed and lay still while he finished, enjoying the feel of his hands and lips on her skin. His touch wasn't sexual right now, but there was a definite possessiveness and certainty to his touch that soothed her on the most primal level. She was his and she wanted him to know it.

When he was done he set the bandages back in place then gently rolled her back over to face him. Before she could touch him he was stripping off his shirt and uniform pants, his underwear. Naked, he reached for the lamp.

"Wait," she said. She sat up and put a hand on his hip, pulled slightly to turn him. "Have you got green footprints back there?"

He huffed out a laugh and turned more, exposing his backside for her inspection. Two small, green footprints were tattooed on one taut butt cheek in the PJ tradition. "How'd you know about those?"

"I read up on PJs once I got back home and was

always curious if you had them." She traced a finger over them, smiling.

"You thought about my ass?"

"I did," she answered, unrepentant.

"Okay, hands off it before you get me all worked up." Nathan switched off the lamp, slid in next to her and pulled her close.

Immediately Taya curled into him, sighing in contentment at the feel of his strong, warm body cradling her in the darkness. "I hurt all over," she said on a small groan. But she was alive. And if she had nightmares tonight, Nathan would be here to banish them. Just as she'd do for him.

"Yeah, I'll bet." He kissed the top of her head. "Did you take anything?"

"A while ago. I don't want anything else but you right now though." She ran her hands over his muscular back, enjoying the closeness, the sense of peace stealing over her. "Are you okay?" she whispered.

His big palm stroked over her hair, down her spine in slow, drugging sweeps. "Now that I'm holding you, yeah."

"I can't even process what happened today." So many people dead or maimed, and the trial still had to happen.

"Don't even try," he murmured. "There'll be plenty of time for that later. Right now just be here with me."

She snuggled deeper into his embrace, smiling a little. "How'd you get to be so wise?"

"I met this incredible woman a few years ago. It was the toughest mission I ever went on, but she battled through everything like a champ. I never forgot her, thought about her all the time and then recently she walked back into my life again."

His fingers stroked up the length of her spine, down again, sending warmth chasing through her. "She's dealt with things so much better than I have and I've already learned a lot from her. She's really rubbed off on me." His arms tightened and he pressed his lips to her forehead. "I don't plan on letting her go, either."

Taya slid her hands into his hair, stroked it while she tipped her head back to look into his eyes, barely visible in the near darkness. "I'm falling in love with you, Nathan."

At her words he groaned and wrapped both arms around her, holding her to his heart. "God, sweetheart, I'm right there with you. And I swear I'll catch you if you'll trust me enough to let yourself fall the rest of the way."

She smiled, kissed the center of his chest where his heart beat strong and steady beneath her lips. "I do trust you." He'd earned her trust in giving him her heart, as well her body.

****

Ten days later Taya walked up the courthouse steps accompanied by a new WITSEC team. The new location for the trial had been kept secret from the media and general public until this morning. Even though she knew The Brethren had been dismantled and the cell responsible for the attack destroyed, she couldn't help the fear building inside her with every stride.

There were no crowds outside this time, and only a handful of media crews, who were kept well away from the pathway to the front doors. Inside her team waited beside her while she gathered herself. She'd made it clear she didn't want to be present in the courtroom until she was actually called to the witness stand.

The attack had left her with a bad case of claustrophobia she was doing her best to tackle but in light of the importance of what she'd come here to do, she didn't want anything distracting her.

She sat outside the courtroom on a wooden bench, using every calming technique she knew of to settle her heart rate. *You're fine. Everything's okay.*

Finally a bailiff came out of the courtroom doors. "Ms. Kostas? It's time."

Taya rose and followed him through the tall mahogany doors. The courtroom was packed. Everyone turned in their seats to stare at her, but she had eyes for only one person.

Her gaze sought and immediately found Nathan seated at the back of the room. He was dressed in a black button-down shirt and khakis, and his welcoming smile was so full of pride she couldn't help but smile back. She knew he was armed, she'd seen him tuck his pistol into his waistband just an hour ago.

They had talked on the phone every day but since the attack she hadn't seen him again until last night, when he'd stayed at the safe house with her. All night he'd done an admirable job of keeping her mind off the trial, leaving her too tired and sated to worry about anything. His team was nearby again at a new staging area, on standby in case they were needed, but DeLuca had given him the okay to come here today. Once her testimony was over she would go back home to help look after her father, and as soon as the trial was over Nathan had promised to come see her, figure out their future from there.

She couldn't wait to move forward in their relationship, together.

Turning her attention to the front of the room, Taya kept her eyes fixed on the judge and the prosecution team waiting there for her, completely ignoring the man dressed in the orange prison suit sitting in the defendant's seat.

She walked to the witness stand, her heels clicking with authority with every step. Placing her hand on the Bible, she took her oath and sat. Meeting Nathan's stare at the back of the room, she held his gaze for a long moment, taking strength from him. He nodded at her, a confident gesture that said *you've got this, little warrior. I'm right here to support you.*

It meant more to her than he'd ever know.

Releasing a slow breath, she raised her chin and finally turned her gaze on Qureshi.

The moment their gazes connected she felt a surge of power go through her. Throughout her nine hellish months of captivity, she'd been forbidden to look him in the eye. She'd known better than to even try, because she'd known what would happen to her if she did.

But they weren't in Afghanistan anymore and he was no longer the one calling the shots. *She* held the authority now. Her life, her opinions, had value here. And her voice, silenced for so long, would now speak for all the victims unable to. Her voice would not only be heard here in this courtroom—it would be his undoing.

In the end, words would prove more powerful than any weapon he'd had at his disposal during his reign of terror. More effective than tyranny, fists, bullets or bombs.

Qureshi stared back at her with an insolent, almost bored disdain on his scratched face, making it clear what he thought of her. To him she was nothing but an infidel whore, a commodity less valuable than a goat or mule, to be bought and sold whenever it suited him, handed out to one of his soldiers as a prize of war.

Well this infidel whore is about to bury you, you son of a bitch.

Holding that cold, hateful gaze in the taut, hushed silence that filled the courtroom, she sent him another silent message. Let him see it in her eyes. *You didn't break me. I'm no longer afraid of you. You no longer have the power to hurt me or anyone I care about. And by God, I'll make sure you never have the chance to hurt anyone else again.*

Giving him one last scathing look to drive her point home, she broke eye contact. Dismissing him, as he'd done to her and her fellow captives countless times.

Elation and a sense of calm flowed through her as she turned her attention to the lead prosecutor and gave him a decisive nod. "I'm ready."

Epilogue

Nate paused at the edge of the paddock in the fading twilight. Ahead of him the barn light was on, leaving a glowing yellow rectangle that spilled out of the half-open doorway. His pulse thudded as he gathered himself. This was the most important mission he'd ever undertaken. He kept telling himself there was no need to be this nervous, but he still was.

So much had happened over the past five weeks. Taya's testimony was the most powerful of the entire trial against Qureshi. It had taken the jury less than a day to convict him, and a few weeks later, the unanimous decision to grant the death penalty had been given. Mahmoud and the other senior leaders of The Brethren were all in jail awaiting their own trials. Agent Duncan was on the mend, although facing months more of physical therapy to regain strength and control of his core muscles.

After spending the night at Nate's place the night of the attack and with the threat against her over, Taya had gone back home to help take care of her dad. It had been hard to be apart from her that long, but he'd been busy at work and then sent out for training this past week. Talking on the phone every day hadn't been enough for either of them. Now he was finally here and he couldn't wait to see her.

The soles of his shoes were nearly silent against the paved path on the way to the door. A horse whickered from inside and the earthy, dusty smell hit him even before he got inside. He glanced around the well-kept barn, noting the stalls and the neat rows of tack and grooming equipment hanging on the walls. The faint sound of rhythmic brushing reached him, mixed with soft feminine humming coming from the last stall.

He headed for it, aware of his heart beating faster with each step. He stopped when he saw Taya. She was in a stall, her back to him, stroking a soft-bristled brush over the side of a bay horse. The animal was half asleep, its eyes half-closed and its ears drooping, but it perked up when it scented him. It lifted its head and Taya looked over her shoulder.

The way her face lit up when she saw him made him the most grateful man on the planet. "Hey, sweetheart."

She dropped the brush, opened the stall and flung herself into his arms. Nate grabbed her tight, chuckling when she wrapped her arms and legs around him, clinging like a monkey. She leaned back to take his face between her hands, covering his face with sweet, frantic kisses. "You're here," she breathed, continuing to rain kisses over him.

"I'm here," he confirmed, sinking a hand into her hair. "Your curls are back. I missed them."

She smiled against his mouth. "Got my hair put back to normal last week." Planting a long, lingering kiss on his lips, she looped one arm around his neck and trailed the fingers of her other hand down his cheek. "You shaved. You've got such a baby face, Nathan."

He wrinkled his nose for show, not minding the teasing. "Yeah, that's why I don't shave very often."

She rubbed her cheek against his, murmured in pleasure. "Don't worry, you're still insanely hot. I like your scruff, but I like this too. Can't wait to feel your smooth face rubbing all over my naked body."

A chuckle burst out of him even as her words made him go rock hard in his jeans. "Hmm, any places in particular?"

"A few very sensitive ones," she murmured, a mischievous twinkle in her eyes when she met his gaze once more. "This is a nice surprise."

"Yeah, I drove down as soon as I got back."

His team had been at a training school in New Mexico for the past eight days. He hadn't been able to call her the entire time, only to send a couple texts here and there when he could. Thankfully she seemed to understand, which was good, because if they were going to make a go of things then she needed to be okay with him being gone a lot, and not always able to be in touch. Because he wouldn't be leaving his job anytime soon.

For the first time in months he felt like his position in the HRT was solid. DeLuca had told him personally that the unofficial probation was over, but not to be afraid to speak up if he needed anything.

So Nate had asked for and received three days off to come here to North Carolina. Before he headed back home, he wanted to make a serious commitment to Taya and take their relationship to the next level.

"I'm glad you did." She leaned in to nibble at his lower lip, her tongue gliding along it and stealing inside his mouth.

Nate groaned and backed her up against the nearest wall, right beside the stall. Taya tightened her legs around his waist and rubbed her pelvis against him. He held her up with his body and kissed her hard and deep, wanting to be inside her. Something ruffled his hair. It took a moment for it to register that both Taya's hands were locked around his shoulders. Which meant someone else was stroking his hair.

He jerked away from the alien touch in time to see the horse throw its head back, eyes wide as it stared back at him in astonishment from over the top of the stall door.

Taya laughed. "Was she putting the moves on you?"

"I think so, yeah." He reached up one hand, touched his hair. None of it seemed to be missing.

"As a female I can't say I blame her. You're pretty irresistible." Her legs slid from around his waist, her expression becoming curious. "What's this?" She reached around to the small of his back, tapped the hard bulge tucked into his waistband.

"Oh. Brought you something." He withdrew the wrapped package and handed it to her.

Taya glanced up at him, a little smile on her lips. "Can I open it now?"

"Sure."

She tore off the paper to reveal the camo print notebook, shot him a questioning glance before opening it. "What is…" She flipped through a few pages, looked up into his eyes. "Is this…?"

"My journal," he said, reaching out to glide a knuckle down her cheek. Her skin was so damn soft. She was a contradiction in terms to him, and one that he found endlessly fascinating: a woman with the inner strength to rival any Spec Ops member he'd ever known, yet she had such a kind, soft heart beneath that hard-won armor. Resilient. Independent yet willing to compromise. Formidable in her confidence and strength of will, yet gentle and loving.

He loved her so hard it hurt.

"I bought it the night after you stayed at my place," he continued. "I knew if I was going to have a real shot with you going forward then I needed to get my shit together once and for all. You said the writing thing really helped you so I called my counselor and talked to her about it. She thought it would be good for me too. So I wrote in it every day since. I've been working hard at it."

Taya leafed through the pages until she came to the end and looked back up into his eyes. "It's full."

"Yeah. Guess I had a lot to say."

The tenderness in her eyes slayed him. "Nathan, I'm so proud of you."

Her pride in him made him feel twenty feet tall. He let out a relieved breath. "I want to read it to you. That's my next step, if you're okay with it."

"Of course it's okay. I'd love for you to read it to me, as long as you feel comfortable doing it."

"That's the thing, I am. And I wouldn't be with anyone else except you. You make me feel…whole." He didn't know how else to say it, how else to explain himself, except he needed her to know he was trying like hell to deal with his issues. "I know I've got a long way to go before I get to the same place you're at, but I'm willing to put in the work to get there. I feel safe with you and I'm ready to move forward, let go of all the stuff that happened before. Like you said, I'm doing it for me. I'm sick of my past having any kind of hold over me. So I'm going to do whatever it takes to make peace with it."

Her answering smile lit up her whole face, made her gray eyes sparkle like gems. "Then I'll gladly listen to whatever you want to say."

Warmth kindled in his chest. She did that; warmed him from the inside out, just by being her. "Good, because I love you."

She froze, her eyes widening slightly.

He nodded, laughed at her shocked expression. "Yep, I love you. That's what I came here to say. I love you and I'm a better man because of it, but not as good a man as I'll be down the road if you stand by me."

Her eyes filled with tears and she flung her arms around him. "I love you too," she blurted out against his neck. "So, so much. And of course I'll stand by you."

Nate felt like his heart might burst. He hugged her hard. "Would you move to Virginia with me? When your dad's strong enough. I know you need to be here for a while longer, but after that, I want you in my bed every night so I can wake up beside you each morning."

She gave a soggy laugh, her face still buried in his neck. "There you go again with the romance."

"Oh, baby, have I got plans for you." He stroked a hand over her back, fascinated by the combination of softness and strength that was uniquely her. Then his stomach rumbled, making her smile. He was starving, hadn't eaten since lunchtime. "Hey, you wouldn't happen to have any bacon in the house, would you? Because I'd kill for a BLT right now."

Laughing, Taya pulled back to wipe at her eyes. "Yeah, I think we've got some bacon. But I'm not serving it to you in just an apron and heels. My father's had enough heart attacks for this lifetime, thanks."

Nate grinned and wiped away the last traces of tears drying on her cheeks. "But I'd be putty in your hands."

Taya flashed him a knowing smile full of such feminine power that it made his heart thud. "Oh, I think you're already there," she said, shooting a sultry look at him over her shoulder as she walked toward the door.

Yeah, she was right. But it went both ways. And by night's end he'd make sure she was putty in his hands as well.

—The End—

Thank you for reading AVENGED. I really hope you enjoyed it and that you'll consider leaving a review at one of your favorite online retailers. It's a great way to help other readers discover new books.

If you liked AVENGED and would like to read more, turn the page for a list of my other books. And if you don't want to miss any future releases, please feel free to join my newsletter: http://kayleacross.com/v2/contact/

Complete Booklist

Historical Romance
The Vacant Chair

Erotic Romance (writing as *Callie Croix*)
Deacon's Touch
Dillon's Claim
No Holds Barred
Touch Me
Let Me In
Covert Seduction

Acknowledgements

Once again a shout out to my A-Team: Katie, Kim, Joan and Todd. Couldn't do this without you.

And to my incredible, unbelievably supportive readers, THANK YOU! If not for you I wouldn't be able to follow my dream and make the characters in my head come to life on the page.

About the Author

NY Times and USA Today Bestselling author Kaylea Cross writes edge-of-your-seat military romantic suspense. Her work has won many awards and has been nominated for both the Daphne du Maurier and the National Readers' Choice Awards. A Registered Massage Therapist by trade, Kaylea is also an avid gardener, artist, Civil War buff, Special Ops aficionado, belly dance enthusiast and former nationally-carded softball pitcher. She lives in Vancouver, BC with her husband and family.

You can visit Kaylea at **www.kayleacross.com.** If you would like to be notified of future releases, please join her newsletter. **http://kayleacross.com/v2/contact/**